SWINDLED IN PARADISE

PARADISE SERIES

BOOK 8

DEBORAH BROWN

SWINDLED IN PARADISE
All Rights Reserved
Copyright © 2015 Deborah Brown

ISBN-13: 978-0-9903166-7-1

Cover: Natasha Brown

PRINTED IN THE UNITED STATES OF AMERICA

SWINDLED IN PARADISE

Chapter One

Automatic gunfire flew into the restaurant from the street, ricocheting off the walls. A steady stream of bullets wreaked havoc everywhere, beginning in the bar, where anything glass shattered and expensive bottles of liquor exploded, sending liquid and shards flying in all directions. Screams echoed throughout the building; hopefully people weren't injured, just scared out of their wits. Furniture overturned as people hit the ground, scrambling in blind fear. The staccato sound went on and on for what seemed like an hour, but it was over in less than a minute, as the destruction moved at a steady pace through the main entrance, into the dining room, and completed its assault on the far end of the wrap patio. Squealing tires signaled the end of the chaos.

* * *

We sat under an umbrella on the patio of an upscale restaurant called B's, the current "in" place, complete with prime people-watching from sidewalk seats. Its Ocean Boulevard location in Miami Beach was in the middle of the Art Deco Historic District, which continued along the water to the southernmost end of the main barrier island.

I sat across the table from my best friend and roommate, Fabiana Merceau, in a midriff top and a flirty above-the-knee tropical print skirt in greens and oranges. I sighed at having to leave my flip-flops in the SUV and change into persimmon color slides. I looked like the girl next door except for the red hair and the whispers of "crazy" everywhere I went.

Fab wore a full short skirt that just begged to twirl and a black halter-neck top, adorned with columns of sparkling crystals at the neckline, that showed off her sculpted, tanned arms. Her feet loved the four-inch designer heels. No one did sexy like this golden-brown-haired, blue-eyed Frenchwoman. The only downside to her outfit? No place to carry her Walther, so she tucked it in her black envelope purse.

"What are we doing here?" I asked.

"The owner, my newest client, wants me to work here." Her eyes scanned the interior of the restaurant.

I whined when Fab said we couldn't sit outside and moved to seats just inside the sliding doors that ran around the perimeter of the restaurant. A warm breeze blew in from the Atlantic Ocean across the street, but it wasn't nearly as invigorating as if we'd stayed at the sidewalk table.

I arched my brows. This wasn't the dress-up girlfriends lunch Fab had sold; this was a job. "Doing what?" Customer service wasn't Fab's strong point; she had no patience. One snotty comment and the patron would end up wearing their food.

I asked her several times where were we going, complaining loudly and questioning why I had to wear uncomfortable shoes. This was another one of her crap surprises, but we never said no to one another.

"Madison…" she began.

The sound of gunfire interrupted her.

Fab and I hit the floor and rolled into an alcove, both of us drawing our weapons. Judging by the sound of the gunshots, which quickly melted into the distance and ceased, it had been a drive-by shooting.

"You listen to me," I barked. "I don't know what's going on, but you're never working here."

"I hate it when you sound like your mother." She grabbed my hand. "Let's get the hell out of here before Miami's finest show up."

We could hear the sirens rapidly approaching. This would be headline news, and we weren't going to be part of the story.

She peered around our upturned table. "Now."

We raced out a side door, across the corner of

the patio to the sidewalk, and blended in with the gaping crowd that had started to gather.

"Should we cut across to the beach?" I looked across the street. The waves breaking on the sugar-white sand had a calming effect.

"We need to get back to the SUV and out of the area before they start cordoning off streets and we're stuck here. If we hang around, someone might recognize us, and the questions will be endless."

I kicked off my shoes; Fab looked disgusted. "Your feet will get dirty."

"That's what your overpriced French shower gel is for."

She took off her shoes, and we ran for the parking garage.

When we got there, Fab slid behind the wheel of my black convertible Hummer. It was the best deal I ever got on a car though I rarely got to drive it. I'd been banned from driving my own vehicle, the common complaint being that I drove too slow. I looked forward to the day when driving the speed limit didn't garner evil looks.

"Start talking about the job duties for this new employment you're forbidden to take."

"Calm down. We got away uninjured."

I glared at her.

"B's is running private poker games in the back room. The owner wants me to check the security, sit in as a player, make sure the games stay friendly, and run checks on the high-rollers and employees."

"First off, gambling is illegal in this state."

"Your mother uses the back room at Jake's for the same illicit operation." She smirked.

"Don't bring Mother into this. Jake's has never been riddled with bullet holes." She gave me a look. "Okay, I admit to the occasional gunshot inside the bar. Anyway, her games are invitation-only to a select few, doctor, lawyer, CPA, all friends of the family."

Jake's was a tropical-themed dive bar I owned in Tarpon Cove, frequented by locals who liked cheap drinks and the best Mexican food at the top of the Keys. I couldn't wait to get back to the Cove; I was tired of overly-impressed-with-itself Miami. Besides, shouldn't you check out the people involved *before* dealing the cards or hiring them?"

"When there's big money on the table, sometimes rules get bent."

One thing about Fab, she knew when to keep a low profile, when not to play chicken at yellow lights or incite a smoking-hot male driver into a game of chase, only to laugh and disappear on them, always ending the game on her own rules.

"Let me guess, your new client screwed someone and got served up some payback. If this was meant to scare him, I'd say mission accomplished unless he's completely stupid. Does this client have a name?"

"Patino," Fab murmured. "It did appear as though the shooter aimed high." She stared at the roadway, lost in thought. "He's probably going to want me to investigate."

"N-O! This Patino person already knows the answers to all his questions, and I bet you he's on a first-name basis with whoever ordered the shooting." I shook my finger at her. "Don't think I won't stoop to telling on you."

"You wouldn't." She frowned.

"I love you. You're the sister I never had. Are you crazy enough to think you can be replaced? We don't allow just anyone into the Westin family."

"Women are having babies later in life; maybe your mother will get preggo by Spoon."

I gasped. "Don't you repeat that to anyone. Brad would have a stroke."

My brother, was coming around slowly to Mother's reformed badass boyfriend, Jimmy Spoon. He liked the man, but wanted Mother to hook up with a stable, less fun, older gentleman, not a younger one with whom she shared cigars and Tennessee whiskey straight up. But babies…

Chapter Two

Fab maneuvered the Hummer onto the Overseas Highway, an exotic road that ran through the lush tropical landscape between Miami and Key West. A colorful Florida scenic highway sign confirmed that home was closer than ever. Tarpon Cove was the first exit at the top of the Keys, a small beach town that housed more full-time residents than flighty tourist traffic. Cars generally passed up the Cove in a cloud of sand, heading to the ultimate playground at the southernmost tip—Key West.

"What are you doing?" Fab snarked.

I had reached over the seat and grabbed the carry bag that I'd left on the floor. "Since I'm not driving, I can change my clothes." I smoothed my hands over my skirt. "You'd owe me a new one if this had gotten covered with blood stains. What the hell happened back there?" and pitched my shoes over the seat, not caring where they landed.

"I don't know, but I'm going to find out." Fab grabbed her cellphone and dialed it one-handed without taking her eyes off the road. After a minute, she made a face and ended the call. "Went to voicemail," she said, tossing her phone back on the console. "I'll call Patino later, and when I do, I bet his answers to my questions will be vague." She tapped her fingers on the steering wheel, an intense look on her face.

"And this is the conversation where you'll be giving your notice, effective immediately? Don't think you're going to pull one over on me." I stripped down to my black lace bra and lace-trimmed hipster underwear. They were a little fancy for the black sweatpants I pulled over my hips, rolling the legs to mid-calf. I grabbed my cropped black sweatshirt with the State of Florida seal embossed on it in a deep silver.

"Yes, Mother." Fab glanced at the pile of clothes between my feet. "Don't forget to pick up your clothes."

I ignored her. "We need to stop by The Cottages, make sure they're still standing."

"More problems?" She snickered. "You wouldn't have so many problems if you stuck to your hard-and-fast rule: no renting to locals."

I pulled my red hair up into a messy upsweep and forced it between the teeth of a clip. "I'm hiring you as the Director of Security. Evict the lot of them and call me when it's done. You're perfect for the job; you never have sympathy for anyone's sob story."

"What's the pay?" From the look on her face, she was giving serious thought to my impromptu idea. "It better be extra if I have to listen to a single problem." She smiled evilly. "Do I get to charge by the person? Just so you understand that I only relocate as far as the curb."

"Best friends don't charge; they offer up their services for free and skip the 'tudiness," I sniffed.

She made a face.

"I saw that." I bent over, sliding my feet into black flip-flops, another new pair. I couldn't resist the crystals on the straps.

* * *

"Slow the hell down, that's a horse," I yelled and shoved my hands against the dash.

Fab jammed on the brakes, screeching to a halt in the entrance to the driveway of The Cottages. "What's that doing here?" She swerved around its rear-end and parked in the visitor space in front of the office.

I had inherited the ten-unit beach-front property from my Aunt Elizabeth. The individual units were painted in an array of the famously bright South Florida colors. The place had always attracted colorful tenants, but during my tenure, I'd managed to rid the place of felons, drunks, and drug addicts. I'd like to say none of their ilk had managed to sneak back in, but that would be a lie. Since I couldn't shoot them all, I had an A-1 eviction service, courtesy of Mother's badass boyfriend.

Mac Lane strolled out of the office as though it was just another day. She'd shown up one day and talked herself into the job of office manager in a matter of minutes. If I had my way, she would never quit. The thought of handling tenant problems gave me a headache.

She was an ample-sized, middle-aged woman who handled everything with patience and calm. When that failed, she also packed a handgun under her clothing. Her style could easily be categorized as bohemian: today, she sported a multi-color checked long skirt gathered together and tied into a knot between her calves to show her legs and ankles. I knew her well enough to know that underneath all that material, she had donned a pair of electric-colored bicycle shorts or obscenely short shorts. Her tops came in one size—too small. Today's shirt had 'Yee Haw' written on the front.

I jumped out of the SUV. "You're fired," I told Mac, pointing to the horse.

"I've been trying to call you to ask what you want me to do with our newest guest. He won't fit through any of the cottage doors." Mac blew a kiss at the chestnut brown, full-grown horse.

"She's been mean to me," Fab whined to Mac as she walked up behind me.

"I…" I stuttered, "I didn't get lunch. And I'm hungry."

Mac tapped her foot, waiting to see if, just this once, we'd get into a hair-pulling, roll-on-the-ground brawl. I knew that if one erupted, every tenant in the place would put their money on Fab.

"Focus." I snapped my fingers at Fab. "Part of your new security detail is getting rid of the horse."

Mac laughed. "I called animal control, and the woman hung up on me after telling me to call back when I sobered up and saying that hopefully then I'd make sense."

"It just wandered up?" I looked up and down the street; not a single person or car in sight. "In a residential neighborhood?" The area was zoned for single and multi-family homes with no exemptions for livestock.

"Miss January 'found it' — " Mac made air quotes. " — and walked it home. It took Score longer than usual to sleep off his drunk, so she went for a walk alone. You know she shouldn't be allowed off the property by herself."

"Can you hurry the story along?" Fab elbowed Mac in the back. "I'm hungry too."

Miss January is/was an original tenant who'd been handed down by my aunt, who'd inherited her from the first owner. She looked eighty but was actually half that age. A tear-jerking life did that to the woman, helped along by being an alcoholic with cancer. The doctors had given her a date with death, but she'd failed to RSVP.

Her boyfriend, Score, also a drunk, actually looked his age: a few years short of ninety. He was another "find" of Miss January, who brought him home one day from a walk on the beach.

She'd whispered to me, "We're perfect for one another — we like to drink and have sex."

To my credit, I managed to make some appropriate noise; it was one of those times I was at a loss for a more fitting response.

I surveyed the property. The cottages reserved for tourists were once again filled, each with a rental car parked in its assigned space. All was calm, which could be very deceiving. Two drunks getting in a fight over which one would get the last swig of the bottle could break out in a hot second, as past experience had proven. Not a single head pushed between the wooden blinds that covered the windows, so the horse had thus far gone unnoticed.

"Miss January strolled up the driveway and tossed me the reins, telling me she needed a cigarette." Mac inclined her head towards the porch, where Miss January lay slumped in a chair. "She had one in her mouth but had forgotten to light it. The horse and I followed her to the door, where she sat down and fell asleep. I took the smoke from her mouth and put it in her pocket, and fished out the matches and kept them for myself. I figured when she sobered up some, she'd have to find another pack of matches, lessening the chances of something accidentally catching on fire, like her muumuu."

"I suggest *you* get rid of it." Fab nudged me and pointed to the horse. "Before it uses your property as a bathroom. One other thing, I quit. The pay sucks, and I don't have animal skills except for my cat."

"That's *my* cat," I said.

The four of us turned at the sound of a car taking the corner too fast and bouncing into the driveway. The horse had come up behind Mac and nudged her shoulder; she reached up and patted his mane. Another qualification for her resume—horse rapport.

Deputy Kevin Cory slammed the door of his patrol car. "Which one of you stole the horse?" he demanded. Sneer in place, he'd perfected a tight-ass look.

His blondish hair, was slicked straight back, unlike its usual off-duty, windblown style. The only plus to Kevin being in uniform was that it showed off his muscular backside. In addition to being good friends with my brother, which had come about when Brad started dating Kevin's sister, he'd recently became a full-time tenant of The Cottages. His previous residence, a duplex, erupted in flames due to a drug-cooking explosion in the neighbor's unit and everything had burned to a crisp.

"None of us." I forced a half-smile that wasn't even remotely friendly. "Miss January found it and here it is. Don't you think you should be a little nicer to your landlord?"

Brad had graciously let Kevin move into my property before informing me, knowing I wasn't rude enough to tell him to get out after he'd unpacked his newly purchased bag of clothing. My brother found it amusing that my name always appeared at the top of Kevin's suspect list when a crime got committed. I secretly got a perverse kick out of the fact that the address that garnered the most police calls in the Cove was the one he now called home.

"The horse was used in the robbery of a liquor store." He struggled to control his irritation.

The three of us laughed.

"I'm going to need to question Miss January," he said, glaring at us.

"Good luck." I pointed to her porch. "She's passed-out drunk. And when you first wake her, she has a tendency to not make any sense. Then she either comes around or goes back to sleep."

"You're enjoying this, aren't you?" His lips pursed in a hard line.

"She mentioned you the other day, told me, 'he's such a nice young man...and hot.'"

Fab and Mac snickered.

"I'm sure she'd love to be dragged from her stupor and grilled about things that she won't have any answers for," I said.

"Did you get a description of the robber?" Fab asked Kevin.

"We've got him in custody. The dogs sniffed

him out behind a dumpster."

"Well good, you got your man and your horse." I turned and walked towards the pool.

Rounding the corner, I came face to face with Professor Crum's chest. Fab and Mac skidded to a stop. Crum was another tenant gift from my brother.

Over a year ago, I had acquired a rundown trailer park. The presence of its only tenant—the professor—had served to keep the squatters out. My first choice was to bulldoze the property, but my brother had other plans. Brad undertook the renovation, turning it into a tourist destination and selling it for a tidy profit. He felt bad when the new owners had made Crum's eviction a condition of the deal. The retired college professor didn't project the right image for their property, probably because the man constantly strutted around in tighty-whities and changed shoes depending on the occasion; for gardening, he chose a dingy pair of mismatched flip-flops.

"Hello, ladies." He gave us a sweeping bow, a garden trowel in one hand. He stood at over six feet, ramrod stiff, with a butch haircut, and a condescending look he had perfected firmly in place.

"Those plants aren't stolen are they?" I pointed to a couple of containers lying in the dirt.

He'd replaced the last gardener by showing up and doing the work. There were no other applicants, and surprisingly, he did a good job.

Who would have guessed that, in addition to his off-the-chart IQ, he had a green thumb?

"How many times do I have to tell you? I don't steal." He looked down his nose at me.

"You and I both know that digging up and relocating plants from someone else's yard is stealing." I lowered my voice. "We've got a sheriff's deputy living here now, and it would amuse him to put you in jail, especially since he didn't take it well when you informed him he was dumber than a stump."

"He's clearly the product of an inferior part of the gene pool," Crum insisted.

Fab laughed, and I wanted to poke her but she stepped out of range.

"How did Kevin get in here anyway?" Crum asked.

"The same way you did," I said in exasperation. "Snuck in by my brother when my back was turned. For familial reasons, I'm trying to warm up to Kevin. You, I have a slight affection for already, but don't think you'll use that to get anything over on me."

Fab looked up at Crum. "Give us the highlights version of what's going on around here, so we can go home and guzzle tequila."

The thought of a margarita—rocks, salt and lime—had me closing my eyes and letting out a small sigh of pleasure. Before we left the driveway, I needed to place a takeout order from my bar.

Crum pointed to the two-story building next door. "Told Huck to stop peeing out the bathroom window."

"The exhibitionist?" I almost snorted. Nothing that man did surprised me.

When I first moved in, I'd asked a few questions of the owner of the building next door and found out that Huck had a perfectly good bathroom with a working toilet. And still he peed out the window. The landlord didn't care— Huck was doing his part to save water.

"Huck's been doing that since I took over." I glanced up at the second floor unit. "What could we plant on this side of the fence to block the view?" I asked Crum. "One of the recent guests complained. She was afraid she might get urine in her hair. I reassured her that, having seen him in action, that wasn't possible."

We catered year-round to tourists from different countries. They came for the warm, beautiful days and nights and blue-green waters, where you could splash mid-calf deep and still see your toes. Returning guests hoped for a little excitement: an arrest, a fight, or the occasional local girl who'd tumble naked into the pool, which the men in particular enjoyed seeing.

Crum craned his neck, scoping out the property, then lowered his voice. "You don't need to worry about Kevin. Since our discussion, he doesn't hang around much. Too busy banging his flavor of the moment at her place. Also, Julie is sneaking around, trying to hide from Liam that she's shagging your brother."

Liam was the only child of Julie, Brad's girlfriend. Mother and I were crazy about the teenager and considered him to be the first grandchild/nephew.

I shook my head. "He's a teenager; he knows what's going on."

"Let's go," Fab said, coming up behind me. She pulled on my arm. "A horse trailer just pulled up."

Chapter Three

Fab pulled into my driveway and slid the Hummer in next to her black Mercedes. When I first met her, she'd traded her cars in regularly, like a pair of shoes she'd grown bored with. But she'd had this particular model for a while, mostly because she drove my Hummer instead.

I'd inherited the two-story white Key West-style home, with its wraparound veranda, from Aunt Elizabeth. Growing up, my brother and I would come and spend our summer vacations playing under the sun. Elizabeth and I would shop all the local nurseries for a variety of tropical plants, mostly hibiscuses. I'd added my own touch once the house was mine, filling the inner courtyard with brightly colored pots, adding more flowers and mulching with seashells from many afternoons scouring the beach.

"I wonder what's up?" I'd skimmed the street when we pulled up, noticing that my brother's and both our boyfriends' vehicles were parked in the street.

"They're working on a super-secret real estate deal."

"I'd ask how you know that, but I already know the answer, you eavesdropper."

Fab pulled the clip from her hair and shook out her long brown hair, letting it fall down her back. "You're just annoyed you don't have the same sneak-around skills I do."

"You've already taught me to pick locks and hotwire cars, but you'll have to have another seminar. I'll invite Mother; she wouldn't want to miss out on anything to do with sneaking around."

Fab opened the front door, and I wiggled in front of her. "Didier, she hit me," she yelled.

I rolled my eyes and grabbed at her, coming up with air as she skated across the kitchen into the arms of her tall, dark-haired, blue-eyed, flawless boyfriend, a highly sought-after male model with only a first name.

"I saw the whole thing," Brad said. "Madison used to do that to me as a kid." He held my long-haired black cat in his arms, spoiling him with a treat that he offered in the palm of his hand. Jazz, who was twenty going on a hundred, took a cautious sniff, then wolfed it down.

My brother was the only fair-haired man in the room, more "boy next door" than anything that smacked of the disreputable. Over six feet, like the other two, he was tanned and brawny from hours spent on the water as a commercial fisherman.

"Damn, no girl brawl?" Creole snapped his fingers.

Creole, AKA Luc Baptiste, was my boyfriend and was sometimes snidely referred to as my cousin, as my aunt had unofficially adopted him as a kid, offering him shelter from an abusive father. The tallest of the bunch, with shoulder-length dark hair, he stood at the kitchen island with his arms crossed and a smirk on his lips.

I dropped my bags on the entry bench and walked into his outstretched arms.

"How was your day, honey?" His deep-blue eyes sparkled with amusement.

He'd ditched his work uniform of ratty blue jeans for shorts and a t-shirt that stretched across his rock-hard abs. As an undercover drug cop, blending in with the seedier element required that he seldom wore shoes. Today, he'd donned boat shoes, showing off his long, tanned legs.

Fab rushed over, hugging me. "I forgive you," she said, then whispered in my ear, "Don't mention the shooting."

I flashed her an evil stare; she knew I hated to keep things from Creole—most of the time, anyway.

Creole pulled me back against his chest. His arms around my waist, he leaned down and whispered, "What's she up to now?"

I looked up into his eyes, happy he was here. "Let's sneak out the patio doors and go make out on the beach."

The kitchen area blended into the living room, making the downstairs area a large open space with a wall of windows running along the back and French doors that opened onto the patio and pool. I'd made few changes inside: adding a coat of fresh paint, rearranging the furniture, and trying to prevent myself from over-accessorizing. All family events were held at my house, as I had the most room and the largest outdoor entertaining space.

The patio had been my personal stamp on the house. I hired a contractor to build an outdoor kitchen with plenty of storage and comfortable seating, which was a high priority. I'd finished the counter top myself, with small seashells for the finishing touch. Brad had contributed a large barbecue that could cook up delicious, aromatic food...if only one knew how to turn it on.

On the left side of the yard, an opening in the side fence led to a pathway and a set of steps that ended on the white, sandy beach a short walk from the shoreline. It had been overgrown with knee-high weeds, but once cleared, the shortcut to the beach was a welcome surprise. Now the small area was filled with brick pavers.

All eyes turned to the garden window over the kitchen sink as a woman with long blond hair wiggled by, a shopping bag in each hand. Phil, the bartender at Jake's, had offered to deliver our takeout order on her way home.

Brad had the door open before Phil could

knock, and she strode right in, setting everything on the counter.

"Thanks for the delivery. You're the best," I said.

"Just kissing up to the boss." She waved to everyone.

Most people who knew Philipa Grey, a curvaceous young woman in short-shorts, also knew that she was a third-year law school student. The real secret was that she ran a side business selling information. Her street sources could be depended on to get the kind of dirt that local law enforcement couldn't coax out of anyone. She and her associates located people reluctant to be found and got them to talk. For an extra fee, they would force a sit-down meeting. Phil always managed to stay under the radar, never attracting unwanted attention. In my experience, she delivered what she promised, which was why Fab and I called her instead of our unreliable street snitches, who traded info for cigarettes.

While Phil took the containers out of the bags, I grabbed plates and silverware. With a shuffling of the stools, there was enough room for all of us, including Phil to sit around the island. My brother got out an assortment of beers—none of the guys could agree on the same brand—and Creole had the blender going for margaritas while Fab's favorite vodka appeared on the counter.

A pounding on the front door brought the activity to a halt. Fab jerked open the junk drawer and grabbed the Beretta that was inside. It sounded to me like a cop knock, which I'd mastered a long time ago. Creole nodded to Brad, who checked the peephole, then turned and shrugged, opening the door.

Kevin crossed the threshold. He never showed up at the house in uniform unless he was on official business. *Now what?* I thought. *Wait until Creole hears about the horse.* I wanted to laugh, but Kevin looked serious.

Kevin stalked into the kitchen, skipped the pleasantries, and ordered, "Didier, would you step outside."

Fab had slipped the gun back into the drawer when Kevin set foot in the house, but she jumped in front of Didier. "I don't think so. What do you want?"

Creole spoke up, his mouth a firm line. "What's going on, Kevin?"

Didier shook his head. "Good question."

"Hands behind your back," Kevin ordered. "You're wanted for the murder of Lauren Grace."

Didier's eyebrows shot up. "Murder?"

The man wasn't a cold-blooded killer, and the look of shock on his face convinced me he had no knowledge of the crime. I'd known him long enough to know he was an honorable, straight-up guy. "Doesn't Didier have the option of telling you to go…stuff it?" I asked.

"I know you think you know the law, since you're always busy trying to skirt around *your* legal issues, but this piece of paper gives me the authority." He held up an official-looking document.

Fab jerked it from his fingers.

"Don't say a word," I told Didier. "I've got the best criminal lawyer in the state on speed dial. Do not speak to *anyone*," I stressed, "without speaking to Cruz Campion first." I tossed a glare at Kevin.

"This isn't cool," Brad told Kevin. "There's no other deputy on duty to make this arrest?"

Kevin, by virtue of his sister and Brad being together, had been included in family get-togethers lately. The same events that Didier had been a part of for longer than him.

Does Kevin have to look pleased when whipping out the cuffs? I thought.

Fab handed me my phone.

I eyed the screen and saw that she'd already dialed the lawyer's office. I was on hold momentarily before he picked up. "Cruz Campion," he said.

I hit the highlights, knowing he liked his information quick and to the point. Cruz only had one question when I was done. "His lawyer wants to know where you're taking him," I barked at Kevin.

"He's going to the local station. Miami is

sending an officer to pick him up," Kevin responded.

I relayed the information to Cruz. "No talking to anyone until you talk to your lawyer," I called out as Kevin cuffed Didier and led him out the door, Creole right behind.

The trio passed the window, Creole talking to Didier. He gave him a pat on the back when they reached the patrol car. I knew he was reassuring Didier that he and I would use every connection between us to make sure he didn't end up in jail and, if the worst happened, that I had bail connections. Creole would be the biggest help since he worked directly for the Miami Chief of Police and if…well, Creole could get Didier jail perks.

Fab's hands shot out in front of her as she demanded, "Who the hell is Lauren Grace?"

Brad shot a look at Didier, still standing in the driveway, before answering, "She's VP for the 100 Ocean Boulevard Corporation, the real estate developer of the new project we're partnering on."

Fab grabbed her keys and ran to the door. "Call me if you hear anything."

I grabbed the back of her shirt before she could disappear out the door. "Where are you going?"

"I'm going to follow Didier, so when he walks out of the police station, he'll have a ride home." Fab looked a wreck, not at all her usual calm and collected self.

I didn't bother to remind her that it might take a while. Instead, I said, "Call if you need company."

Kevin put Didier into the back of his car and, without a word to Creole, got behind the wheel and sped away.

Chapter Four

"Do you have something to write on?" Phil asked.

I'd forgotten that she had stood off to one side, listening intently. I knew that if there'd been any illegality on Kevin's part, she would have spoken up. I pointed to the junk drawer, which really should be labeled "multi-purpose," as it held a number of useful items, the Beretta, a switchblade, and the large plastic zip ties that could function as handcuffs.

To keep busy, I reclosed the lids on the takeout containers and made room for them in the refrigerator. Good thing everyone enjoyed leftovers, except Fab, who complained but ate them anyway.

"Lauren Grace." Phil scribbled. "What do you want to know?"

"Who killed her? It's not Didier; I know that much, it's not in his character," I said. "Unearth every piece of information about the deceased and her life and get a list of those who might want her dead. Hopefully the list is short."

I leaned over the sink to scan the driveway,

figuring Creole had left, but I saw him leaning against the fence as he talked on his phone. He would call in favors for his friend and cycling partner. The two of them loved to ramp up the testosterone, taking exercising to a new level, and recently, they'd included my brother in their insanity.

"Partner?" I said to myself. I locked eyes with Brad. "On what?"

"We planned to bring you up to speed tonight." He ran his fingers through his sun-bleached hair, blowing out a frustrated breath. "Didier and I started talking about working on a project together before I sold the trailer court. He got a tip about a couple of condo developments in Miami Beach that could be had for dirt cheap because the developer went bankrupt before completing them. So we put together a group of investors. You're one of them."

I shook my head and let out a sigh. "I know we discussed doing something but I didn't realize it was already in the works. Who's Lauren and how does she fit in?"

"Didier's friend Patino Balcazar is the real estate developer who gave him a heads up on the deal. Lauren is his VP. A new title; she just recently got promoted from assistant." Brad paused to finish his beer.

Patino? I thought. So there was a connection between B's—the restaurant with all the bullet holes in it—and Fab's boyfriend, and she'd kept that tidbit to herself.

Brad continued, "Nothing gets done without Lauren. She's the brains of the outfit; Balcazar doesn't get hands dirty with the details. We were in negotiations to acquire one of the bankrupt properties before it went to auction."

"Don't auctions have pesky requirements—like cash? Are we talking beachfront?" I realized I was holding my breath at the thought of how much the asking price might be and let out a whoosh of air.

Brad nodded. "With Balcazar's connections, our bid was accepted before auction. We secured financing from a short-term lender, had a lawyer read the fine print of the contracts, and were waiting for the title company to schedule a closing. Lauren was a bit abrasive and snooty, but she handled the details with extreme efficiency."

"Who's we? How many people are in this investor group?" I slurped down the last of my margarita.

"Would you like another, Boss?" Phil reached for the glass.

I put my hand over it. "You're a guest."

"It's a bad habit." She smiled.

"The group's all family: me, you, Creole, Didier, Mother, and Spoon. You do remember we talked about reinvesting the profits from the trailer court? You said you were content with being a silent partner." Brad sounded defensive.

Good riddance to the trailer park, I thought. "I trust you, and I knew that once you found something, you'd fill me in. A family affair. Are you sure you can work with all the diverse personalities?"

"Just call me ring master." Brad cracked an imaginary whip. "I like ordering people around. Most are silent partners, like yourself, and will be given regular reports and financials. No background checks necessary since we know every one." He glanced at Phil, who stopped taking notes. "I'd have wagered my..." He paused, turning red. "Only Didier and I have had dealings with Lauren. None of the others even know her, let alone have reason to kill her."

I opened the refrigerator and took out a bottled water, holding one up for Phil and raising my eyebrows in a silent question. She nodded, and I handed her the water.

"It's a bigger project than I'd originally planned and definitely required more investment capital. Truthfully, once Didier pitched the idea, I didn't want to be left out. It was a big ego boost to find out that I could contribute more than brawn." Brad flexed his bicep. "I used old connections from when Aunt Elizabeth and I had a few business deals going to arrange the financial backing we needed."

"Elizabeth would be very proud of you." I thought of the woman who had changed all our lives. She'd known how to bring out the best in each of us, and because of her, I'd found out I could hold my own in a tight situation. "How is this partnership going to work? Once the deal closes, who takes on the responsibility of construction? The *silent* partners just sit back and rake in the profits?" That seemed out of balance to me.

"Didier and I are going to be general contractors on the deal. We've already lined up sub-contractors through Spoon's connections. Creole offered up brawn. All of us but Didier have a background in construction, and we'll soon toughen up those callous-free hands of his."

"I'm available anytime," I said. "I can't sling a hammer with finesse, but I can be on hand to check in shipments and run errands." My ex-husband and I had flipped several houses, and I had learned a lot about how to be useful.

"We'll want you for decorator decisions."

"My taste runs more to beach casual than waterfront high-rise chic. But I'll start looking for a decorator, a name with cachet that will look good on the marketing materials."

I shook my head when Brad held out a plate. It surprised me that either Brad or Phil had an appetite; my stomach had gotten queasy when Kevin showed up and stayed that way.

"What evidence could the police possibly have that would give them cause to arrest Didier?" I asked.

Brad shook his head. "No clue. Didier's a

straight-up guy. The man I know would never murder anyone. He told me that he and Balcazar have been friends for a few years; they were introduced through mutual friends in South Beach during Didier's rise to fame." He drained the last of his beer. "Lauren informed us that she'd gotten our offer moved to the top of the list for consideration with the bank representative and indicated that the bank was salivating to make a deal and get the property off their balance sheet. The bid process went faster than we expected; the bank seemed to be on top of it and accepted our offer rather quickly."

I eyed Phil, who sat in silence, taking in every word and making the occasional note. "Find out everything you can about Lauren, Balcazar, and 100 Ocean Boulevard." I took the notepad from Phil and pushed it at Brad. "Write down all the phone numbers you have for them."

He tapped the pen against the notepad as he flipped through his phone. "I've got a couple of phone numbers here for the business." He began writing on the pad.

"Are the company's name and address one and the same?"

"Yes, and Balcazar owns the building. You're not going break in, are you?" He frowned at me.

I crossed my arms and scowled at him. "How am I supposed to perfect my burglary skills if no one will let me practice?"

"Thank goodness that little French spitfire

keeps you out of trouble. For the most part, anyway."

"Fab's the funnest friend I've ever had."

Brad and Phil laughed.

"Find out what evidence the police have on Didier," I told Phil.

Creole slammed the front door. "I've got Harder making discreet inquiries. Kevin just got the call that he'll be the one transporting Didier to Miami for questioning."

Chief Harder was Creole's boss, and they swapped favors on a regular basis.

Creole opened the refrigerator, grabbing a beer. "Cruz has already been in contact with the district attorney and will meet Didier at the station." He smiled at me. "Harder grouched that Cruz doesn't take *his* phone calls as fast as he does yours."

"Ask the chief what's in it for the lawyer. If it's nothing, then there's his answer," I said.

Cruz Campion— "lawyer extraordinaire," his billboards boasted, —had helped me out of more than one difficult situation. In return, I entertained his visiting family members at The Cottages and had Mac put on her trip-planner hat and arrange sight-seeing adventures and reservations for local restaurants. Once word spread through his extended family about the occasional shooting, brawl, or arrest, they came for the entertainment.

Creole grabbed me into a bear hug. "I'm going

in to the office, just in case anything happens and Didier needs a friend. Give Brick a call and give him a heads up that bail money might be needed; he'd better come through, and at a reasonable rate. Tell him I said that if he doesn't, neither you nor Fab will take another one of his crappy jobs."

Fab had worked for Brick since long before she met me and still did on an on-call basis. One of the perks? A flashy car for her to drive. Not me. I'd bought my Hummer through Brick and paid cash, holding out for the used car discount. That way, I had the option to turn down jobs.

I had worked for him for a time to obtain my private investigator's license. On most jobs, I was assigned a backup role, but since most of his cases degenerated into an exchange of bullets, my good aim with a Glock was an asset.

Creole nodded to Brad. "Make sure your sister doesn't get in any trouble until I get back."

Brad groaned. "Why me? Madison's the sneaky one. Growing up, she was always the instigator."

"You had a few shining moments of your own, bro. Remember when you stole the blinking traffic sign and hooked it to the bumper? You're lucky the Chief of Police's son in the car when you and your posse got hauled in."

"Mother picked me up at the police station and chain smoked all the way home. Didn't utter a syllable to me for a week."

My brother and I laughed. It was a rare

instance when mother went silent, as she preferred heaping on the guilt through long, torturous lectures, during which, to make sure we heard her, she repeated herself frequently.

Creole took my hand and hauled me to the front door. "Keep your phone close; I'll be calling and talking dirty to you later. Hang in there—I've got a long weekend coming up, and I have plans for just the two of us."

"You'll be looking for a murderer." I grimaced and wrapped my arms around him.

"Is that a step up from rousting drug dealers?" he chuckled.

He bent his head and kissed me firmly, teasing, coaxing a response, and I leaned in and kissed him back. I wanted the kiss to remind me for the rest of the day of what was to come when we had that promised alone time.

"Thank you for using your connections," I whispered against his lips.

"Didier's family. He'd help any of us if he could."

Chapter Five

The only sound that could be heard were the birds chirping outside the window; new babies insistent upon being fed. I woke up by myself and lay in bed, listening for anyone moving around and trying to smell coffee brewing, which would be impossible since my door was closed. The house was eerily silent. I jumped up and hustled into the shower. I finished in record time, threw on my favorite black t-shirt dress, grabbed my phone and Glock, and headed out the door to The Cottages. Fab would call when there was news, good or bad.

On my way, I detoured across the highway and whizzed through the coffee shop drive-thru, picking up my favorite latte. I had them add extra whipped cream and caramel. With no traffic, I made good time and rocketed into the first available parking space, in front of the cottage next to the entrance, which currently didn't have a guest. I peeked around the side of the unit before dashing across the driveway, not wanting to be forced into chitchat before my coffee. I entered the code to the security gate, a new addition to keep out uninvited passersby, and entered the empty pool area. After kicking off my flip-flops, I plopped down at the top of the steps, slipped my feet into the warm water, then lifted the lid on my cup and savored the aroma before taking a much-needed sip.

Mac had called earlier and mumbled that she'd be in late, giving a vague excuse about an appointment, which she didn't want to discuss. She'd been secretive of late. I was sure it wasn't anything illegal; she'd assured me once that she had an aversion to going to jail. She'd visited a friend there a time or two but didn't want to take up residence and therefore never did anything to risk making it happen.

When I inherited The Cottages, I jumped into the manager's role with the eagerness of a person who had no clue what the position entailed. It didn't take long to realize that I was ill-suited for the job, so I hired someone else to handle it and got busy doing what I enjoyed — overseeing much-needed updates and clearing out overgrown foliage.

The pool showed signs of use from the previous night. I finished off my coffee, stepped out of the water, and started dragging chaises back into place. With an annoyed sigh, I fished a chair out of the pool with the leaf catcher and wiped down the bar area. I tossed a couple of beach towels, which had been left behind in a chair, over next to the gate.

"Dumb bitch," floated across the driveway in

an angry male voice.

I slipped into my flip-flops and quietly unlatched the pool gate, slipping between two cottages where I could see the driveway without being seen.

Julie Cory, a tenant and my brother's girlfriend, struggled in the arms of an oversized man. One of his beefy hands was clamped across the petite blonde's mouth as he dragged her to the door of her cottage. She'd gone limp, and the toes of her shoes scraped the ground. Her lack of cooperation had him frustrated, and he continued to spew a litany of curse words.

"Get your grimy hands off her," I yelled, clearing the distance between them and me until I stood a dozen feet away.

He turned and dropped one hand from her mouth, but the other maintained a firm grip on her arm. "Mind your own business," he snarled, his eyes giving me the once-over.

Before he could blink, I pulled my Glock from behind my back, having drawn it from my thigh holster before I approached, and pointed it between his eyes. "Let. Go. Now. I'm a damn good shot; I can put a bullet right between those beady eyes of yours."

"I'm not as good a shot as her." Mac came around the other side of the building from the direction of the office. "But I always hit my target...somewhere," she promised, her Beretta pointed at him.

He shoved Julie away, and she struggled to stay on her feet.

"Call the sheriff," I said to Mac over my shoulder.

"No," Julie yelped. "This is just a misunderstanding. Striker is an old friend. You can put your gun away."

"I don't think so." I mimicked Fab's creepy smile for Striker's benefit. "He's not *my* friend. What he's doing is trespassing on my property. Striker, word of warning, you come back here again and I'll shoot you."

"Ohhh… I'm scared." He gyrated.

I dismissed shooting at his feet to watch him dance. "You familiar with the name Jimmy Spoon?" There were perks to throwing Mother's boyfriend's name around.

His suddenly rounded eyes gave me my answer and let me know that he must be a local or have lived in the Cove in the past.

"Julie's under his protection." I wrinkled my nose as though he smelled. Bad. "Think about that before you come skulking around again. I won't have to waste a bullet. One word from me, and you'll disappear. Spoon takes family seriously, and it won't be pretty."

The last sentence definitely caught him off guard.

Striker jerked Julie back to his side and whispered something. She nodded, and he let her go.

"You're trying my patience," I told him.

He looked ready to spit nails but must have had some sense, since he turned and stalked down the driveway without a word. I didn't hear a car start up, which meant he was another shiftless local, but how did Julie know him?

Mac followed him to the road to see which direction he went. She'd wait a few minutes to see if he doubled back to throw us off his trail. She knew her criminals.

Maybe this situation would soften Julie's feelings towards me. She didn't approve of my partnership with Fab, thinking we stirred up situations more than we helped. Mostly, she didn't want her teenage son, Liam, to think it was cool to chase bad guys. However, judging by her demeanor, there wouldn't be any bonding over this situation.

"I could've handled this," Julie said, hands on her hips. "We need to keep this between the two of us." She glared at me.

Brad would flip if one of us didn't tell him.

I counted to three before answering. "If you break my brother's heart for the likes of someone like him—" I tossed a glance in the direction of the street. "—I will kick your ass."

Surprised by my threat, she said, "Striker is an old boyfriend, and he's disappointed that I've moved on. He understands the situation and won't be bothering me again."

Baloney. I did a mental eye roll. "Next time

someone grabs you, I suggest you kick, scream, bite, and put up the fight of your life. Once he gets you inside a car or house, all bets are off and you're at a severe disadvantage that usually doesn't bode well."

"He wouldn't hurt me."

"He already did." I pointed to the finger impressions on her arms. "Striker will be back; he didn't get whatever it was he wanted. I suggest you be on the lookout. You have to tell Brad. I can't keep it from him; it would be bad for our relationship. Trust me, this will come out sooner or later."

"Oh please!" she snorted. "You keep things from Brad all the time. I can take care of this myself, and at least no one will get hurt."

"The secret-keeping days are over. When I promised months ago to keep him in the loop, I meant it. I keep my promises."

Julie blew out her frustration. "All right, all right, I'll tell him. But not one word to Liam!"

"You're a great mother. Have you thought what might happen if Striker shows back up and Liam's the only one home?"

She paled despite her suntan.

"You have my number. Fab and I would do anything to help you. Or you can call if you just need a sounding board."

Mac came trudging up, her handgun tucked away somewhere under her voluminous ankle-length white ruffled skirt. She'd stuffed her double-sized friends into an electric-blue, glittery t-shirt that appeared to be straining at the seams. When she stopped next to us, her green garden clogs started tapping impatiently on the pavement.

"Your friend," Mac said to Julie, "went left and then looped over to the dead-end. He looked this way before using the public path to the street. We both waved, my gesture friendlier than his."

Generally, only locals knew about the neighborhood short cuts.

The Cottages were part of a several-block residential neighborhood. Most of the residences were owned by investors or out-of-state landlords and handled by the vacation rental businesses that were now on every other corner.

"I've got a gig to get to," Julie said. "Don't worry. Striker is harmless."

"Another cartoon?" I asked.

She nodded, clearly annoyed with me.

Julie supported herself and Liam as a voice-over actress specializing in animation, and often entertained the family with a wide range of different voices. She'd gotten so popular, she had bookings nearly every day. It surprised me that she continued to live at The Cottages when she'd expressed a desire to move several times and now had the money to do it, but having her brother living here and Brad staying in whatever empty unit was available must have changed her mind.

"Have fun." I linked my arm through Mac's, and we headed in the direction of the office until a shrill whistle brought us to an abrupt halt.

Chapter Six

Joseph waved his arms, staggering from the opposite end of the driveway and acting like he'd gotten his drunk on early. He was another inherited tenant from my aunt and, like Miss January, had been given a signed death warrant by his doctors. He suffered from cancer and a variety of ailments, and also like Miss January, he thumbed his nose at them and overindulged in cigarettes and liquor. Lately, he'd started to look a tad healthier. Ignoring his expiration date, he'd even put a few pounds on his boney frame.

I started in his direction, but Mac jerked my arm. "Oh no you don't. You're not going anywhere without me. I'm listening in."

"Did you get his girlfriend back from the doctor?" I asked.

"That's another thing I deserve a raise for. I boxed Svetlana up and shipped her to Los Angeles. Martin at the doll hospital assured me that if he couldn't patch her thigh like new, he'd cut off her leg and give her a new one."

Joseph had inherited the rubber doll from a friend, she came with a complete wardrobe and shoes. Another of his friends, mad because he

45

wouldn't share, deliberately burned a hole in the sexy blonde's leg. Svet had a positive effect on his surly attitude. There had been a time when he'd wanted to marry her, and when he got turned down by the court clerk and a couple preachers in town, he went into a funk and went back to hardcore drinking.

Mac continued, "You had to pay extra to jump to the top of the list and get expedited service. Apparently Dr. Martin has a waiting list for his talent." She grimaced at the thought. "But it was worth it. Svet just came back, and Joseph's been all smiles. I forgave him for moping the whole time she was gone and frankly for acting like a prick."

"Did you actually call him that?" I asked.

"Heck yes, and his response was, 'I get called that every other day.'"

"What's up?" I asked Joseph as we came to a stop in front of the fold-up beach chair he'd dragged out into the driveway. "Happy to see you're not in jail."

Joseph had cut back on his felonious activity when I cut off the twenty-four hour jail pickup service and made him wait until business hours for a ride home. It limited his options to walking or taking a snooze in the bushes.

"Striker's a bad dude," he said in a stage whisper that the neighbors could hear. "Hope you're not renting to him."

I shook my head. *That's all I need.* "How does

he know Julie?" I asked.

Joseph had his ear to the street, and if he wanted to find out information about people, he could, especially the low-life element. But he couldn't be depended on to produce in a timely fashion and not cop an attitude, or worse, sell you out to a higher bidder.

He looked around as though he expected someone to be eavesdropping. Seeing no one milling about, he continued, "Those two dated a long time ago, long before your brother. Striker got arrested for trying to buy drugs from an undercover cop. He got free room and board for a couple of years—end of romance." He brushed his hands together. "He just got released. Probably won't take him long to get sent back to prison since it's like a second home. He's one of those guys that can only stay out of trouble for a short time and then gets sent back. He needs the structure."

I breathed a sigh of relief, knowing that Creole had had nothing to do with any of his arrests. He'd moved back to the Cove long after Striker was incarcerated. Besides, he didn't deal with the bottom of the food chain. He worked the middle, which made it more likely he could get seriously hurt or worse. I tried not to think about the danger that surrounded his job.

Joseph downed his beer and stomped on the can, throwing it through his open door onto the living room floor. "Striker has a heavy hand with the ladies, if you know what I mean. He speaks, expects the woman to dance, and if not, he gets real mean. So be careful."

"You're being nice." I eyed him and didn't feel guilty for thinking he wanted something. "How are you and the professor getting along?"

"He told me that I was a dim-wit and added that that was being generous." Joseph snorted. "Just wait, he'll want something, and I'll slam the door in his face. I will admit that I admire that he can bag a woman in his underwear."

"Don't even think about wandering around half-dressed. We now have a dress code — pants, shorts, or skirt. Mac has informed him of the new rules and *anyone* caught breaking it moves." I gestured to the street.

"Don't get all worked up, thinking I'm going to be a copycat. I'm not putting my treasure on display like that. Sorry ladies, I gotta to pee." He went inside, slamming the door behind him.

"At least he didn't do it in the bushes," Mac whispered as we headed back towards the office.

"The last tenant that did that killed my flowers," I grumbled.

"Joseph is right about one thing, the professor brought some painfully thin... ah... older woman back the other night. She was wearing a fifties polka dot full-skirt dress. I wouldn't mind one myself, but I think it would make my butt look big."

I bit my lip, controlling the laugh that

threatened to burst out. How would a fifties dress fit into her retro-hippie look?

"For an old gal, she rocked those four-inch heels, but the hat...someone needed to tell her that the flowers and bird on the brim were a bit much. She clung to his arm, giggling. I got the impression she'd already sampled his... um... goods."

"Did anyone die?" I asked, not wanting to think about his, or anyone's, goods.

She sucked in a breath. "I would've been hot on the phone if that had happened."

"I probably don't say it enough, but I appreciate you."

"Ha," she snorted. "I love my job, and I'm not going anywhere. I never got to pull my gun at my last place of employment."

"If you want to show me your appreciation, you could fix me up with one of Creole or Didier's friends."

Her innocent smile made me give her a second look. "When are you going to tell me what's going on with you? Did you kick your husband to the curb?"

She looked momentarily sad, then replaced it with her contagious smile. "I haven't told Shirl; she has to be the first. Best friend and all. Then I'll tell you."

Shirl, another tenant, had come to The Cottages temporarily after an ugly breakup with her boyfriend. A highly respected registered nurse at Cove Hospital, she'd just been promoted and hadn't been around much lately. She'd become the cottage nurse, and with her easy manner, the tenants and guests loved her. She too had been banned from ever moving out.

"Call anytime." I climbed into the Hummer and waved.

Chapter Seven

Carrying my heels in one hand, I descended the stairs and dumped my shoes in the entryway.

Mother sat at the kitchen island smoking a cigar, Fab waving the smoke in the direction of the living room. She and Didier stood at the island, coffee in hand. The man knew how to rock a suit; he looked delicious in all black. Fab, also in all black, had on a short dress with cap sleeves.

I pecked Didier's cheek, reaching for a coffee mug. "Mornings wouldn't be the same without your pretty face." I smiled at him. "Get your own cell? The uniforms are ugly," I scrunched my nose, "but they have matching shoes."

He smiled back at me. "I was in a holding cell, praying they wouldn't call my name and order me into more permanent accommodation. Thank you for getting me the lawyer. Cruz says I'm a huge step up from your usual referrals. He's damn good; he talked with me privately and then had me answer all the questions the detectives put to me. They release me with certain conditions, which I readily agreed to."

Fab hugged him. "Don't worry, we'll keep you out of jail."

"It's times like these you find out what kind of friends you have—and I have the best." Didier brushed her cheek with his lips.

"He also can't leave town." Fab winked up at him.

He looked at her with such love in his eyes that I had to look away. Just giving them some privacy, I told myself. "You know smoking is not allowed in my house." I frowned at Mother and opened the side panels in the garden window.

Mother ground out her hand-rolled Cuban in an ashtray that she must have brought with her. Her dark-brown eyes scowled at me. "Why did I have to hear from Spoon that Didier got arrested?"

"Fab…" I turned to her and dropped onto a barstool.

She glared at me, letting me know she didn't appreciate being thrown under the bus. I tried not to laugh at her discomfort; she hated being on the hot seat with Mother. "Today's the funeral for Lauren," she told Mother. "I planned on stopping by afterwards to take you out for lunch and tell you all about it. It's been a hectic couple of days." Fab turned to me. "How come you're dressed in black?"

"I'm coming along. You need someone to schmooze with the mourners. You know you don't do friendly."

"I can do friendly," said Mother raising her hand. She'd obviously known all along about the funeral, as she was also dressed in black, her blond bob in place, eyes sparkling. She also knew that no one would be rude enough to tell her she couldn't crash the funeral in the company of her daughter.

Didier laughed and put his arm around Mother, giving her a hug. "I love all of you, but you need to stay out of this. My hotshot lawyer has hired an investigator."

Fab, hands on hips, rattled off something in French.

"As usual, I don't know what she said. Are you familiar with the phrase 'fat chance'?" I asked Didier. "Friends help friends."

Fab huffed and tossed her hair. "I called Raul this morning and asked if he had any connections at that snotty funeral home in Miami, and he did. He's going to call his friend and get us as much information as he can. Didier forbid me to break in and search the records myself."

I winked at her. "Good idea, though."

Fab and I had a good relationship with the owners of the local funeral home, Tropical Slumber. Dickie and Raul could always be depended on to sleuth out information from the coroner and their competition. Who knew funeral directors were a close-knit bunch?

"You two need to stay out of trouble." Didier shook his finger at us. "I'll tell Creole."

"That's not a very good threat; I tell Creole everything. We share, starting with 'How was your day, honey?'"

"We'll be out past curfew; we're staying overnight in Miami," Fab informed me.

"I'll ride with Madison," Mother said. "Spoon's coming back tonight, and he can pick me up here."

"While you two mourn the deceased, Mother and I will play girl spies. You wouldn't threaten to tell on Mother to Spoon, would you?" I eyed Didier.

He groaned.

* * *

Memorial Park sat in the middle of the city of Miami, with not a whiff of an ocean breeze on this hot, humid day. The service was held in a non-descript chapel, the stained glass window the only stand-out. Mother and I sat in an uncomfortable pew at the back and people-watched. There wasn't a vacant seat in sight. Most of the people in attendance were well-dressed, in expensive suits and dresses with lots of gold and bling, unlike at a beach funeral, where they gave new meaning to casual.

The service had been short. One person strode to the podium to read his prepared remarks, which sounded impersonal, then everyone adjourned to the graveside. A short line formed, and roses were handed out to drop on the closed casket. Once again, Mother and I hovered in the back. I had no intention of participating.

Mother poked me in the side and motioned for me to get in line. "Go," she hissed. "You would if you'd ever met her."

My stomach grumbled, reminding me that I preferred to attend funerals at Tropical Slumber, where they served food. A free sandwich or two is a good way to loiter and make small talk.

Mother and I walked by Fab, who wiped the corner of her eye and smirked.

"Don't throw the rose," Mother whispered. "Lay it on top, all nice like."

"How do you know this stuff?" I asked, crossing the manicured lawn to say my good-byes, thankful it was a closed casket.

"At my age, people die." Mother looked younger than her sixty years, her blond bob now windblown and looking sassy and flirty, her knee-length dress showing off her long, tan legs. Since she'd started dating a younger man, she looked fit and better than ever.

I leaned over and kissed her cheek. "Well, you're forbidden to have any thoughts of your own demise. I'll always need you around."

"I wish your father could see you now, that you and your brother have grown into fine adults."

Brad and I were devastated when Father died in our early teen years. Mother, in her usual style, jumped in and became both parents, holding our family together.

"He knows." I smiled at her. "Dad and Elizabeth are watching out for us and our happiness."

"We should split up," Mother said in my ear, after we'd laid our roses on the casket. "We'll work the outer edges, where the loners like to hide. What kind of questions are we asking?"

"Pretend the deceased is someone we know, make vague comments about the loss of a dear friend." I brushed a lock of Mother's hair behind her ear. "Pay attention for inappropriate responses, anyone acting odd; you know, the ones you wouldn't think would normally act that way. We're looking for a chatty co-worker of Lauren's. Try to avoid questions like 'did you murder her or know who did?'"

Mother and I separated and went in opposite directions. I homed in on an unremarkable-looking young man doing his best to go unnoticed. His shaggy brown hair hung in greasy clumps, his expensive suit jacket and wrinkled khaki pants didn't even remotely go together, and the ensemble was finished off with scuffed, cheap shoes.

"Sad about Lauren." I frowned and sidled up next to him.

"Female?" He looked confused. "Yeah, I

didn't… Yes, very sad." His eyes flitted around the grassy area, and he looked ready to bolt.

I ditched the niceties. "If you didn't know the deceased, why are you here?"

"Keep your voice down," he shushed. He tugged on the sleeves of his jacket, casting an eye around before looking at the ground. "This is my job. I'm a paid mourner," he said in a voice barely above a whisper.

"Pay well?"

"It's part-time, and I need the work." He reached into his pants pocket, taking out his keys.

"How many of these people are professional mourners?"

He toed the grass, kicking up a small divot. "Half maybe. We're forbidden to disclose any details, including anything about payment."

"Did you know the deceased was murdered?" I asked.

"Eww!" He jumped back. "That's bad karma." He continued stepping backward. "Gotta go. Please don't tell anyone about me or that we talked."

Mother walked across the grass, a smirk on her face. "Did you know there are paid mourners here?" she asked when she got close enough that no one else would hear.

I was shocked that she'd found out and a little annoyed I couldn't be the first to share that little detail. "Yes, how did you find out?"

She pulled a business card out of her clutch. "I got this."

I grabbed it from her fingers and read it. "You're forbidden to call." I shoved it in my purse. "Don't give me your innocent look. This is just the kind of weirdness you and your friend Jean would sign up for. Now tell me how you got the card."

"This well-dressed woman who came solo sought me out—another woman alone, I suppose—and asked me if I knew the deceased. I told her no, that I'd come for the food."

"Really, Mother," I clucked. "Next time, we'll rehearse appropriate responses ahead of time."

"That funeral friend of yours serves food and lots of it. Anyway, the woman—Mali was her name—told me that this service is always looking to hire. The only requirement is dressing professional. She says you can wear the same outfit every time; it's not as if you're going to run into the same people."

Once you wore a black dress to a couple of funerals, it would lose its appeal for any other function. I squirmed at the idea that being a professional mourner was a career choice.

"I'm starving." I grabbed her arm. "Let's get out of here. My guess is the ones that know her are in that small group over there." I pointed to where a dozen people stood under a towering oak tree. "We won't be able infiltrate and make headway with that bunch. Looks like a high school clique—invitation only. I don't see Fab and Didier; they must have left already. Let's go snag a window table at the Crab Shack."

Chapter Eight

The baby blue sky was filled with white, fluffy clouds; a great day for a drive. And the view only got better once we hit the Keys, the whitecap waves crashing onshore on both sides of the highway — the Atlantic and the Gulf of Mexico.

The Crab Shack was a family favorite; it sat off the main highway in Tarpon Cove and overlooked the darker blue waters of the Atlantic. The restaurant was low-key, decorated in nautical décor and served the best seafood in town.

The sun shone brightly through the floor-to-ceiling windows. Mother, like daughter, would only accept a waterfront table. Before sitting down, I took a moment to enjoy the waves, which were heavier than usual, breaking on the sand below and washing up under the stilted building. I ordered drinks while Mother had a short conversation with someone on her cell.

"Who did you just ask to meet us here?" I asked after she dropped the phone back in her purse.

"Your brother. It's been a while since the three

of us got together."

I wrinkled my nose. This would be the first time I'd seen him since the incident with Striker, who, according to Mac, hadn't been back. I'd suggested that if he showed his face, she should anonymously tip off Julie's overprotective, cop brother. He tended to keep an eagle eye on his sister and nephew.

"Mother..." I winced at the whininess in my voice. "I need your advice."

"Is it too much to hope that you're going to announce that you're getting married and need my help to find a dress? I suppose you'll want to wear flip-flops." She sniffed. "Did you know they have white ones with pearls?"

"Oh, Mother," I sighed. "Your best bet for marriage and babies is Brad and Julie. You need to work that angle. I'm begging you, please don't mention the 'M' word to Creole."

"Most women my age have grandchildren." She gave me a forlorn stare. "You and your brother need to work on it; think about making your mother happy."

"That is so manipulative." For the most part, I was hardened to her attempts to make me feel guilty and this was no exception.

She smiled and tapped her glass, letting the server know she wanted another Jack on the rocks.

Babies. I need to rent one and see how that goes first.

"My problem is Julie." I went on to tell her about Julie's ex showing up and how she didn't want me to say anything to Brad. My sixth sense told me she'd never say a word unless she was forced.

"I can tell Brad," Mother offered. "But let's give her time to say something first. If she doesn't, I'll tell Brad, and if it comes out, you can blame me. I'll throw myself in her arms and beg forgiveness. What's she going to say?"

"That could backfire. She could get mad and refuse to speak to you. I'll take your suggestion to wait, and then tell him myself." I smiled at her. "It would be cowardly of me to make you the bad guy."

"You'd owe me."

It was clear that she liked the idea of me owing her, and I could tell she was already figuring out the best way to redeem such an IOU. "You want a wedding? An opportunity to play dress-up? What about Spoon making an honest woman out of you? Brad can walk you down the aisle."

Brad had come a long way from wanting to throw Spoon in the Gulf. Now he could be in the same room with the man and not growl when Spoon hugged Mother or kissed her on the cheek.

Mother's cheeks flushed hot pink. "I'm enjoying playing the bad girl. Ssh." She looked around. "He bought me a black leather motorcycle jacket."

Sometimes I wanted to strangle her for doing things she'd never allow me to do. "Okay, I'm going to be the mother here. Wear the jacket all over town, to the beach, wherever, but I don't ever want you draping your body over his motorcycle and cruising around town." I wagged my finger. "Do you hear me, young lady?"

"I never sound all bossy like that."

"No, *you* can be scarier." I leaned in and repeated the question, growling out each word.

"Oh, okay." She pointed. "Look who's here."

I turned to see Brad and Fab coming through the door. Fab tapped his arm and pointed to our table. I found it amusing that the women at the table were dressed up and all in black, whereas my brother was in beach casual: shorts and a tropical shirt, briefcase in hand.

"What happened?" I stood and hugged Fab, who tried to hide a yawn behind her hand.

Brad pulled Mother out of her chair and wrapped her in a bear hug, letting go when she grunted.

Fab sighed. "Didier got a call from Cruz, who made him available to the police for more questioning. At least this time, it was at his office. Didier took the Mercedes, and Brad invited me to tag along with him."

"You were in Miami today?" I asked Brad.

"I had business to take care of and called to ask Didier a question. I wasn't far away, and offered the ride."

"I'm intruding on a family threesome, aren't I?" Fab asked.

"Don't be ridiculous, sister from parents I've never met," I said and gently shoved her into the chair next to mine.

Fab grimaced. She rarely spoke about her parents or growing up in France. They'd turned their backs on her adventurous lifestyle, slamming the door on a relationship, and I knew she wasn't as blasé about the estrangement as she pretended. Their loss was our family's gain.

She and I met officially when she picked the lock of my house and made herself comfortable. I'd had to harangue her to get her to believe that although other friends had let her down in the past, I would not. We had a good relationship of covering each other's backs. Her skills outshone mine, but thankfully, most of the time I didn't feel like a slacker.

Our initial drinks arrived while Brad and Fab placed their drink order with the hostess, who brought them in short order. Fab leaned over and kissed Mother.

"What are you doing to find the killer?" Mother asked Fab. "You know my services are always available."

"No, they are not," Brad snapped, and guzzled his beer. "What services?" He pinned me with a stare. "You're not encouraging Mother to hunt criminals, are you?"

"Mother's got a nice, silver-handled .22; why not put it to good use?" I teased.

Fab banged her glass on the table. "Of course we don't. We take her on the flea market jobs. You don't know how excruciating it is for me to watch these two shoppers comb through junk."

"Yes, Miss Haggle Queen, and who steps in when the price isn't low enough in her opinion?" I didn't bother to remind Fab that Mother and I had told her she could stay home but she'd refused.

Fab turned to me. "You're the planner. Do we have one yet?"

I gave Mother and Fab a quick recap of everything Brad had told me about Lauren. "Do you have anything to add, bro?"

"No, but I'm available to help out, and I'd prefer it be legal," he said as he signaled the waiter. It only took a minute to order, as we almost always ordered the same thing. We knew what we liked and rarely deviated.

When the waiter had gone, Brad opened his case and fished out a contract, which he handed to me.

I glanced at the paperwork for the new project, and it appeared standard. Nothing unusual stood out. "Is this moving forward, or is it on hold?"

"I knew Balcazar would be at the funeral, but I dropped by his office to see who was in charge in his absence. The doors were locked, and no one answered my knock," Brad said.

"Good work, bro. I told our favorite investigator to blow the skeletons out of all the players' closets, including the company's. My hope was that we'd locate a friend or two of Lauren's with inside knowledge that would help us."

"I watched you and Mother flitting around the grave, haranguing people in their time of grief." Fab barely succeeded in not laughing. "How many of those people did you unleash your charm on, getting them to spill their guts?"

"Madison's had that annoying gift since her teenage years. She won't ever cut anyone off and tell them to get a drink and sleep it off," Brad said.

I ignored my brother. "Big dead end. The majority of the people in attendance were rented mourners."

Brad laughed. "That's a good one."

Fab rolled her eyes. "Your made-up crap is usually better."

The food arrived on a large tray, and my stomach grumbled at the veritable feast.

"Two appletinis," Fab told the waiter. She handed over her glass. "I hate funerals."

Chapter Nine

Creole cruised into the driveway just as Fab and Didier were pulling out for a weekend getaway. He scooped me off my feet, put me in his truck, and sped off to his beach hideaway, secreted away at the end of a dead-end road that overlooked the western coastline of the Gulf, the nearest neighbor a half-mile away.

He had purchased a run-down house and ripped the inside walls doing most of the work himself to turn the choppy rooms into one large living space that included a kitchen, living room, and a king-size bed with a bit of privacy behind a bamboo screen. The side facing the road had no windows; the other side had sliding pocket doors that opened out onto the pool and private beach. The large bathroom was my favorite, with its sunken tub, walk-in shower, and decadent water view.

* * *

For the entire weekend, we'd blocked out the world and, best of all, turned off our phones. We stayed in bed until noon, walked on the beach, read, talked, and cooked our own meals. We worked well together in the kitchen, and we used all fresh ingredients that we'd picked up at the Farmer's Market. Most meals were eaten outside on the patio overlooking the blue-green water. I wasn't looking forward to ending our two days together.

The second we turned our phones back on, both of them beeped several times, letting us know we had messages. Creole was summoned to a big meeting at the Miami Police Department, and Fab had left me a message that Brick Famosa had called and demanded our presence in his office.

Fab and I had done many jobs for Brick, and they were seldom straight up, in and out, clean and no bullets. Fab had more tolerance for the man than I did.

Creole leaned over my shoulder to read the message. "I don't like Famosa; he's smarmy. He doesn't look out for your safety, and his apologies after the fact are weak. Makes me want to pound his face in." He turned me around. "Promise me you're going to start saying no to your volatile best friend. You can assess a situation; you know when you're in over your head."

I sighed. "I'm working on that. It would help if you could install a tamper-proof GPS on the SUV that stays in working order."

He picked up my bag, and we headed out the

door. When we got to his truck, he swung me around, scooped me up in his arms, and set me on the front seat, planting a kiss on my lips. Then he reached around and fastened the seat belt in a sweet, protective move.

The GPS was a big issue between Fab and Creole. He wanted us to stay safe and had programmed an alarm into the GPS to alert us when we entered a crime-infested neighborhood, which was intended to prompt us to turn around.

Fab saw it as a control issue. The woman had more tricks up her sleeve to disable it and make it look like just another malfunctioning unit…except the times she removed it, threw it in the street, and ran over it several times. He never had to ask what had happened to the unit, as she finished by throwing it in his truck bed or on the front seat.

Creole's snarky laugh surprised me, and I stared over at him, a little uh-oh bell going off in my head. "What have you done?"

"I've got a surprise for Miss Fabiana the next time the alarm goes off. You watch her reaction and report back in excruciating detail."

"Promise me she's not going to get hurt." I frowned.

"If I wanted to hurt her, I would wring her neck."

The traffic on the Overseas Highway was light this early in the morning—a few locals and tourists breezing through town to get to Key West and enjoy the day. I scooted over and put my head on his shoulder.

"Which snitch are you using to dig up info on Lauren Grace?" he asked.

"I expect a call anytime with an update. I'll share what I find out."

"You didn't answer my question."

I hadn't thought I'd get away with not giving up a name, but it was worth a try. "I'd have to ask before revealing the name. Don't worry, it's not the homeless guy at the liquor store."

"I've used Bosco a few times myself. Sometimes you get desperate."

Just as Creole turned onto my street, both of our phones chimed. Fab had texted me that she'd extracted a promise from Brick that the job was local. She knew that I loathed driving all over the state.

Creole pulled to a stop half in and half out of my driveway and returned his call. "You okay?"

I leaned over and tried to listen. After all, Fab employed the same strategy.

He gave me a toothy grin and shook his finger. "I won't be back until late tonight. Catch up with you over morning coffee." I watched as he frowned at the phone and made a few grunting noises, his shoulders relaxing a little. He hung up. "Lucky Didier." He shoved his phone in his pocket. "He has an alibi for the time the coroner estimated for Lauren's death. He's not off the hook, but the investigation is going his way."

"The killer has to be found. Didier's reputation is being smeared in the tabloids. His long-time agent took a step back and suggested he take a vacation. This is when he'll find out who his real friends are." I leaned back against the seat, not eager to go inside and find out what kind of drama awaited. "Why did the police suspect Didier right from the start?"

"Lauren was found dead in her living room, single gunshot to the forehead. No defensive wounds, which suggests she knew her killer. Didier's jacket lay over a chair."

I shuddered, my mouth forming an O. "How frightening for Lauren. To stare death in the face and have no way out."

"Hey." He wrapped his arms around me. "We're going to solve this murder and keep Didier out of the slammer."

He got out of his truck and ran around to my side. When he reached for me, I wrapped my legs around his torso and pulled him down on top of me. I needed a final make-out session to jumpstart my day.

"We need to stop before I drive you around the corner and molest you in public," he whispered against my lips.

I clutched his shirt and pulled him against me. "We need to do this again—and again—very soon."

He lifted me out and set me on my feet. The

only other way for me to get out of the truck was to roll on my stomach and slide down to the ground. I'd once suggested a stepladder, but he about spit out the water he was drinking.

"Behave yourself," he said with a low growl.

I wagged my finger. "You need to watch your back. No getting shot."

He bit the tip of my finger and swooped in for a quick kiss. "I'll track you down later." He slid behind the wheel and waved.

A loud whistle echoed across the driveway. Fab, hand on her hip, motioned to me. "We don't have all day," she yelled.

Chapter Ten

Fab nearly missed the driveway into Famosa Motors, but she'd never admit to not paying attention. A bundle of pure frustration, she hadn't taken her eyes off the Miami patrol car that had followed her for blocks before we reached our destination. She'd started tapping her fingernails on the steering wheel when the officer pulled up behind her, waiting for his lights to start flashing, but he'd cruised along patiently.

Brick specialized in the sale and rental of high-end cars in this well-located, upscale area of Miami. In addition, he owned pawn shops, bail bonds agencies, and a strip joint in Alligator Alley.

One salesman dogged a mangy-looking guy around the lot, probably afraid he'd touch one of the sports cars. If the would-be buyer was stupid enough to steal it, Brick would have us chase the auto down. The other salesman, who was guarding the front door, straightened up and gave the Hummer a once over. Recognizing us, he nodded and went back to rubbing his back up and down against a pole, a cup of coffee in one hand and a phone in the other.

We walked under the double roll-up doors, both of us admiring the sleek black Lamborghini with red leather interior on display.

"Do you suppose Bitsy's hiding under the desk?" I eyed the empty chair at the receptionist's desk.

Fab looked around. "Where is our least-favorite bosomy blonde?"

Brick had promoted his favorite stripper from pole dancer to receptionist; he swore she was an asset to the showroom. What he meant was her double D's were an attention-getter for his mostly male clientele. Fab and I had had an aversion to her ever since she screwed us on a business deal and bullets were exchanged.

I looked up at Brick's second-floor office window. Usually, the man stood there surveying his kingdom, but not today. "Shall we scream our arrival from down here or surprise the boss man?"

"I dare you." Fab quirked her brow.

She knew I'd never make a scene. I ran to the stairs and got there one step ahead of her. We swung our hips back and forth, knocking into one another, laughing all the way to the top.

"Just once," Brick huffed out a growl, slapping his fist on his desk, "could the two of you not play on the stairs and stay off the damn banister?"

I glanced around the office, checking the tops

of the cabinets and the side table before turning to Brick and demanding, "Where's the candy bowl?"

Fab leaned against the window ledge and scrutinized the busy boulevard below. She liked to scope out all of the exit routes wherever we went. In this office, it was the door or the window, but you'd have to knock out the glass and then risk the long jump and hope for the best.

"Got rid of it. Too much sugar puts on weight."

The dark-haired, sexy Cuban boxed five days a week at a local gym for badasses. There wasn't a scintilla of fat on his rock-hard body. His dark brown eyes turned beady as he returned my stare.

"I'll go sit in the car. Hurry up," I told Fab and marched to the door.

"You get back here," he roared. He turned in his chair, opening the credenza, and slammed my favorite bowl on his desk, mini candy bars and, my favorite, a bag of Oreos falling over the side. "I don't know why you can't buy your own."

"I've already told you, they don't taste as good when you have to pay for them yourself." *Everyone knew that,* I thought.

I picked out a mini Mars bar, which I knew was one of his favorites, and put it in front of him. "Do you have a bag? I forgot my purse." I fingered the snacks.

"Such a shame. I bet next time you won't forget your purse." He rolled his eyes. "Sit down, you two." He pointed to the leather chairs in front of his over-sized desk.

He kicked back in the chair that comfortably held his considerable, over-six-foot frame. Above his head hung his newest plaque, announcing him to be a Chamber of Commerce Man of the Year. The committee must have overlooked the fact that his businesses ran to the seedy. He stood out from his competition in that he gave back to the community and supported local charities.

Brick sucked down the last of his water. "I suppose you want one of these?" He wiggled the empty water bottle before pitching it in the trash.

I held up two fingers.

His lips turned up on the sides as he struggled to keep from laughing. "This is a simple case of lost and found. There's to be no confrontation. You're to recover said items and quietly relocate them to a storage unit that is already rented and waiting." He pushed a brand-new heavy duty lock across the desk. "Use this to secure the stuff."

I ripped open a piece of candy and devoured it, squashed the wrapper, and pushed it across his desk. "Thank you." Annoying him was too much fun today.

He glared at it before flicking it into the trash.

"Simply put, we're stealing back something

that's already been stolen. Does that sum it up?" I asked. "Have the police been involved *in any way*?"

"Sort of," he hedged.

Fab and I groaned.

"Ian Neal is the client and a friend of mine, and I can't stress enough that this has to get done ASAP."

"How is it that all your clients are so-called friends? You're certainly popular." I finished off my water and tossed it over Brick's shoulder and into the trash. I made a fist pump.

Brick glowered at me. "It's my sunny, warm personality. I'm a people person."

"Yeah, me too...people person, that is." I smiled.

Fab snorted. "Skip to the good part; the part about how the police are involved."

"Ian broke up with his live-in girlfriend, Ursula Richards. I never liked her." He spit the last part out. "Ian takes an annual ski trip with his eleven-year-old daughter to Vermont for ten days. He and Ursula had been arguing non-stop and agreed that it was a good time for Ursula to move her things out of the house and that he'd use the time to explain everything to his daughter. When Ian returned, he got the shock of his life. Ursula had moved out all right; she gutted the entire house. She took *everything*— fixtures, appliances, clothing, furniture. She didn't leave behind a single personal possession, only leaving his daughter's bedroom untouched." He shook his head, still not believing what had happened.

"Wonder why she spared the daughter?" I asked.

"Who the hell knows. They did have a good relationship. Ian tried to keep everything from his daughter and make an adventure out of staying in a hotel. When she started asking too many questions, though, he had to lie or fess up, and he chose the latter. She took the news better than him."

"It must have been quite a shock when he opened the front door," I said.

"Ha," Brick said in disgust. "Ian told me it took a minute to register that the front door was missing. When he crossed the threshold, he found that the house had been stripped to the drywall. He scooped up his daughter and took her to the car, ran back in, and surveyed the damage."

"Is this where the police show up?" Fab tapped her foot impatiently. She preferred cut-to-the-chase explanations.

"Ian didn't call law enforcement until the next day. They met him at the house. Can you believe she even took the cabinets? Anything that could be removed was gone, and if removing it wasn't an option, she inflicted damage that left the word 'repair' out of the equation."

"Why so vindictive?" Fab asked.

Brick shrugged. "Bitter over the break-up. I get that Ursula was unhappy—the relationship didn't work out—but who destroys an entire house?"

"What did the police have to say about this lovely family drama?" I asked.

He pulled a file out of his drawer, shuffling through papers. "Here's the best part. The officers claimed there wasn't anything they could do. Referred him to civil court even after they said they'd never seen damage the likes of what had been done. As far as they were concerned, it was a new twist on he said/she said unless he could provide receipts for all the missing items."

"Did they speak to Ursula?" Fab asked.

"My brother spoke to one of the detectives assigned to the case." Brick's brother, Casio, worked for the Miami Police Department as a decorated detective, and there were whispers that he wasn't a man to screw with. "He reported that she was cooperative, claimed most of the household items belonged to her, and stated that she had left behind anything that belonged to him and had no clue who caused the destruction inflicted on the house. Suggested it might be one of his unsavory connections and that he had low standards when it came to choosing friends."

"Any prior clues that Ursula was crazy-vindictive?" I asked.

Brick shook his head.

I shouldn't be so cynical about Brick's new

forthcoming attitude about disclosing unpleasant facts in their grim detail. In the past, one had to read between the lines. I wondered if the confrontation with Creole had made him rethink sending us on jobs in complete ignorance of what to expect.

"Any eyewitnesses?" Fab asked. "What you're describing took a long time to execute, hours if not an entire day, and certainly could not be done by one lone woman."

"Several neighbors reported seeing a moving van and four men loading it up. Ursula, calm as can be, walked around the neighborhood, saying her goodbyes and informing anyone that would listen—and they all did—that Ian was a bastard of the worst sort. That he abused her and she feared she'd be killed if she didn't leave. She claimed she was running for her life."

Brick opened his refrigerator and took out another bottle of water. "She reported all these claims to the police, and in addition to her friend theory, she offered up another theory that it was a hoax orchestrated by Ian to provoke sympathy. According to Ian, the police acted like they deserved each other and were happy to refer the happy couple to the courts and let them figure it out."

"Any truth to her claims?" I asked.

"No." He slammed his water bottle down on the desk. It sprang a leak, water dribbling across his desk. The bottle took flight and landed in the trash with a bang. "Now that Ian is over the shock, he wants to get back at Ursula by stealing his stuff back. Forget the thrift stores. He hit those up, looking for anything familiar, and didn't find anything. No one could remember seeing her either, but they did confirm that there had been no large donations of household goods recently. Ian figures she's got it stored somewhere."

"There's always the trash," I said. "But disposing of an entire household in bins without anyone noticing would be nearly impossible. She'd have to do a dump run. Not sure they allow moving vans out there."

"Ursula wouldn't ruin her fingernails at the dump," Brick sneered.

"Why is Ian so certain she still has the stuff?" Fab got up and started to pace.

"I tried to tell him this was a lost cause, but he wants answers. Before contacting me, he hired a feckless detective to tail her," Brick grouched. "Why not call me first? Ian figured Ursula spotted the detective, because she never slipped up."

"Sounds like she's a clever one. We'll have to factor that into any plan we come up with." Fab massaged the back of her neck.

"What makes you think Ursula's still in the area?" I asked.

"She's been sighted a few times in various parts of the Keys. It surprised me that she didn't skip town. First, you need to find her. She gave my guy the slip and then showed back up right under his nose. I've got two addresses you can check out." He turned his glare on me. "Miss Schmoozy here can shake the information out of Ursula's neighbors, acquaintances, whoever you can find. I'm not sure how you get people to spill their guts, but if it can be used to Ian's advantage, it works for me." He passed me a notepad with the addresses on it.

I flicked the page. "We need a list of names, other pertinent information, something besides two measly addresses."

He opened a desk drawer and produced a sheet of scribbled notes across the desk. "Make the most of it; it's better than nothing," he grumped.

I held the page at arm's length and squinted. "You could use a handwriting class."

"Smart a…" he mumbled. "Ian's a single father. His wife died of cancer a few years back, and he's raised one happy little girl." He paused to glare at us before continuing, "And another thing…if you two are inclined to side with your own sex and believe the crap Ursula spews about Ian, you should ask around about him. No one is going to say an unkind word about him because it wouldn't be the truth. Even the neighbors took Ian's side and didn't believe Ursula. When they found out what happened, they gathered replacement household and clothing items for him."

Fab passed her empty water bottle over my shoulder, I tossed it in the direction of the can but this time I missed, sending it flipping off the rim.

"You have terrible manners." Brick eyed me.

"Call and complain to Mother." I said, knowing full well she scared him. "You could part with one of your Cubans, and I'll give it to her with your regards." I eyed the humidor.

"No thanks. She'll talk you out of working for me, and then I'll have problems with Princess here." He smiled at Fab.

What was the secret to their relationship? I wondered. *He always has her back.*

"Where can we find Ian?" Fab asked.

"Insurance is covering their stay at a residential hotel until repairs can be made to the house. They approved the claim pretty quickly. He called the contractor and had a few of the boards over the windows removed. The neighbors keep an eye out to discourage undesirables. Last thing Ian needs is for someone to camp out and set the house on fire."

I tapped my finger on the note he'd given me. "Write down the name of his hotel and the address of the trashed house."

"You need to talk to Ian, you can do it by appointment here at my office. You shouldn't have a problem finding the house, it should be crawling with workmen, repairs just got started."

Fab bent across his desk. "Just so we're in agreement, anything goes wrong and our fee is quadrupled."

Brick slammed his hand down. "Listen, you two money-suckers, ever since you thought up this enhanced fee, you've charged it on every case. This time, there will be *no* guns, no violence, no one so much as stubs their toe. Fab…" His tone suddenly changed to one of concern. "Sorry to hear about the boyfriend. My resources are available. He needs bail, I'll get it posted. Reassure him that if he's booked, he won't have to spend a minute in a cell. I'll handle this one myself."

I liked the caring side of Brick. I hadn't believed it when Fab assured me it existed until I saw it for myself.

"Thanks," she said softly. "Right now, he's hopping one hurdle at a time. He's got Cruz in his corner. You run in those circles. Ask around, find out who wanted Lauren Grace dead."

"I've got some feelers out now; I'll keep you informed," he reassured her.

Fab stood up and nudged me. "Don't forget the snacks."

I stood and plunged my hand into the candy bowl.

"Stay off the damn banisters," Brick yelled as Fab disappeared out the office door.

I waved a fistful of treats at him and followed her out.

Fab looked like she had the weight of the world on her slender frame. There hadn't been an update from Didier, and I knew she'd worry until she heard from him, assuring her Cruz was living up to his reputation and keeping him out of jail.

"What next?" I asked. "Stakeout?"

She turned up her nose. There wasn't anything exciting about a stakeout—just a bunch of waiting, eating junk food, and nowhere to go to the bathroom.

"That option is way down on the list," she said. "Since Ursula's so good at spotting a tail, we need to be extra vigilant. I refuse to follow her all over town when all we'll get is a big fat nothing. We'll wait outside her house. When she leaves, you follow her, and park at the end of the block. If she turns around and comes back, call me. Hopefully, by the time she gets back, I'll have had a look around inside and found a clue as to what she did with Ian's stuff."

"Creole gets attitudinal when we commit felonies. I haven't had a lecture in a while, and I'd like to keep it that way. It kills the getting-frisky mood."

Fab's laugh conveyed that she didn't care what he thought. "We need to take care of this case fast. I want to be available for Didier. I'm not taking any new clients right now, not criminal ones anyway. My full attention is going to be on Didier."

"I made a little checklist that could bring our felony count to an all-time high, starting with Lauren's house. Next stop, snoop through Balcazar's corporate offices. We need to hurry, in case someone decides to clean out her desk and any personal belongings, if they haven't already. I weaseled a little info out of Brad—Didier was the connection to Lauren through her boss, Balcazar—but I asked too many questions, and he clammed up, making it clear he didn't want me nosing around."

"Call our Information Coordinator. Tell her we need a rush job—two in fact. This Ursula chick and a thorough investigation on anyone who knew Lauren Grace."

"That's a fancy title; Phil hears that and she'll raise her prices. She's already working on Didier's case."

Fab stepped on the gas. "We need to get home. I need a glass of wine out by the pool before we go to dinner."

Chapter Eleven

Looking in the mirror, I sighed. Another date night with Fab and Didier, which meant dress-up, painful shoes, and dining with nameless people with a need to be seen. Who could be so important that you'd be willing to eat at an overpriced restaurant where the food sometimes made you wish for a greasy hamburger?

One afternoon, while I was shopping with Fab, she'd chosen a low-cut, black dress for me that required a strapless bra, which I was now adjusting. The owner of the lingerie store I frequented had talked me into the newest addition to the bra line, the ultimate push-up, instantly adding two cup sizes. I poked the top of my cleavage, knowing it would disappear as soon as I unhooked the back.

Fab had insisted that the dress was a must-have—every woman needed more than one in her closet. I tried to curb her enthusiasm pointing out that I had three such dresses, but she wasn't listening. So I bought it with every intention of returning it, but soon discovered she'd thrown away the receipt. I slid my wincing toes into two-inch black heels, the highest I could manage without falling. They had been a gift from Fab, along with a threat that if I didn't wear them, she would burn my flip-flops.

Creole, who was standing at the bottom of the stairs, looked up when my foot hit the first step. His eyes glittered with heat, turning deep blue, promising an interesting evening. I flew into his open arms, and the rush of his breath on my neck calmed me.

I wanted to whisper, *Throw me over your shoulder and take me to your lair.* Instead, I pushed my diamond encrusted heart necklace, a recent gift from Creole, into his palm and turned, holding up my hair.

"It's about time," Fab muttered. Draped across Didier's lap, she flicked her watch. Didier tugged on her hair.

I winked at her, tactfully not reminding her of all the times she kept us waiting. The woman wasn't acquainted with "on time." She looked perfectly put together, as usual. Her long brown hair cascaded down her back in loose curls, and her black designer dress clung to her slender frame like a glove.

"How is it that you got to pick the restaurant twice in a row?" Creole asked Fab in a suspicion-laced voice.

"The restaurant is owned by Didier's friend, Balcazar, and we're going to support him. What's wrong, Neanderthal? Too much dress up for you?" Fab snickered.

This should be interesting, I thought.

"Babe, I think you look hot-hot," I said with admiration, leisurely perusing him from head to toe before turning to Didier. "You come in a very close second."

Both men were dressed in black dress pants and Italian loafers, only differing in shirt choice. Didier wore a long-sleeved black dress shirt and Creole had on the shirt Mother had got him from an upscale boutique that had become a favorite now that she had men in her life to dress.

Fab buried her head in Didier's chest and made an unidentifiable noise. Didier laughed and jerked her to his side, clamping an arm around her. He whispered something in her ear, and she cooed up at him. "I apologize. It seems my girlfriend forgot to give you all the details." He looked down at Fab. "I appreciate your going. Not sure why I got the invite, as the relationship between Balcazar and me has been strained since Lauren's death."

"Let's go." Fab grabbed Didier's arm and practically dragged him out the door.

It surprised me when Fab jumped behind the wheel of the Hummer. I would've thought she'd choose her Mercedes.

I snuggled up to Creole in the backseat, and we did little talking, sneaking a kiss or two.

* * *

Fab was a completely different driver with her boyfriend sitting next to her; she didn't turn unless there was plenty of room, slowed at every yellow light, and ran only slightly over the speed limit. Finally, she pulled up in front of a valet stand, and the door was quickly opened by a young hottie. Fab handed the keys to the twenty-something with beach boy looks.

"You joyride," she said, glaring at the guy, "and I'll have you arrested."

He looked surprised at her bluntness.

"Her father is the Chief of Police here in Miami," I lied convincingly. Harder would kill me if that ever got back to him. At fiftyish, he liked them young, and he'd be insulted at the father label. He was old enough, but he'd deny it.

"I'm going to tell him you said that," Creole said. He held his arm out. I linked mine in his and turned, noticing for the first time that the lit-up restaurant with sidewalk seating was the scene of the shooting, B's. I skidded to a stop.

"I'm not setting foot inside there. Why didn't you tell me about this?" I practically shouted at Fab. Heads turned at my outburst, but I didn't care. "Don't you think you owe it to me to let me decide if I wanted to come back here or not?"

Creole cut off her response and turned me to face him. "What happened that I don't know about?"

"Fab and I were almost gunned down in this restaurant. Remember the day I texted that I had something to tell you? At the time, I thought getting shot at should wait until we were face to face. Then Didier got arrested." I pulled away and marched over to the valet, who was getting ready to drive off in the Hummer. I jerked the door open and held my hand out. "Give me the keys. Please."

"No can do. It's her car." He tossed his head in Fab's direction.

"It's registered to me." I leaned in, jerking the keys from his hand. The valet got out, shrugged and walked away.

Didier lowered his head and whispered in Fab's ear. He dragged her to the curb, arguing in French. Whatever lie she came up with placated him, and his anger dissipated somewhat.

"I should have told you, but I didn't think you would come," Fab said. "The odds are good it won't happen again tonight."

"We're leaving," I fumed.

Didier and Creole edged off to one side and huddled together.

"Are we okay?" Fab asked.

"Of course we are," I said.

She nodded.

"What did Balcazar say when you told him you wouldn't be back?" I dragged her over to an empty outside table, trying to keep my voice down. "You left out a few pertinent details that day, such as his relationship with Didier. Does your boyfriend know his friend tried to hook you into something illegal?"

"It doesn't matter. Balcazar's shutting down the games until the investigation into Lauren's death is over. Word on the street is that they hit the wrong restaurant; the message was meant for someone else."

"I can't believe you spouted that drivel with a straight face. Heads up—I didn't tell Creole before, but I'm relaying the gruesome details on the way home. Working for this Balcazar character could get you killed. Think about that."

It annoyed me that Fab wasn't taking this seriously. Right now, her attention was on her boyfriend and she was looking frustrated that she wasn't close enough to eavesdrop.

I nudged her out of her reverie. "I suppose if they decide that Lauren was killed by mistake, you'll believe that too?"

"At this point, all I want is for them to no longer consider Didier a person of interest. Once they do that, they'll start looking for the real murderer." Fab tucked a stray lock of my hair behind my shoulder. "I knew this dress would look great on you."

"Was there any doubt? You picked it out." I smiled at her. "Don't try to change the subject. We're not cats; we only have one life, and we take too many chances as it is."

Didier wrapped his arms around me from behind and whispered, "I guess this dinner wasn't meant to happen. Turns out there's another reason for you to leave; Creole will explain. Go ahead and go. Fab and I will take a cab home."

Creole was already behind the wheel of my Hummer. The valet stood at the passenger door and helped me in, and without a word between us, we eased into traffic.

"I'm sorry, I probably overreacted. But when I realized where we were, it freaked me out. Should we be leaving them here?" I looked out the back window, but they had already disappeared inside. "What did Didier mean when he mentioned a second reason for leaving?"

"There were two maggots at the bar from a previous case, I hadn't realized that they were back in town. They won't be staying long," he barked. "Overreaction—that's the same word Fab used in her vague explanation to Didier." Creole's angry face glared at me. "Didier hasn't figured out yet that his girlfriend is light on the truth. When the color drained from your face and you refused to set foot in the place, it pissed me off that she'd set up this stupid dinner. Besides, although I'd like to meet Balcazar, it's better that I continue to operate in the background. Now spill," he demanded.

"If you need any info on your maggot acquaintances, I can hand their names off to our Information Coordinator." Then I told him in exacting detail what had happened that day, backing up a couple of times to make sure I didn't leave anything out. I told him that the day had started out as a job from one of Fab's corporate clients, but we hadn't even had time to order a drink before the bullets flew, and that we'd snuck out at the first opportunity. "It was never my intention to hide anything," I said. "I didn't think a 'just shot at' text message was appropriate. And I really had planned to tell you the day Didier got arrested. Then, with so much going on, I forgot."

He entwined his fingers with mine and squeezed. "Didier told me about the shooting, but not a word about the two of you being there, and believe me, he would have if he'd known, which means Fab didn't tell him. Something about his friend must not be sitting right. He asked me to nose around, check out the kind of people Balcazar does business with and why someone would shoot up the restaurant...also why someone might want to kill Lauren and whether there was a link. He wanted his questions answered before signing off on the condo complex deal."

I scooted closer to him and leaned my head on his arm. "I had a bunch of questions myself. I went online and read everything I could find on both shootings. The articles were light on specifics, and most of the stories were reposted from the original AP posts with barely a mention by the local press. I also looked for any references to witnesses sneaking off, which would have made us look guilty as opposed to not wanting to make the local news."

Creole grabbed a quick kiss at the red light. "According to the detectives assigned to the case, the employees at B's haven't been cooperative. One detective summed up the case as 'Balcazar screwed someone, and since no one got killed, it was a warning.' Didier doesn't want to believe his friend is hanging with the wrong crowd, and my advice was to stay far away, no matter what the explanation is. Anyone bold enough to carry off that job in broad daylight could have killed everyone in the restaurant. Who knows what they'd do next."

I kicked off my shoes as we rode in silence back to the Cove, happy when the headlights flashed on the city limit sign.

Creole finally broke the long silence. "Balcazar sucks as a friend. He thinks Didier killed Lauren."

I gasped. "I'll bet Fab doesn't know that."

"I don't understand why Didier wanted to go to B's. He doesn't need a free dinner. I'd have told Balcazar to shove it up his…" Creole fumed and laid his arm across my shoulders. "I want you to stay away from anything that has to do with Balcazar unless I know the details *in advance*. I find it interesting that he hired Fab to do a job when he could have had a high profile security firm do his dirty work." He held up his hand. "I know she's good, but Balcazar is all about appearance, according to Didier. I suggested that he put the real estate deal on hold until we find out who Balcazar really is and who murdered Lauren. The last thing we need is to get involved in something illegal."

A Mercedes SUV swerved around the Hummer, honking its horn and coming dangerously close to the bumper before speeding off. Creole gave a half-laugh but didn't react. A minute later, flashing lights came out of nowhere and the chase was on to catch the speeding car.

"Can I roll down the window and wave when we pass?" I asked.

Creole grabbed my hand. "The officer might see you and radio ahead to his partner, and we'd get the next ticket."

"Are you mad that I made a scene at the restaurant?" I asked in a quiet voice.

"Hell, no. I didn't want to go, but when a good friend asks, how do you say no? Change of plans just means I can get you naked that much sooner."

"Are you planning on feeding me first?"

He handed me his phone. "Call in a takeout order anywhere you want."

Chapter Twelve

Returning from a coffee run to our favorite bakery, I parked in the driveway and ran around to the passenger side, leaning across to lay on the horn. An annoying reminder to Fab to speed it up. I hit the horn again on the off-chance she hadn't heard me the first time.

The front door banged open. Fab shook her finger at me as she marched across the driveway. Didier waved from the kitchen garden window. He held Jazz and waved his paw. I waited to see if the cat bit him.

"Really?" Fab said as she slid into the driver's seat. "That racket isn't very neighborly."

"One of them is old and hardly ever wears his hearing-aid; he enjoys shouting. I don't see any of the others standing outside looking for the noise offender. You should thank me for thinking about you and not wanting you to drink a lukewarm double espresso." I pointed to the cup.

She popped the lid off and took a sniff. "Hmm, my favorite."

"Did you finally cough up the whole truth to Didier about what went down at B's when you showed up for your dubious job interview?"

She banged her fist on the steering wheel, letting out a big sigh. "Why didn't I just tell him the whole truth the first time?" She frowned. "Didier told me he was tired of having a liar for a girlfriend and that we've been together long enough that I should trust him. If not, what are we doing together?"

Didier had replaced my brother in the last-to-know department. Another added heap of humiliation for Fab was that everyone in the family knew that her first confession of an incident was always heavily edited.

"Did you have an answer?" I asked.

"I didn't get the chance. He issued an edict: next time it happens, we're over." She whispered the last word as though she couldn't believe he would leave her.

"Do you love him?"

"Of course I do," she snapped. "I can't imagine my life with someone else, and I don't want to. He's the first man I'm certain I can trust with my secrets and that he won't throw them back in my face, and yet I never seem to remember that in the moment. My usual excuse of wanting to protect him sounds lame even to me."

I reached across and gently tugged on a strand of her hair. My best friend looked ready to cry, and I wasn't sure what to do. "You listen to me," I scolded. "Tell as much of the truth as you can spit out, then add, 'I may have forgotten something and reserve the right to amend it later.' Works with Creole. You might want to mention that changing overnight is a tad unrealistic, but you're going to make every effort. Here's the most important part—you have to be the one to fill him in on any missed details before anyone else does."

"We're not breaking up! I can start by sharing something every day. That way, he'll see I'm making an effort." Fab turned slightly and stared out the window. "We sat through dinner as though we were on an awkward first date. I don't know how much more polite chit-chat I can stand."

"Just be your charming, kinky self. I'll go to Creole's, and you can have the house to yourselves. That way, you can make all the noise you want."

Fab's eyes were glued to the road as she drove in a way I'd never seen, staying in one lane, holding the SUV to a tad above the speed limit. I'd never admit out loud that I liked her nauseating style of driving better than the brooding woman she was today.

"How was your dinner with Balcazar?"

"I'd mct him several times when I was with Didier but never exchanged more than a few words in person. The job offer was transacted over the phone. Slimy—that was my impression of him. He wants me to come back and finish the job of checking out his employees, but before I could come up with a way to blow him off, Didier told him no and didn't offer an explanation."

"Good for Didier. Mad or not, the man loves you. I still don't get why Balcazar extended the dinner invitation. Creole told me that Balcazar told Didier to his face that he thought he murdered Lauren."

"Didier thought he would apologize or offer an explanation as to what the..." She shook her head, finished off her latte and handed it to me. "Didier had an interesting observation: that he'd never known his friend at all. Thinks Balcazar collects people, calls them friends. After all, they may be useful down the line."

"I've had a couple of friends like that, and when they found out I'd never be of any help to their agenda, I never heard from them again. It used to hurt my feelings; now it's good riddance."

We fist-bumped.

"Did Lauren's death make it into the conversation?" I asked.

"I brought up the topic, asking if he knew anyone who would want Lauren dead. Balcazar dodged the question, and when I pressed him, he struggled to control his anger. About the time Didier pinched my thigh to try to get me to shut up, Balcazar suddenly remembered he was under orders from his attorney not to talk to anyone about the case."

"Did Balcazar act like he was hiding anything?" I pointed to the sign indicating that our turnoff was coming up.

"More like he talked about his reputation and clearly didn't want anything to tarnish his pristine image."

Chapter Thirteen

Fab pulled off the Overseas Highway and into a winding cul-de-sac. The houses were all cookie cutter, two story, and waterfront; the only thing differentiating them was the color. We cruised down the street. At the turn-around, residents shared a large, green, grassy park that hosted a few picnic tables, some playground equipment, and a boat launch ramp. Ian's home stuck out in the well-manicured area. Thanks to the vindictive girlfriend, it looked sadly neglected and fallen into disrepair. A contractor's sign poked out of the brown and weed-filled lawn, no sign of any workers.

In place of a front door, a sheet of plywood had been nailed over the opening, a "do not enter" sign prominently displayed on it. The double-paned windows that ran along the front were newly installed, the stickers still in place.

We sat at the curb and checked out the neighboring properties.

"I suppose we have permission to enter the property in case anyone should ask?" I patted my Glock where it rested at the small of my back.

Breaking into a vacant house could easily bring an unpleasant surprise.

Fab glanced over her shoulder. "Then I'm pulling into the driveway. You can handle any police issues."

"Hopefully that doesn't happen. Let's check out the back first. Maybe we'll get lucky and there will be a lock we can pick. I doubt Ian would appreciate us breaking a new window."

Just as we slammed the doors of the SUV, a neighbor from the adjoining property walked out from under his carport and headed straight for us. "What are you two doing?" the older man asked. I guessed him to be a retiree, enjoying the sunshine in Bermuda shorts and tennis shoes.

Fab excelled at dealing with older men. I wanted to smack her when she didn't step forward, leaving me to take the initiative. "We were hired to make regular checks on the property."

From his look of disbelief, he clearly didn't believe a word. "We'll see about that. If you're lying, I'll have you arrested. I've already got your license plate number," he warned as he removed his phone from his shirt pocket and dialed a number. "You hire two girls to check out your property?" he said into the phone. Whatever the other person said made it clear we were liars, and he shook his head at us. "Don't worry, I'll take care of this. They're headed to jail."

"Tell Ian to call Brick Famosa," Fab yelled in

frustration. "Maybe he didn't get the message."

The old man gave us a nod and waved us back. "I'll keep an eye out," he said and ended the call. "Ian could hear you yelling; he's going to check it out."

"Did you know Ursula?" I asked. He gave me a skeptical look as I went on. "She didn't do all this damage by herself. Got a clue who helped?"

He hesitated for so long, I didn't think he'd respond. He checked us out carefully from head to toe before answering. "There were two moving vans that day, showed up at the same time, both from one of those u-rent places. The first one filled up in a couple of hours and left; the second one didn't leave until late. I counted four men; two of them left with the first truck and showed back up several hours later, after which, none of them left until after dark. The second truck had been backed up flush to the garage, and I had no clue they were gutting the inside of the house."

"Any sign of Ursula since?" Fab asked.

His phone rang, and he glanced at the screen, stepped back, and answered. The conversation was short, and he ended with, "I'll call you later."

He inclined his head and motioned for us to follow him as he took a walkway around to the back of Ian's house. He pulled a wad of keys out of his pocket and turned towards us. "Ian told me to let you in."

I eyed the plain wood, temporary door that had been installed, knowing a good swift kick would leave it hanging off the hinges.

He noticed my scornful look. "New doors are on order. They should be installed next week."

To the left of the door, a cement pad that had once held the air conditioner unit was now empty, the wires cut and left dangling. Most people didn't know the units were a popular target for theft for the resale value of the copper. Had Ian bolted it down, who knows what the spiteful Ursula might have done next.

We walked into what was once a kitchen. The large space looked naked without a single cabinet or fixture, wiring dangling where appliances had once been. Although we had heard about the extensive damage, Fab and I exchanged shocked looks.

Every room had been stripped and left with gaping holes in the drywall. If Ursula's intent had been to inflict extensive damage, she'd succeeded, leaving only the pink bedroom at the end of the hall untouched. Brick had told us that Ursula had left it completely intact, but now it stood empty.

The man noticed me lingering in the doorway and said, "Ian had his daughter's room packed up the next day. He was afraid that dreadful woman would change her mind, come back, and finish taking everything. He's storing the furniture in a friend's garage since they're staying in a hotel."

Fab gave the neighbor a hard look. "Did you know Ursula?"

I nudged Fab. "Anything you can tell us about her would helpful," I said, smiling at him.

"Ursula's pretty to look at: tall, blond, fashion-model looks. But her eyes are cold as ice; blue, like icicles that never thaw. Me and the missus never felt comfortable around her; she always had an appraising look, which was always followed up by another one that let a person know that they didn't measure up to her standards. I never understood what Ian saw in her. At least his little girl liked her. Whenever I saw them together, they seemed to have a lot to laugh about."

Fab stuck her head into the empty shell of the hall bathroom and gasped at the giant holes where there had once been a shower and bathtub, and at the rock-hard cement that over-flowed out of the drains. The sewer pipe exposed where there had once been a toilet, and it too brimmed over with cement. "Was Ursula friendly with anyone in the neighborhood? Someone with whom she might have left a forwarding?"

"As you might imagine, this drama has been the talk of the neighborhood. This—" he swept his arm around. "—has eclipsed the last big news: the Curtis couple getting a divorce. That turned ugly when Mrs. Curtis found out that her husband was a serial cheater, and they ended up selling the house and moving away." He looked at his watch and cleared his throat, then took the lead and walked back into the living room.

I poked Fab and mouthed, "Let's go."

"I spoke to each of the neighbors myself." He thrust his chest out. "Not a one of them figured she was capable of this kind of destruction, even the ones that didn't think much of her." He waved his arms around, his voice rising in irritation. "Before she made her getaway, she went door-to-door with dire warnings, accusing Ian of everything but murder. Scared, she said, for her life, the child's life. Swore he had a volatile temper, which no one had ever witnessed. Went on that he was an abuser of women and children, and for her own safety, she had to move while he was out of town."

"Did you believe any or all of what Ursula said?" I nudged Fab towards the door.

"My wife and I were skeptical, but we also discussed whether or not we'd turned a blind eye to Ian's real personality because we liked him. We decided that her description didn't jibe with the man we had come to know over the years, who'd always been nice to everyone."

"Any clue where Ursula moved to?" Fab asked.

"Ursula told us she was moving to the panhandle and asked us to keep her whereabouts a secret. But a week ago, my wife swore she saw her come out of that pricey grocery store in Marathon, one of them healthy kind. My wife had just pulled into the parking lot and spotted her walking across the lot. She got into the passenger side of a BMW sedan, and the car took off. My wife didn't get a look at the driver, because the car had dark-tinted windows, which my wife claims are illegal. She'd know, since she worked for the Transportation Department for twenty-five years; got herself a nice retirement."

Fab thanked him and shook his hand. I scooted out the door and raced back to the SUV before he stuck his hand in my direction. People who knew me knew better than to expect a handshake. The whole ritual freaked me out.

"Really, Madison." Fab shook her head and climbed behind the wheel. "Where are your manners?"

"If you're trying to imitate Mother's voice, you need to work on it."

Fab backed out of the driveway and sat at the stop sign for a moment. She snapped a couple of photos before heading back to the main highway. "Another nutjob case. We need to be careful; whatever plan we come up with includes never meeting Ursula."

"I knew when Brick told us about the job that if she did this, she wasn't the picture of mental health." I fished my ringing phone out of my pocket. "Yeah, what?" I asked and hit the speaker button.

"Are you two close by?" Phil asked.

I glanced at the clock on the dash. I never set the time on the watches I wore; they were more of a fashion accessory. "An hour away, but you can cut that in half, the way the wild one drives."

Fab revved the engine.

"That works. Let's meet at your office. I've got an update on Lauren. Don't dally; if I get bored, I'm leaving."

"Order some food, have a drink, we're on our way," Fab shouted.

Chapter Fourteen

Jake's was my favorite bar, and not just because I owned it. The original Jake had left town a few steps ahead of loan sharks who wanted their money or, if he didn't have it, to kill him to serve as an example to other non-payers. Jake had about run the bar into the ground when he sold to me. Since then, the longtime customers had stopped complaining about the bad attitude of the management and the subpar service.

It still maintained its dive bar status but was way less rundown. It had been power-washed, cleaned from top to bottom, and freshly painted. I added another pool table, darts, and hired someone to get the jukebox running. I commandeered the corner table on the outside deck for my office because I didn't care for the broom closet-sized one in the back hall that was now used for extra storage. That office had a small dingy window, but this one had a view of the inlet of water that ran along the back of the property, not to mention the fresh breezes. I'd marked my territory with a custom-made "Don't sit here" sign. The only exceptions were family and friends.

Mother and I had turned the private meeting room into a card room, where she held poker games on a regular basis to an invitation-only list. My original plan was to rent it out for parties, but so far, there had been zero interest. I couldn't complain; the house got a cut off Mother's friends, which made the bottom line happy.

I owned the whole block. In addition to Jake's, it included four dubious businesses: the trailer court, Fab's office, a roach coach and the gas station. The trailer court at the back had been sold off in a deal put together by Brad.

The newest addition, Fab's office, was housed in an old lighthouse, white with a red weathered roof, that was delivered one day on the back of a gigantic flatbed. I never got a straight answer about where it had come from, the only explanation offered being, "Some guy had an extra one and here it is." But since the police never showed up, asking questions about possible felonies, I figured it must be legal. Besides, I couldn't imagine even Fab managing to steal an entire building.

If I could have found someone to take the wager, I'd have bet that Fab wouldn't use the new office more than a handful of times. And I'd have won. Once it was freshly painted inside and decorated, she lost interest. As predicted, she rarely used the upper level space, which held two desks and chairs. She had to be where the food and action was — the bar. I had a plan for the lighthouse: restore it to its former glory and turn it into a gift shop. The slight wrinkle to my plan was getting Fab to agree.

The biggest eyesore, the old deserted gas station, sat at the opposite end of the property. It wouldn't get a facelift, just a good cleaning. I didn't want to diminish the character. I'd recently partnered with Junker, an old man in town I befriended after spying his yard of junk, and we were in the process of filling the old building with garden collectibles and antiques, or as Fab would say, "crap that no one in their right mind would want."

In the front, next to the curb, the brightly painted lime roach coach, "Twinkie Princesses," sat parked. It advertised that they would deep fry anything. Now if only the two women who owned it would actually show up and open for business. In the time I'd owned the property, I'd met them once. They were extremely vague on their entrepreneurial plans but paid their rent on the first of every month. The other plus, not a single sheriff's-response call.

Fab parked at the back door of Jake's, and we cut through the kitchen door. I yelled at the cook over the noise coming from the television airing his telenovela. "Two usuals," I said, holding up my fingers. My eyes wandered to the TV screen. Poor Lucia — divorcing her fifth husband.

Two old sandy tomcats, who looked like

they'd been sleeping on the beach, wandered into the bar from the deck. One shouted, "Here's your tip, bitch," as he stuck out an empty hand.

The bar went silent. At this time of day, it was the regular half-dozen locals, who shifted on their barstools almost in unison.

Phil flashed him the middle finger. "Next time either of you comes back here, be careful what you drink." She leveled a glare. "I'll get Bud here to take a pee in your glass."

A man I presumed was Bud smiled widely, nodded, and made a rude gesture from between his legs.

The other bum stepped in Phil's direction, and Fab cut him off. "Just so you know before you pick a fight, management has shot customers in the past. Check out the sign." She pointed to a prominently displayed metal sign that read, "In case of disagreement, we shoot unruly patrons." It was an old sign Mother had found at a flea market.

The two men looked at one another and came to an unspoken agreement. One grabbed the other's shirt and said, "Let's get out of this hellhole." He glared at Phil. "We ain't never coming back," he spit.

"So sad." Phil sniffed as they scuttled out the door.

Now that the show had ended, everyone went back to talking and drinking.

"Really, Philipa," I tsked. "The finger? To non-tipping customers?"

"First off, I told those two that the reserved sign on the table meant don't sit there. Did they move? No. I told them that they'd get their drinks when they moved their fat asses." She moved out to the deck and stretched her long legs across one of the vacant chairs.

Fab and I slid into our usual seats. All of us had our backs to the side wall so we could keep our eyes peeled to see anything that went down inside the bar.

I pulled a beat-up notepad from my canvas bag, which I'd dumped on the floor, ripped out several sheets, and pushed them across the table. "Here are some more names that I need you to check out. The second sheet is for a new case from Brick."

Phil had prepped a serving tray with a pitcher of margaritas and a bowl of chips and had it waiting for us. She filled our glasses, garnishing with a lime.

"Did you find anything helpful on Didier's case?" Fab held up her glass in a silent toast.

"Lauren was found dead in the living room of her condo, a pricey unit that overlooks Biscayne Bay, lying in the doorway of her sliding doors, no defensive wounds. The blood stains on the carpet were a nice contrast to the all-white decor."

"How do you know?" I asked. "Did you get a

look inside?" I didn't get why colorless décor was so popular when there were fabulous colors from which to choose.

"Friends and associates," she said slyly. "I can't do everything myself."

I reached over and flipped the switches for the overhead ceiling fans and the strands of lights that wrapped around the deck.

Phil continued, "There are several reasons the cops think Didier pulled the trigger. According to the security tapes, he was the last person to see her alive, and they found a man's jacket draped over a chair. It was spattered in her blood, and in addition to his monogram inside, it had a business card holder in the pocket with Didier's cards in it. The cops believe the motive was the cancellation of the contract for the sale of the condo. They found a letter about that balled up under the desk."

Fab hissed and banged her fist on the table, almost knocking the glasses over.

I put my hand over Fab's. "What? Neither Brad, Creole, nor Didier mentioned that."

"My police informant told me they reviewed a month's worth of security tapes from her condo, and he's not on a single one, other than the night she died and they've sent that one off for further investigation as a couple of skips in the time stamp were noted. The tapes from the office show them meeting several times, but every time, Brad was there. A couple of times, there was a tall man with dark, shoulder-length hair, who managed to keep his face off-camera. Imagine that?" She looked at me and winked.

"Do they have any other suspects?" Fab asked.

"None. My source tells me they're taking a closer look at the 100 Ocean Boulevard Corporation, as they filed for bankruptcy a month ago. It's rumored their deals weren't always on the up."

"Maybe we're looking for a disgruntled client. The deal Brad and Didier were putting together was for big money. With that kind of cash on the line, if an investor were to get screwed, it might make someone mad enough to kill. Do you have a pen?" I asked Phil.

She pulled one out of her back pocket and grabbed a napkin off the table.

"Check out the corporation and its CEO, Patino Balcazar. We need this info ASAP." I nudged Fab. "Knowing Didier's lawyer, he's probably already warned your boyfriend not to say a word, but I'd like a peek at what his investigators found."

Fab shook her head. "Didier would flip if I broke into his lawyer's offices. He'd leave me for sure."

I slurped the last of my margarita, licked my lips, and turned the glass upside down. "I guess I need a refill," I stated and handed the glass to Fab.

"We're going home after this," Fab reminded

me. "I'm planning a surprise for Didier tonight."

I made kissy noises, and Phil laughed.

"No more tequila for you. You're totally annoying when you start with the sound effects. Didier doesn't get that when he laughs, you only get more outrageous."

"I'll behave," I sulked.

"No, you won't; you're already starting."

"Find me a boyfriend, and then we can do a couples thing," Phil said.

Fab and I exchanged looks. "If a woman who looks like you can't find someone…" I said.

"I can have sex, but I want someone who leaves me wanting to cook them breakfast, not checking my watch, waiting for them to leave."

Fab banged on the table. "Can we focus and get back to the case at hand?"

"I almost forgot the good part—Miss Lauren was more than a VP. She and Balcazar had a torrid affair going on under his wife's nose. Lauren earned a salary in the low six figures but lived in a five-million-dollar waterfront penthouse bought by the partnership, and the deed was in her name."

"That's a nice piece of real estate for a mistress. Did Mrs. Balcazar know of her husband's activities?" I asked. It wouldn't be the first time a wife decided to end the affair permanently.

"I'm working on that. Interesting tidbit about Tina Balcazar. She owns her own property management company in the same building as her husband's corporation; it's ranked in the top five in Miami Beach. In addition to managing her husband's properties, she has accounts of her own. One of her employees called her snooty, but they were confident in saying there were no shady business dealings."

"Why isn't Patino Balcazar a suspect?" Fab dumped the remaining contents of the margarita pitcher over the banister, giving me a satisfied smile. If only I'd been a tad quicker.

"Like your boyfriend, Balcazar may have an alibi. He had a business meeting that went late; so far only one has verified his attendance, haven't been able to reach the rest of the attendees," Phil told her. "My source uncovered this tidbit, though: it was Balcazar who fingered Didier and suggested that the cops check him out. He told them that Didier and Lauren were having an affair."

"That's ridiculous," Fab scowled. "Trust me, I'm not a woman who'd be the last to know if her lover was cheating on her."

I smiled at her and mentally agreed. We wouldn't be sitting here talking about Didier murdering anyone, he'd already be dead.

"For an extra fee, you can add an upgrade: Lauren's residence and office can both be tossed." Phil scribbled circles on her notepad.

Fab cut in. "You know that's my job," she grumped.

I shook my head, surprised by Phil's offer. I wasn't sure which one of the dozen nosy questions I had on the tip of my tongue I should ask first. Before I could ask, Phil went on without waiting for an answer to her offer.

"This is what I've pieced together about the business so far. Balcazar assembled a group of rich, well-connected, crony friends to form a corporation for real estate deals, and in the beginning, everyone made money. They were set up to buy condo developments from financially distressed developers who were one step away from bankruptcy. A buyout price was negotiated, and before the deal closed, they would inflate the sales price, find a different buyer, and do a reassignment. Their names never showed up on the title. They had vendors in their pockets that they used at every step, so the numbers always worked out right."

"So the bank thinks they're dealing with Balcazar, and they're unaware of who the real buyer is. Well, that's legal," I said. "On the closing date, they just schedule a double escrow, with the seller none the wiser. The rest is fraud. I'd be livid to find out after the fact about the inflated numbers. The buyer's already overpaying from a phony appraisal. Add in the cost of construction, and they'd be lucky to break even. More like financial ruin." It surprised me that Balcazar wasn't the one found dead.

"Anyone lose their shirt?" Fab asked.

"Just so happens that the previous owner of the building you folks are under contract to buy found out rather quickly that he was in the hole and tried to unload. Balcazar, being the benevolent businessman, stepped in and negotiated with his lender for pennies on the dollar."

This wasn't the time to do a little dance that our deal hadn't been signed and delivered.

"Where is this slimy group now?" Fab asked.

"The other officers got a tip-off that their business model was about to be investigated by state regulators. Some resigned, and others disappeared. Rumor has it that the bank accounts no longer have the healthy balances they once did."

"It's business practices like these that led to Miami-Dade County getting the reputation of fraud capital of the country. Though I'm not sure if they still retain that distinguished title," I said.

Fab's special ring for Didier sounded. She looked at her phone. "He's home." She smiled.

"Go ahead and go. I'll get a ride. That will give you two some alone time." I breathed out a heavy sigh, certain that Fab could get her relationship back on track.

She frowned at me.

"I'll give her a ride," Phil offered.

Fab shook her finger at me. "You are forbidden to have any fun when I'm not around. Got it?"

"I would never do that, now go." I pointed to the door.

Chapter Fifteen

The bar had filled up with locals who'd just gotten off work and needed a cool one before heading home. One man beat another in a game of pool, slapping his friend on the back and making a scene that, after a first glance, everyone sitting nearby ignored in favor of going back to their beverages.

"You whore bastard," screamed a female voice.

I turned in time to see a short, rotund woman fist the shirt of a man seated at the bar and drag him backwards off his stool into a heap on the floor. The barstool tipped over and banged him in the head.

She kicked the stool out of the way, sending it flying, then jumped on him, pummeling and kicking, a string of foul words, mostly having to do with his parentage, tumbling out of her mouth.

"It doesn't look like she's going to stop beating on him anytime soon. We should break it up." Phil stood, pulling on my arm. "If I'm getting dirty, so are you."

I credited the man for trying to roll out from under his attacker, but when she clocked him on the side of the head with her fist, he stopped his struggle and covered his face with both hands.

"Dirty doesn't work for me." I grabbed a full pitcher of water off a side table. "If drenching her doesn't work, we put a bullet in her ass."

A dozen steps later, I upended the pitcher and jumped back. She came up screeching, water running down the sides of her face, some puddling between her massive boobs. She jumped up, fists raised.

I didn't hesitate, and drew my Glock. "Don't make me shoot you. Get a grip, or you're going to jail." I motioned for her to sit.

Phil grabbed the back of the man's collar. Two men bolted off their barstools, grabbed his arms, and pulled him around the side of the bar.

"You don't understand." She backhanded the water from her face. "That whore dog is my husband, and he parks his dick in any vacant space he can find!" she screamed. "Do I ever say no, Hunter? Don't I always say yes to every unnatural sex act you suggest?"

I looked down the bar; no one had a response for her. "Sit your ass back down until you can stop with all the noise. You're giving me a headache and that makes me trigger happy." I leveled my fiercest glare at her.

Phil had disappeared momentarily through the front door; she returned and said, "Hunter's gone. A friend took him home."

I caught movement out of the corner of my eye as the woman on the floor launched herself on another woman, who was either making her way to the bathroom or sneaking out the back door. Mrs. Hunter, or whatever her name was, grabbed a fistful of the woman's long brown hair and whipped her around, getting a kick off every few steps. "Bitch." She spit in her face. She couldn't be more than five feet tall, yet she hurled the other woman back and forth. Under her ugly flowered shift, I suspected she was all muscle.

"Your turn." I poked Phil. "I can't get hurt; I'm the boss."

"Watch and learn." Phil pointed at three of her regulars, who hadn't relinquished their ring side seats.

The three of them lifted their beer mugs in unison, saluted one another, and tossed it all over the scrabbling women.

Mrs. Hunter fell back on her butt again, and the other woman, realizing she was free, raced down the hall for the back door. Mrs. Hunter jumped straight up and took one step after the fleeing woman, but Phil grabbed her dress and dumped her back on the floor.

The woman let out a loud humph.

"If you get up before I give you permission, I'll call the sheriff myself," Phil barked.

At that moment, Kevin strutted in the front door. He was decked out in his uniform, which meant someone had already placed a 911 call. The hooting and hollering came to a halt, and the bar went silent.

Just great, I thought. *A few more minutes, and we could have sent the woman home to beat on her husband.*

"Got a bar fight call. Did I miss the fun?" Kevin's eyes searched every corner of the room.

The patrons turned back to their drinks. There were a few who wouldn't want to get into a friendly chat with law enforcement and risk having a warrant or two uncovered.

"Nothing to see here." I flashed my patient smile. "A few words were exchanged, but it all worked out. The parties involved left."

Kevin's eyes settled on the woman on the floor. He crossed over to her and helped her to her feet. "Ash, you okay?" He enveloped her in a hug, not seeming the least worried about getting his uniform soaked in beer. "What's Hunter done now?"

Ash pressed her face into his chest and collapsed into his arms in a sobbing mess. Kevin led her to a table in the corner. Pulling out a chair, he settled her in his lap, stroked her hair, and whispered something in her ear.

Phil nudged me. "What's that all about?" she whispered.

"I'm disappointed that you don't have the answer for me." The noise level rose when a man filled the jukebox with quarters. "I want to go home, but I'll wait until Kevin leaves."

I had never experienced the compassionate side of Kevin. He had a new girlfriend every time I ran into him on his days off. They tended to look alike: tanned, blond, and well-endowed. The only one I met had been a stripper. Mrs. Hunter was none of those things, and quite frankly didn't look his type. I wondered why he cared.

"Buy you another drink?" Phil looped her arm through mine, and we went back outside.

"I'll stick with water on the off-chance a totally hot guy sneaks into my bed. I don't want to sleep through the whole thing."

"The occasional bar fight is good for business. We'll be standing-room only for the next few days."

I scrunched up my nose, took a breath, and asked her something I'd been wondering about. "What do you know about Creole?"

There was a long pause as Phil stared at me before finally answering, "I know he's undercover, and one of the good guys, and the hot guy you were talking about."

I was a little shocked that she knew he was a cop and not sure what to say.

"As close as you two are, I can't imagine I've said anything you didn't know." She looked at me for confirmation. "I'm the best secret-keeper you'll ever meet. I was the only one of my friends growing up that never ratted anyone out.

Although I got the tables turned on me a few times."

"Did you get sweet revenge?" I felt certain that she would never out Creole's undercover status.

"I learned early on that revenge isn't so sweet," she said with a touch of sadness. "Now I just end the friendship and never look back."

"That's adult of you. The only one I trusted growing up was my brother, and if he ever told on me, he knew I'd put bugs in his bed. Or worse."

"I can't see you collecting bugs." Phil laughed.

"Good call," I chuckled. "I would have had to buy them, and even then, I'm not sure I'd have touched the container."

The dish washer delivered our drinks. I glanced at the bar. All the seats were filled and so were half the tables. Word must have spread faster than usual. I peeked around the corner and saw Kevin still administering affection.

"Why did you ask about Creole? Do you need me to dig around in his background?" Phil clinked the edge of my glass with hers.

I thought about him finding out I'd had him investigated, and his probable reaction made me squirm in my chair. He'd be livid. "He's looking for an information procurer. His street snitches have been totally unreliable of late."

Phil's eyebrows rose. "Can the department afford my rates?"

"Haggle with him, make him feel like he's getting a deal. It doesn't matter to me one way or the other, so you don't have to factor that into your decision. Think about it, and if you're interested, let him know next time he comes in."

"I'm surprised he doesn't know about me already."

"You're not the only one that can keep a secret. I know it irks Creole that I get better info than him. We both know how unreliable snitches can be, and their working hours are sporadic at best. Just so you know, I'm sharing all the Didier information I get with him."

"I've been wanting to talk to you about my info procurement business." The worried look on Phil's face made me groan inside. I hoped the next words out of her mouth weren't going to be "I'm closing up shop," or worse, that she was giving her notice. "My business has picked up, and I recently got several clients. I'd like to run the business out of the bar. I could afford to quit and work from home, but I don't want to because then I'd just go to school and never socialize with anyone."

"How would that work? Anything illegal?" The last thing I wanted was to give local law enforcement a reason to shut me down.

"Oh hell no. Nothing illegal. I just need a place to meet clients; I refuse to have them come to my home. I don't give out my address to anyone, and it's not always convenient to go to them.

This would be a low-key operation; I would book all my appointments before the bar opens. Most of my business can be handled at a table out here on the deck, but I'd like the option of reserving the private room. I'd prefer a monthly rate instead of the percentage your mother pays."

"Or we can swap services," I said.

"I was hoping you'd suggest that. I can promise you I won't invite trouble, but that doesn't mean it won't show up—like those two situations earlier. I did consider shooting the two guys, but they didn't take their obnoxious act far enough."

"You're a Fab in the making, and that scares me."

"Will you think about it and let me know?"

"No," I said evenly. "I've made up my mind. You can open for business tomorrow. If you need the poker room, reserve it with Mother. Tip for dealing with her—take her into your confidence and share whatever details you can. She's the queen of secret-keeping and will eat up the attention. Another perk—she'll always have your back."

"I love your mother, but who doesn't." She laughed. "We get along great. Thanks to her, whoever bartends for one of her games makes good money, so she established herself as a favorite pretty early on. I told her once that gambling was illegal, and she looked me square in the eye and said, 'Prove we're not playing Old

Maid.' Then she went on to tell me that poker was legal as long as there were no winnings involved."

"Mother dear was trotting down the wrong road. She needed a diversion, so I came up with the game room. I still can't believe that I had to nag her to at least think about the idea. It keeps her out of trouble, for the most part." Selfishly, I liked that she was in the Cove almost every day and stopping by the house, always with food. Mother's motto was: *There's no problem that can't be solved over food or shopping.* "I don't ask for specifics. The group is made up of friends, and they deserve to have fun. They order top-shelf liquor, and mother made regular trips to Miami to refill the humidor. She's a boost to the local economy." I was proud that she had made a bigger success out of the room than I'd imagined.

They gambled with chips, and any money transactions took place off-property. As long as no one got arrested and Jake's didn't get shut down, I minded my own business. Besides, if she was in the back room, she wasn't out riding motorcycles.

"There is a catch — non-negotiable," I said.

Phil gave me her version of a scary face, which rivaled Fab's. She waited in silence for me to utter what she was clearly certain would be a deal killer.

"You tell Fab. She's another one to confide in and keep happy."

"I think I'll liquor her up with one her favorites—an apple martini. We're friendly, but you can never gauge how she's going to react to something."

"If she pulls her Walther, she's definitely not happy." I smiled. "Oh, and if you're looking for a boyfriend, drop that tidbit into a conversation with Mother; she'll have your date card filled in no time. Just be *very* specific in your wants."

"She wouldn't mind?"

"Oh trust me, she'd love to fix you up. She's a regular little cupid." I hoped the suggestion wouldn't blow up in my face. When I didn't have a boyfriend, she fixed me up with some real ass-clowns. It would be years before I thought back on those "dates" and found them amusing. I really shouldn't be putting Phil through all that, but hey, you do what you have to get a reprieve from the baby talk.

Chapter Sixteen

I stood briefly at the top of the stairs, not sure which I'd noticed first: the sound of voices coming from the kitchen or the aroma of fresh-brewed coffee that had me quickening my step.

The lovers had apparently made up, as they stood entwined, giggling and sharing the same oversized mug of brew. Didier, I swear, was hotter in the morning—shirtless and with bedhead sticking on end—than when he wore custom-made suits.

I grabbed my favorite shell mug out of the cupboard and banged it down on the island. My eyes on Fab, I said, "I need coffee. Will you fix it for me?"

Didier laughed, tousled her hair with one hand, and reached for my cup with the other.

Jazz had prowled into the kitchen and was headed my way, seeing an opportunity for another treat. The two easy marks had already given him one, and he wasn't wasting any time. I bent down and picked him up before he could start howling, but he'd have to settle for having his neck scratched.

I pointed to Fab in a dramatic fashion. "I want her to do it."

"If I put water in the microwave, will you stop whining?" She glared. "I don't know how to make the crap you drink, and I'm not learning."

Didier scowled at her, which made me happy. My irritation level, which had been on high when I walked into the kitchen thanks to Creole slipping into bed late and leaving early, had all but subsided. I'd felt neglected and grouched at him that he needed to take another day off, and soon, but kissed him on his way out of the bedroom anyway.

Fab, hands on her hips, leaned forward. Before she could start yelling, my phone rang. I looked at the screen and groaned; a call from our pal Dickie this early in the morning wouldn't be good news. Dickie and Raul had bought Tropical Slumber Funeral Home several years ago, and I met them at the funeral for my Aunt Elizabeth. The men could always be depended on if we were in a tight spot and we returned the favor whenever called upon.

"Good morning," I said with cheer I didn't feel.

"We have a problem and need your help." Dickie breathed heavily into the phone.

I hit the speaker button. "Fab is here, too. Speak up so she can hear you." I gestured to Didier and put my finger across my lips; Dickie didn't need to know about him.

"Two people broke into one of the garages, and they're still out there. Raul saw them go in, and so far, we haven't seen anyone leave," Dickie panted. "Raul wants to go out and confront whoever it is, but I don't think that's a good idea."

"That's a terrible idea," Fab yelled. "You tell Raul to keep his ass inside and the door locked." Didier looked at her in surprise. He covered his mouth to hold back the laugh that was eager to escape.

"Why not call the police?" I asked. "They'll arrest the trespassers, and hopefully they won't like jail food and won't come back."

"We can't do that," Dickie said in horror. "Bad publicity isn't good for our kind of business. We offer respectful send-offs for loved ones, not prowlers and thieves."

He did have a point. "Is there anything in the garage besides the car and the hearse?" I asked.

"Not that garage," Dickie huffed. "The one where we store the caskets."

This time, Didier ducked his head under the counter and laughed. Fab and I exchanged looks, and she fell face down on the island.

"We'll be right over," I said.

"I told Raul we could count on you," Dickie said, and hung up.

"Do you think he was afraid you'd change your mind, and that's why he didn't bother with good-bye?" Didier laughed.

"Look, pretty boy, you want to come along and help us catch a... a... casket robber or whatever?" I asked.

Didier shook his head. "What is it your brother says? 'Sorry, gotta go.'"

I passed Jazz, who had fallen asleep, off to Didier. "You take care of the child while we go to work. Come along, girlfriend." I hooked my arm in hers. "This won't take long. We'll shoot the intruders and be right back."

"Nooo!" Didier yelled as I opened the front door. "One almost-felon in the house is enough."

Fab pressed her face against the garden window and made a smooch face. I grabbed the back of her shirt and pushed her in the direction of the SUV.

Chapter Seventeen

The funeral home sat back off the road on the main street that ran through town. Originally an old hot dog drive-thru restaurant, the property had undergone multiple expansion projects. Since Dickie and Raul bought the place, they'd turned the ratty carport into a six-car garage and built a two-story home, attached at the rear of the main building. More recently, they added the crematorium.

Fab pulled up alongside the red carpet that ran from the parking lot to the front door. Somehow, they managed to keep it clean and tire-mark free. Raul had the front door to the main entrance open before we could get out of the SUV.

Before opening the passenger door, I said, "Keep in mind that if someone gets shot, we'll be sitting here all day."

Coming through the entrance, my eyes landed on a new display. An antique round wooden table in the middle of the room that normally held a vase of freshly arranged flowers now displayed busts of people in all mediums from bronze to hand-painted, but no one famous that I recognized.

"What's going on?" Fab asked as she prowled around the room, sticking her head into all the viewing rooms.

I dropped down in my favorite plastic-covered, red brocade chair, positioned next to the door in case a dead person woke up and came strolling out of one of the rooms. In that event, I'd be long gone; every woman for herself. I sighed when Raul closed the door and turned the lock. It sent a shiver up my spine, knowing it was just us and deceased folks.

Raul stopped his pacing and leaned against the entranceway to the main room, where final services were held. "Last night, I spotted a man skulking along the fence at the back of the property. I didn't think much of it; thought he was a tattoo parlor or pawn shop customer using it as a short cut," he said in disgust. "This morning, I saw what I'm pretty sure was the same man using the side wall as a restroom."

I laughed, and Raul and Fab turned and stared. There was a certain segment of Floridian men who thought nothing of watering a tree, bush or plant whenever nature called. The appearance of Dickie diverted the conversation and saved me from having to come up with an explanation for my "inappropriate" behavior. He came down the long hall from his workroom, where he gave the dead their final primping.

He'd brought flavored bottled water with him and handed me one. I looked at the label and, seeing that I got orange, nodded and smiled up at him.

Raul and Dickie couldn't be more different, looks-wise. Raul was the bodybuilder, with olive skin and a medium build, big biceps and well-defined abs. He ran the customer service side of the business. Dickie, his skin tone pale and bordering on unhealthy looking, was over six feet and stick-thin, with long, thin fingers.

The first time he stuck out his hand and those bony tentacles reached for mine, I jumped back. I hope in retrospect that I was polite enough when I said something akin to "no way."

Fab gave me an evil stare. "What did he look like?" she asked Raul.

Fab and Raul had bonded over late-night games of chess when the funeral home duo had graciously allowed her to lie low at their place and appear for a chat with police on her own terms.

"I only saw the back of him: a thirtyish man, dirty brown hair, with pants that hung down and exposed his butt crack. Someone should tell him tell to pull them up; it's a dreadful look. I assumed he was by himself until a woman crept around the corner. At least, I think it was a woman, as she had on a skirt," Raul said.

Dickie interrupted, "Don't forget the part where she squatted and relieved herself."

An inappropriate laugh escaped my lips, and this time, I had a hard time getting myself under control. The three of them turned on me, not seeing the humor.

Raul humphed, clearly stressed. "The man opened the side door to the garage, and they both disappeared inside. I kept watch at the kitchen window, and it didn't take long before they both came back outside, backpacks slung over their shoulders, and hightailed it in the direction of the tattoo parlor. It was closed at the time, so it wasn't their destination."

Dickie twisted in his chair. "We took turns manning the window. That's how we know they weren't gone very long. They looked comfortable coming and going; never once looked over their shoulders."

"Dickie wouldn't let me go and check out the building."

"I don't give a damn about the inventory," Dickie almost yelled. "I worried you might get hurt. What if there were others inside?" His outburst came as a surprise to me; I'd never heard him raise his voice or lose his cool.

"Why the casket room?" Raul said. "There's nothing to steal. Every coffin requires a forklift to move."

If they weren't such good friends, I'd block their calls, I thought.

"We need the two of you to investigate and take care of the problem," Dickie said, wringing his hands in his lap. "We would prefer no gun shots, BUT your safety is top priority. If the choice is you or them, don't hesitate. We don't want either one of you to get hurt."

"If anything were to happen to either of you... Well, selfishly, you're our only friends." Raul smiled at Fab. "We should've called the sheriff. We almost did. Then Dickie and I discussed the lurid headlines that would dominate the local newspaper for who knows how long. New customers might avoid us. Even returning ones might not use us in the future and choose to take their business out of the Keys instead."

"Are you certain they're in there now?" I asked.

Both men nodded.

"What do you want us to do with them?" We could get rid of them easily enough, but what about afterwards? "Do you want them arrested? Or Fab could do what she does best—scare the hell out of them."

They both smiled affectionately at her. I rolled my eyes and wished for something cold and caffeinated.

"I'll get the keys." Raul excused himself. Fab trailed behind him.

"Come on." I motioned to Dickie, and we walked to the kitchen and peered out the infamous window. Nothing outside was moving. I didn't hear anyone come into the room, but suddenly there was a yank on my hair.

"Oww." I turned and Fab let go of my hair.

"I've got a plan." She grabbed my arm and jerked me out the door.

"Well?" I skidded to a stop, refusing to budge.

"You fling the door open on three," she directed. "I'll take the lead, gun drawn, and hopefully we catch them off guard. If they're carrying, they'll have no time to go for their guns. But from the description of those two, I'd be surprised if they had weapons. When I give you the all-clear, you do whatever annoying thing it is that you do to get them to talk."

"You should be more appreciative; it's a useful tool that's helped us out in the past," I whispered. We crept across the concrete, stopped to listen for any activity, and slunk around the side.

"Look, I just don't want to hang out with the coffins any longer than necessary."

"Amen." I whooshed out a breath. I hoped this would be some sort of misunderstanding, but figured there was zero chance of it turning out that way.

Hand on the door knob, I waited for Fab to give the signal. She held up her fingers one after the other; when she got to three, I yanked the door open, and Fab charged in. I was right behind her, Glock in hand. The woman spotted us first; her eyes locked on our guns, and she screamed, her hands flying into the air.

The two had been sitting on the floor, leaning

back against a casket, playing cards and munching on crackers. The man spit out a mouthful of soda, the purple mixture dribbling down his shirt.

"You." Fab looked at the man and motioned with the muzzle of the gun. "Hands up. Either one of you moves, I'll shoot one and then the other. If I miss, my friend here is an excellent shot."

I felt sorry for the frightened couple. The woman started bawling, gasping for breath, and the man looked on the verge of barfing up the contents of his stomach. I'd guess them to be in their mid-thirties and pegged them as homeless. I hadn't spotted any signs of criminal behavior.

Fab skirted the aisle, walking between the casket displays from front to back. She lingered at the back a little too long for my nerves, then shook her head and gave me the thumbs up.

"You two are trespassing," I said, pointing out the obvious.

"We didn't steal nuttin," the scraggly blonde blurted.

"Shush, Mandy," her partner hissed. "We don't want no trouble. We'll just go."

Fab and I exchanged a look that translated into "what now?"

"I don't think so." Fab returned to the front and waved her Walther at the two.

"Put your hands down," I said gruffly. "Don't do anything stupid. Now start talking—tell us what you're doing here." I looked at Fab and she nodded.

Mandy made keening noises and laid her head on the man's chest. He petted her head like she was a dog.

"Start with your name," Fab barked.

"Charlie P-P-Panker," the man stuttered. "We needed a comfortable place to stay for a few nights."

Fab gave Charlie her mean stare and said, "You two are living here?"

Thank goodness one of us had people skills.

"We… uh…" He shifted around on the floor. "…only used the one coffin. Both of us fit in real good."

I took a short breath; it felt like my heart actually skipped a beat. If I were a fainter, this would be where I'd hit the floor. "You slept in one of the coffins?" I squirmed. "Why?"

"Don't call the sheriff," Charlie implored.

"I don't like jail," Mandy wailed, "and we don't got bail money."

Charlie squeezed her tighter. "We're homeless. I lost my job, and I haven't been able to get another one. If it's money you want, I can't pay anything, but I can do odd jobs."

"What happened to your last job?" I could easily get him a job, but first I'd like to be sure he wasn't hiding something. Frankly, neither one looked smart enough. But the jails were filled with stupid criminals.

"I cooked at the Pancake Joint and it burned to the ground," Charlie said.

I'd heard about that and also knew that the owner was under investigation, suspected for the arson. He certainly had motive if the rumors were true—he needed the insurance money to pay off gambling debt to unsavory characters.

Fab moved to the front, propping open the door. "Drugs? Alcoholics?" she asked.

Charlie shook his head. "My wife has asthma." He looked down at her. "If we went to jail, you could get a new inhaler."

"Please," she moaned. "Last time, I had to stand in line at the infirmary, and when I got released, I didn't get to take it with me."

"Stop it, you two," I said, louder than I'd meant to. "You're not going to jail." I asked Charlie, "Can you pass a background check?"

"I've been arrested for loitering a couple of times. There's some places folks don't want you sleeping," he said. "Most serious was a vandalism charge when I was sixteen."

"What did you do?" Fab asked.

"Me and two other guys threw toilet paper all over the neighbor's house and in the trees. The girl's father didn't seem to think it was funny when he caught us and turned us over to the cops. The girl spread it all over school, and the kids laughed at what dumbasses we were for the rest of the school year. My friend, who really liked the girl, never looked at her again."

I smiled, thinking about how many times my girlfriends and I had snuck out in the middle of the night and thrown rolls of toilet paper on a boy's lawn. That was until my mother found out and made us go clean up the mess. Me, anyway. "Pack up your stuff and clean this place up. It better look like you were never here," I told them. "Don't go anywhere."

"Clean up in aisle 5." Fab laughed at her joke.

My lips quirked as I glared at her.

"I know you want to laugh." Fab elbowed me.

"You stand guard." I winked at Fab.

"You're not going to throw our stuff out, are you?" Mandy wheezed out the last word.

"We're going to come to a compromise." I lifted my skirt and reholstered my Glock in my thigh holster.

"That's what the cops did," Mandy said sullenly.

Before I stepped outside, Fab leaned in and whispered to me, "We'll give them some cash and report back that the poachers have left the property."

The coffin storage room had become claustrophobic and I was never happier to breathe in fresh air. I pulled my phone out of my bra—my go-to pocket when my skirt had none—and called the only person I knew who had extensive experience helping people get their lives back on track.

"Hello stepdaddy," I said when the call connected.

A deep, growly laugh filled my ear. "Whatever it is you want, the answer is yes."

"What if I ask you to off someone?"

"You know the answer would be 'what's his name?' I'm putting you on speaker; your mother's giving me an evil stare."

"Hi, honey, you in trouble?" she asked.

"Not this time, but I need Spoon's help." I told him about Charlie and Mandy.

"You make me proud," Mother said. "I would've given them money and told them not to come back."

"That was Fabiana's idea," I told her. "You two could be related."

"They were really sleeping in a coffin?" Spoon asked in shock.

"Turns out they're comfortable. That's good to know, don't you think?"

"Really, Madison. No one wants to think about that," Mother said.

I hoped I would never outgrow inappropriate talk.

"Tell them to wait out front," Spoon said. "I'll have Billy come by and pick them up. I can get them an interim place to stay until Charlie finds employment. If he's a decent cook, I can get him a job. After that, I'll give them a couple of addresses that won't demand first and last month's rent if I vouch for them."

"You're the best," I said.

"You owe me." Spoon laughed. "And don't think I'll forget that. Ouch," he yelped.

I grinned, knowing Mother had done something painful.

"You need anything else, call." He clicked off.

Raul and Dickie had the window open and their faces pressed to the screen. I waved and shook my head for them to stay inside. Fab had reholstered her gun, confident that she could take the two of them, even at the same time.

I relayed the happy news to Fab and informed her that she'd be the one to share it with the couple. "It will be good for your people skills." As hard as I tried, I couldn't maintain a straight face.

She tugged on my arm. "You're coming with me."

"I'm not going back in there." I stared at the open door. "I've had enough of the coffins. What I need is a drink."

"I'll go get them," Fab whispered. "You tell them." She stuck her head across the threshold and yelled, "Get out here. Time to leave."

I shook my head.

The young couple shuffled out into the sunshine, fear written on their faces. They were about to get a big break, and I hoped they didn't squander it.

"Your ride will be here in a few. My friend, Spoon, has arranged for a place for you to stay and has a possible lead on a job."

"Jimmy Spoon?" Mandy shrieked. "He hurts people."

"Breathe deep," I mumbled to myself. "You have nothing to worry about if you take this opportunity and make the most of it. If it's something you're not interested in, say so. I'll give you a few dollars, and you can be on your way."

Charlie leaned down and whispered something to his wife. Instead of a reply, she buried her head in his chest. "Thank you," he said. "For everything. You won't be sorry. Once I get a cooking job, you come in, and I'll make you something special."

"There's one more thing." Fab glowered at the duo. "Don't come back here unless you need funeral services—that you can pay for."

"Your ride is here." I motioned for them to follow me.

Billy, one of Spoon's long-time employees, jumped out of his pickup truck. He opened the back door, and before they got in, I made the introductions.

I whispered to Billy, "Free meal at Jake's, anytime. Just tell the bartender."

He half-laughed. "Stay out of trouble."

I ran to catch up with Fab. We barreled back into the funeral home, and I plunked myself in the chair reserved for me, leaning back as she explained the situation, hoping she had fast exit plans. I liked the guys but the funeral home gave me the creeps.

"Are you collecting busts now?" Fab ran her hand over one bust's head. "New art collection? They look hand-sculpted."

"That's our newest service," Raul boasted. "You give us a picture of your loved one, and we commission the urn in the deceased's image. Dates back to the Egyptian pharaohs. This way, you can have the statue as an art piece to put on display."

Fab jerked her hand back. "There's a dead person in here?"

"They're just for display. Our clients prefer to see their choices up close. A catalog is so impersonal."

"I don't care for cremation," Dickie said, frowning at the urns. Everyone knew he felt cheated when he didn't get to give the deceased the sendoff he felt they deserved. He prided himself on his attention to detail.

Fab lifted the head off the brightly painted ceramic one and peered inside. She tipped it my way so I could see.

"We cremate the loved one, store the ashes until the urn arrives, and then present it to the client. We're thinking of a very short handing-over ceremony to mark the moment as a pleasant memory," Raul said.

I waited until both men were distracted by something and glared at Fab, jerking my head towards the door.

"We've got another appointment," Fab said as she slipped over to Raul and hugged him. "I'll send over a friend to install a security system on the garage. Locked doors aren't enough. I'll come back once it's installed and check it out."

Chapter Eighteen

It was the perfect afternoon to lie back on an inflated chair sipping a margarita. The blue sky overhead was filled with fluffy white clouds, but in the distance, grey clouds were getting darker by the minute. Hopefully, the impending storm would veer west and stay out in the Gulf.

I paddled to the side of the pool. "I deserve this after a long day at the funeral home," I said, setting down my glass.

"Two hours." Fab stood over me, holding up her fingers. "Shortest job we've ever had."

I swept my arm through the water and sent a blast of water her way. She jumped back, but not before it soaked her shorts.

She kicked off her obscenely high wedge sandals and sat on the side, sticking her feet in the water and shaking her finger at me. "Remember the rules, no drinking and floating."

"Once I've sucked the rest of this one down, I'll get my drunk on inside, on the couch."

"We need to talk before you get all happy and loud." She looked over her shoulder.

We had the house to ourselves. Didier had an appointment, and Creole had promised he'd sneak into my bed later. He never discussed the details of his assignments, but stayed in touch mostly by random texts so I wouldn't worry.

"I've got a couple of appointments tomorrow, and I'll be gone all day," Fab announced.

My heart sped up; I knew this could be big trouble. "Who? What? Where?" I planned to push the issue and not let her out of my sight.

Fab skimmed her hand along the surface of the water, blasting me with water and reveling in the payback. "You know damn well I have my own company, or have you forgotten about FM Associates? I get the occasional client that doesn't want me teaming up."

"Is that the same business I'm a supposed partner in? If you think you're going to sneak something by me and then call from jail, forget it. Spit it out." I paddled over to the steps.

Fab stood up and dragged a chaise over to the poolside. "Just a little corporate espionage. In, plant a bug, then out. First, I'm meeting with the client to get the details."

"The first trick to selling a lie is to not look down." I wrapped myself in a towel and sat down next to her. "It would have been slightly less hurtful if you'd said, 'None of your business.' I don't understand why you don't trust me. Some would say it's not that big a deal, but funny, I feel differently."

"Seriously, you know how to heap the guilt on, and it's not attractive." She shrugged and met my gaze. "I'm going to commit several felonies, not least breaking and entering, and I don't want you getting in trouble."

"You know I have talents other than providing bail money," I huffed.

Fab banged her head on my shoulder and sighed heavily.

"Oww," I mouthed, surprised that I managed to stay silent.

"I overheard Creole telling Didier that he'd like to get a look around Lauren's condo but his boss told him no. It could mean his job if he got caught."

"Did you happen to *overhear* what it is he's hoping to find?"

Fab ran her fingers through her long hair. "No," she said in frustration. "You know that if I even hint at going myself, they'll both forbid me. Better for them to be upset after the fact."

How many times had we used that tactic? They still got mad. Then they extracted promises that we wouldn't sneak around again, which lasted until the next time Fab needed information. "Have you forgotten no matter how many GPS devices you destroy, he just installs another one? I don't know how closely he monitors it when we're on the move. Although Lauren's condo isn't in a bad neighborhood, so maybe our location will escape his notice."

I didn't find the tracking as intrusive as Fab did. I liked that someone always knew where we were. There had been a few times I didn't think we'd make it out alive.

Fab had plans that Creole would hate written all over her face. "We'll rent a car." She looked proud of herself.

"We?" I glared at her.

"I feel a strong-arm tactic coming. A threat of some sort—something involving your mother?" She raised her eyebrows. "Can't you be gracious?"

"Don't even think about going by yourself. Forget the rental car, we'll use the Hummer," I said as I stood up. "Do you know if the police have finished their investigation? The police tape gone?"

"Lauren wasn't high profile. Once the investigation of the scene was over, they wouldn't leave an officer behind to stand guard."

"You always do these jobs at night. Why the change?" I refused to lecture about unnecessary risks when I knew she'd do anything for Didier, including going to jail.

"We're going in the early morning hours. It will still be dark out, and hopefully no one will be milling around. Didier's in New York; what's your slug up to?"

I flashed her a dirty look and started for the house.

"Okay…boyfriend. Happy now?" Fab called.

I turned in the doorway. "I thought you two were growing on one another?"

She jumped up and followed me inside. "Like a rash." She laughed behind me. "We like each other fine. You and I both know that Creole won't like what I'm about to do. He'll be mad I dragged you into a crime with a chance of us ending up in matching orange jumpsuits."

"You're in luck." I opened the refrigerator, taking out my conch shell-shaped glass pitcher, a flea market find that I'd filled earlier with apple water that I made myself. "Creole won't be here tonight to put his foot down or, as my father used to threaten, 'Do I need to put my foot up your ass?'"

"Did you and Brad get the foot?" She kicked her foot in the air, laughing.

"When he used that threat, we stopped horsing around. He was the easiest-going man until we irked his last nerve."

"I grew up with rules. When I broke them, I got punished, a lot of times banished to my room, which I hated. Now I live to break all the rules."

I felt bad that Fab didn't have a relationship with her parents, but there was no forgiveness on either side. They'd turned their backs on her and her wild ways, and the only chance of them making up was if Fab turned into another person. They had a mold of the perfect daughter, and she would need to be an exact fit. It had surprised me when she told me that they'd never approve of Didier.

"No more alcohol." I filled both of our glasses with apple water.

Fab sniffed hers, then took a sip.

"Stop doing that, it's so rude." I mimicked her evil eye. "You know I hate early—so wake me in the morning. You better give me time to get dressed, not some last-minute, hurry up deal."

Her disturbing laugh trailed behind her as she disappeared up the stairs.

Chapter Nineteen

Huddled behind the wheel of the Hummer, I noticed the South Beach revelers had already made their way home to sleep off their alcohol-induced states. In the dark, it looked like any other neighborhood. I groaned when my phone rang, knowing by the ringtone that it was Creole. I held my finger over the disconnect button, debating, but finally decided to take the call. He'd just call back anyway. The ringing stopped.

"Shoo." My fist shot into the air. The smile on my face disappeared when the phone started ringing again. "Damn him," I mumbled. "Hi, honey," I answered with overblown cheerfulness, then flinched, certain that would alert him that something was up.

"Honey, my backside." He rumbled out a deep laugh. "Where the hell are you?"

"We're in a great neighborhood; no criminals here. White-collar ones, perhaps. If you were here, we could walk on the beach," I rambled.

Total silence—I knew he hadn't hung up; I could hear him breathing. I blew into the phone to restart the conversation.

"Damn it, that's my ear," he grouched.

"There's no pleasing you today. Talk to you later."

"Don't you dare hang up, or I'll call in your license plate. Now where are you?" His voice had taken on a serious edge.

I wanted to end the call, to weasel out of the questions, but I wouldn't hang up. The thought of sleeping by myself for several days was an effective deterrent. "Did you miss the meeting on misusing police resources?"

Silence again.

"Oh, all right." I heaved a sigh. "We're at Lauren's condo. One of us is tossing the joint; the other sitting in the SUV."

"How long has Fab been up there?" He sounded surprisingly calm, and that surprised me.

"Less than five, not counting the time it takes to get up there and all."

"Do you have a way to contact her—the one committing felonies, breaking and entering, fucking with a crime scene, etcetera?"

"Language," I said in a shocked voice, covering the phone so he didn't hear me chuckle. "Yes to your question."

"I want pictures of every single room. And anything else she thinks I need to see. Tell her if she gets caught and jeopardizes the case, I'll knock Didier out of the way to strangle her first. Call me back when you've made contact."

"Hanging up now." I clicked off and sent the

message, asking her to confirm so there would be no misunderstanding.

It took too long, in my opinion, before I got back a thumbs-up text. In fact, it took so long that I started to think something had gone wrong. We hadn't discussed a plan for how I'd come to the rescue, and I knew that was on purpose.

I called Creole back. "Done," I said when he answered.

"Where are you? Exactly!" He'd reached his limit of stalling and attempts at evasive answers.

"Sitting across the street at metered parking, listening to the waves pound on the shore." Under the last bit of moonlight, they looked high, racing over one another to crash on the sand. The surfers were coming out in droves and gathering in groups.

"Listen to me. Don't make some excuse later that you weren't paying attention. If police cars show up, leave. Fab will text you when she gets out. There's not a single reason why both of you should get arrested. Driving the getaway car is a crime." His voice was controlled, but I knew he wasn't happy.

"Fab always has my back. You know she would never ditch me in a similar situation. Why can't I help her out?" My voice trailed off as I leaned back against the seat.

"You are helping. I wasn't suggesting you ditch her. It would take days, or more, to walk back to the Cove from Lauderdale. Fab is a pro.

She'll come walking out any minute, and you'll be there to give her a ride."

"Did you just give Fab a compliment?" I kept my eyes glued on the lobby door, occasionally checking out the side of the building in case she came out through the garage.

"Don't tell her," he said with humor in his voice. "Promise me you won't take any unnecessary chances."

"I won't. Are you mad?"

"I'd rather have searched the place myself, but pictures will work. The last thing I'd do is ask Didier's girlfriend to put herself in jeopardy, but now that it's happened, I'm anxious to see what she's got. I tried hitting up a friend for a favor to get my hands on the file, but he turned me down. 'Nothing personal,' he said, but apparently there's a password required for access," he said, his voice laced with frustration. "Text me when she gets back."

It didn't take long before my phone rang again. This time it was Fab. "You okay?" I whispered.

"I'm up the street on the beach side. Come pick me up. I'll be the one standing in the street with my thumb out."

I threw my phone on the console and squealed out of the parking space. All the waiting had made me jittery. Instead of subtly pointing her thumb out to the road, she started jumping up and down and waving when she saw the SUV.

She looked fresh off the beach—white shorts, navy-and-white button-down shirt, floppy hat, and a cotton bag over her shoulder. To my surprise, she didn't run around to the driver's side and demand that I move over.

"Am I dropping you off at another location?" I asked. When she shook her head, I pulled over into a parking space. "Let's switch sides now. Your instructive driving techniques give me a headache."

She shook her finger. "Don't say I never let you drive."

"You should call Creole. He wanted me to call when you showed up, but I don't have the answers to his questions," I told her.

"How did he find out?" She quickly pulled away from the curb. This early near the beach, the streets were deserted, and even the bars that stayed open until the early morning hours were closed.

"He called, asked where we were, and I didn't lie. He'd find out sooner or later, and when he did, why should I be the one to go without sex?" I stuck out my lower lip.

"Men! It doesn't matter. I planned to bring it up somehow, tell Didier when he got home—I thought maybe liquor would help." Fab picked up my phone and hit redial. "Got what you wanted," she said, then hit the speaker button.

"Thanks," Creole said. "I'm assuming you weren't arrested. Did anyone see you, coming, going, or otherwise?"

"I didn't see a single person. I kept the brim of my sun hat down, didn't take off my dark glasses, and avoided cameras."

"I'll be over later for dinner. You two cooking?" He laughed.

Fab and I made faces at the phone. Neither of us found him amusing. I was once a great cook, but it no longer held any interest for me, and it didn't help that Mother had gotten me addicted to take-out. I'd never seen Fab touch a pot or pan.

"I'm almost out of frozen waffles," I said. "We'll stop at the market and get more."

"I'll call you when I'm headed in that direction. You call in the takeout order."

"Fine." I winked at Fab.

"Ease my mind and tell me that the two of you are going home," he sighed.

"Yes, we're headed that way," Fab assured him, and hung up.

"I'm not waiting until tonight; I want details now," I said after she tossed the phone at me.

"You would have loved her place: open floor plan, one-hundred-eighty-degree view of the Atlantic Ocean, decorated in comfortable slip-covered furniture, beach chic. You two could have collected shells together." Fab hated that I collected shells. I took a bucket or two with me when I went for walks on the beach, brought them back full, and used them as mulch in the potted plants.

"The places we usually break into are all uptight chrome and glass, where it looks like no one has ever sat on the furniture." A couple of times, I'd wanted to leave my butt-print on the pristine leather couch but figured the owner would notice.

"It was a clean crime scene, no signs anyone had tossed the place, and nothing looked out of place, except in the living room. You know, plenty of dried blood stains on the carpet." Fab flew onto the interstate in record time, just ahead of morning rush hour.

"The rest of the condo?" I asked.

"Lauren had great organizational skills; everything had its place, all the drawers and closets were organized, even her bed had been made. Not like at your house, with the ginormous junk drawer that a person can't find anything in."

"There's a fully-loaded Beretta in there, just in case," I said. "What's in the bag?" I tossed a glance over my shoulder to the back seat.

"I found a couple of files and several journals that she'd hidden in the bookcase behind some legal books."

"Apparently not well enough." A grin slid across my lips.

Chapter Twenty

Lost in thought, Fab almost missed our street and turned hard, squealing around the corner. "Look who just pulled up to the curb." She looked in the rearview mirror.

"Mother." I glanced at the dash clock. "Five bucks says she's got dinner."

Fab shook her head as though I'd lost my mind. "When does she show up without food?"

Mother's horn sounded.

"That's code for she needs help."

"You go. I'm going to sneak this stuff into the house so she doesn't ask questions." Fab grabbed her tote bag.

We'd stopped at The Cottages on the way home. There was no one around, so Fab went into the office and copied the files she'd lifted from Lauren's condo. One held several real estate contracts, the top one for the deal Brad and Didier had been negotiating. The most interesting file had handwritten notes stuffed inside it and a thumb drive taped to the cover. Knowing Mac kept extras of every kind of office supplies, I reached into the cabinet and handed Fab another drive to make a copy, thereby expediting Creole's chances of seeing it sooner, rather than later.

Mother stood holding open the back door of her black SUV and looking impatient. You couldn't get into this family unless you drove a black automobile. I skimmed over her knee-length hot pink shorts to her wedge flip-flops and enveloped her in a hug.

"I recognize that silver bow." I pointed to her shoes, the designer insignia catching my attention. "Did you get me a pair?"

"Only one pair left, and they're mine." She wiggled her pink-manicured toes.

"Maybe I can borrow them?" I asked wistfully.

She shook her head and frowned. "You already have enough of my shoes in your closet. Where's Fab?"

I ignored her question and reached for the two shopping bags with the large red crab insignia on them, sticking my nose in for a sniff. "Yum, smells great."

"I brought everyone's favorites. Did you forget that Spoon and I were coming for early dinner?" Mother grabbed two pink boxes from everyone's favorite bakery.

"I did." I made a pouty face. "Your timing is perfect though—everyone's going to be home tonight." I eyed the pink boxes. "I love that you always remember dessert."

Mother looped her arm through mine and walked across the driveway. I frowned when I saw that Fab had left the front door open. I didn't think Jazz would go for a stroll, but it might be an invitation he couldn't ignore. I never let him out the front; he could hang out in the backyard on comfortable patio furniture.

I set the bags on the kitchen counter, looking out the garden window, and was surprised to see Creole's truck parked in the neighbor's driveway across the street. The couple that owned the house used it as a vacation getaway and had told me once that I could use their driveway for extra parking so the house didn't appear vacant.

Fab could be heard jumping down the stairs, one of her favorite things to do. She slid into the kitchen, kissed Mother's cheek, and opened the refrigerator. "Cold drinks, anyone?" She looked pleased with herself, which meant she was up to something.

"Creole's here…somewhere," I told her.

Mother eyed the two of us, looking us over from head to toe. "What have you two been doing today? Skip the shopping excuse and any other made-up story; I know you were out on a job. Madison has tennis shoes on."

Having been on more than one job with us, Mother knew my shoes of choice were flip-flops, and that tennis shoes were reserved for business attire, worn where running might be the only option.

I arched my brow at Fab in question. It was her boyfriend and her story to tell, not mine.

Mother shifted her gaze to Fab, and they engaged in a stare-off. My money was on Fab breaking first.

Creole and Didier burst through the French doors drenched in sweat. Judging by their attire, they'd had one of their marathon runs on the beach. Creole had once suggested that we run together, and I'd laughed at him. I sometimes accompanied him down to the sand, where he would leave me. I'd walk until I was tired, and he would pick me up on the way back.

"There you are." Creole crooked his finger at Fab. "I want to see the pictures," he said as he crossed the room to stand by her side.

Fab wore a deer-in-the-headlights look. She knew he couldn't see Mother from his vantage point, and she didn't want to spill the day's felonious activities before she had a chance to tell Didier.

"Don't be mad," Creole whispered to Fab. "I told pretty boy what you were up to. I had it half blurted out before I realized that he didn't know."

"Fabiana," Didier said in a soft voice and held out his arms, "you could have gone to jail."

Fab ran across the room. Didier enveloped her in his arms and murmured something in her ear. He must have used the right words, as her body visibly relaxed.

Mother stepped out, shaking her finger at Creole and Didier. "You two go shower. You're getting sand on the floor." She used the voice that always got Brad and me motivated. "The food will be ready when you two come back downstairs," she added.

Creole broke the silence that had filled the room. "Fab, would you send a copy to my personal email? Madison will give you the address," he said hastily, then scurried up the stairs.

Didier gave Fab a quick kiss and followed Creole.

Mother turned on us. "Just maybe I'll find out what's going on and what's so important about these pictures," she said loudly. "And you two better not end up in jail!" She ended in a yell.

Fab poked me. "Calm her down. Please."

Spoon pressed his face to the kitchen window and waved. I, for one, was happy to see him. Spoon could keep Mother calm. Mother met him at the door before he could get it open.

I opened a drawer and pulled out some colorful napkins. "Spoon, send Mother back over here when you're done making out. I need help setting the table."

Mother turned, her cheeks turning pink. "Madison, a nice kiss is not making out." Brad didn't like the PDAs, but it pleased me to see the affection Spoon showed Mother and how she glowed under his attentive eye.

"Anybody object to sitting outside?" I asked.

I needed to tell Fab that she should sit at the

opposite end of the table from Mother, thereby cutting off her opportunity to grill Fab. The only option other than outside was the kitchen island, and it would be too intimate a space with so many people, not to mention uncomfortable with all of us squeezed together.

I motioned to Fab to go upstairs. She turned up her nose but went anyway. She needed the time to explain to Didier that our adventure today had been to help him, glossing over the part where he hadn't found out until after the fact.

Why waste beautiful Florida weather eating inside? The table outside sat twelve, which easily accommodated my family, and I set it with colorful mix-and-match dishes. My newest find, small round vases wrapped in rope, were each stuffed with a string of battery lights.

I bypassed the timer and flooded the backyard with light. The palm tree trunks were wrapped in white Christmas lights, and the potted plants held two solar stakes each, which glowed in the dark. Mother had found globes for the pool that turned different colors while floating on the water, and I tossed in some colored floating LED lights.

Creole walked up and wrapped his arms around me from behind, kissing my neck. "Can we sneak out of here later?" His voice, deep and rich, made me smile.

"If we want any privacy, we'll have to sneak

down to the beach." I turned in his arms. "My laptop is on the desk, help yourself."

"I checked before I came out. Fab hasn't sent them yet." His voice spiked with irritation.

"Why did you rat Fab out?" I schooled my voice to not let *my* irritation show. "She should have been the one to tell Didier."

"It didn't happen that way," he snapped. "I was putting in a good word about her bravery and how she'd put herself on the line for him. I knew in an instant that he had no idea what I was talking about, and I couldn't lie or leave him hanging." He took hold of my shoulders and looked me in the eye. "Didier was never mad. More like awed by her bravery."

We turned as Fab and Didier approached. I wanted a signal that all was good between her and Didier. She nodded, and I breathed a sigh of relief.

Fab handed Creole a folder. "This is from Lauren's home office; projects she was working on, including the one she was working on with you guys. I forwarded the pictures right before we came out, along with a video."

Creole nodded and thumbed through the paperwork. "Thank you. I appreciate this."

"I propose we share information," Creole offered and stared at Fab intently, waiting for her answer.

"I'm tapped out of info. I shared what I had."

Trust was hard for Fab. Creole would have to

have her back more than a few times for her to warm up. From the beginning, our relationship had taken sheer determination on my part that we were going to be friends. I had to convince her I wouldn't be like her previous so-called friends and screw her over. Creole would have to do the same.

Not acknowledging the silence, Fab continued, "I'd like to search the office, go through her personal files. The files I found today were carefully hidden, and I'd like to be sure that I didn't miss anything that would be helpful to Didier, although I'm sure Balcazar is smart enough not to keep anything incriminating around. Any idea what the security is like?" she asked Creole.

Didier, his arm around Fab, wrapped his fingers in her hair and pulled her head back to face him. "I don't like your idea, *chérie*."

Fab pushed away and crossed her arms. "I will not sit around and do nothing. Don't ask me to." Her face radiated frustration and anger.

"We'll discuss all of our operations later. Madeline is headed this way." Creole closed the space between them and hugged Fab. "Good find." He smiled down at her. "I can't believe top investigators went over her place and left these behind."

"I excel at finding things that people want to keep hidden." She breathed in to calm herself.

Mother joined us. "Dinner's ready."

If someone didn't know better, they would have thought Mother had cooked the veritable feast herself, instead of taking it out of containers, reheating it, and serving it on pretty dishes.

Fab took center stage, telling everyone about her day, making it sound quite ordinary. She confessed to eavesdropping on a conversation between Creole and Didier and said she'd known she could get the information if there was any to get. Turns out, she excelled at storytelling; everyone at the table hung on her every word.

Chapter Twenty-One

It was early morning and the house eerily quiet, which made me wonder if anyone was home. I didn't want to face anyone, embarrassed that I'd fallen asleep so early last night. Tired of endless chit-chat I wasn't listening to anyway, I'd escaped to my bedroom for a few minutes of alone time and made the mistake of lying on my bed to stare at the ceiling.

As I passed by Fab's closed bedroom door, I sniffed the air, hoping to be greeted by the scent of coffee, or maybe breakfast — Didier might have decided to cook — but sighed in disappointment.

Fab sat at the island, hand-feeding Jazz tuna, his new favorite. "You're so rude." She handed me a coffee mug.

I turned it upside down. "Isn't there something missing?"

Fab jerked it back, filled it with water, and handed it back. "Here's your morning coffee."

I shoved the mug in the microwave. "I didn't mean to fall asleep. I sat down, and the next thing I knew, I got a hard slap on the ass."

Creole had pulled off my clothes and tossed them in the air. They'd ended up in various places on the floor. He turned back the covers, picked me up, and slid between the sheets, pulling me against his chest. Then we fell asleep. As usual, he had to leave early; he left me with a thorough kiss and a promise to return tonight.

Before leaving, he'd said, "I told everyone you weren't feeling well and didn't want to stop the party."

With a wink, I'd offered to cover his ass if he ever needed me to. He responded with a deep, growly laugh and left.

"I love those good-girl spankings," Fab sighed.

"Please." I rolled my eyes and made a choking noise. "It's too early to hear about your sex life." My phone started ringing annoyingly, and I hit the button to stop it. If only I could send a message: "call after I've had my coffee." Mac's face beamed at me from the tiny screen. "Ye-es," I answered.

Fab motioned irritably for me to hit the speaker button. She didn't involve herself in cottage affairs unless a gun was required, but she also didn't tolerate being the last to know about something.

"Hope you're sitting, problem time. I'm almost certain it involves a stolen car." Mac exhaled loudly.

"Joseph?" I squeezed my eyes shut and counted to three.

Stolen anything had Joseph's name on it. No

one else had the nerve to dump cars at The Cottages. We had yet to have a tourist turn into a felon. In the past, Joseph had escaped being charged with a felony, and I'd hate for his first major charge to be grand theft auto. With his rap sheet of misdemeanor annoying crimes a grown man should know better than to commit, this newest one could carry serious jail time.

"There's a newish Escalade sitting in his parking spot."

"A what?" I banged my fist on the counter. "That's a fifty-thousand-dollar-plus SUV!" I'd never make it through the morning without aspirin.

"Joseph ignored my polite knock, so I yelled and pounded on the door. Everyone else heard me—all our guests had their heads poked through the blinds—but he didn't make a peep. When I finally yelled, 'Fine, I'll get the key,' he responded, 'Go away. Your noise makes my head hurt.'"

I lowered my voice, not wanting to take my irritation out on my manager. "Has his feeble mind forgotten that a deputy lives at The Cottages?"

"We caught a break there. Kevin has two days off, and he's banging his latest girlfriend at her house. Trying to set a good example for Liam, as though teenagers don't know about sex." She snorted. "It's not like he's a backwards convent girl."

"I can hear you," Fab half-yelled.

"I knew it." Mac laughed, followed by two loud bangs in the background as she kicked the desk. I hoped she had on tennis shoes and didn't kick a hole in it.

"I should never have let Joseph keep his parking space," I said. The last car that had appeared out of nowhere had had suspicious origins, having no title and not having been registered in years. I'd managed to convince him to return that one before the police showed up.

How did Joseph repay me? He used his parking space as his personal patio, dragging out a rickety chaise and chair for the occasional friend, more rescues from the trash, something he and the professor had in common. He made it his mission to guard the driveway as though it was his personal domain and kept his eyes peeled for the occasional drunk stumbling by on the street. Like a cat, he fell asleep in seconds, snoring so loudly it could be heard down the block.

"You relay a message—tell him I'm on my way," I fumed. "If he can't produce a current title with his name on it, I'm calling a tow truck. Then I'll give serious thought to bagging up his personal belongings and having him pitched to the curb. Spoon thinks he's a weasel; he'd probably come do it himself and for free." Joseph knew that I knew he couldn't get a car registered in his name. He didn't have a driver's license; it had been revoked.

I hung up and called Joseph—who naturally didn't answer—and left a message: "On my way."

Fab shook the car keys, eyeing me up and down. "Are you going like that?"

I looked down at my black sweat shorts and t-shirt. I looked at her and crinkled my nose. She rocked her skinny jeans and the black cotton top that hung longer in the back to hide her Walther.

My outfit is new and cute, not to mention comfortable, I thought with a sniff.

"If you expected me to pull sexy out of my ass, it won't be today. We can't all look like you early in the morning." I bent over, tousled my hair, and slipped into a pair of flip-flops. "Better? Look." I pointed to my shoes. "They match my outfit."

"I hope we're always best friends," she said, then grabbed my arm and pulled me out the door.

"Now you say that. In the beginning, you treated me like the nerdy girl who was in over her head."

"I'll admit that I thought you over-hyped the whole friend idea, but I believe I was mistaken."

"Wow." I clutched my chest. "That's quite an admission, and I didn't even have to drag it out of your skinny self."

Chapter Twenty-Two

Fab pulled out of the driveway like a normal person and made a complete stop at the sign.

I sucked in my breath, wide-eyed. "Ha, you're an imposter. What did you do with my friend, the one that drives like a crazy person?"

"The sheriff's deputies are out in force. They set up speed traps and are writing tickets. Two days ago, one started sitting around the corner, and on occasion, two sit there and yell back and forth through their windows."

"You wouldn't have to worry about that if—"

"Stop. No accidents, no tickets, stop complaining." She glared at me.

It never got old to irritate Fab. Amused, I continued, "I've come up with a compromise on who gets to drive the Hummer."

Her eyes narrowed to slits.

"I'll give up haggling over who drives and concede to you in exchange for unspecified favors."

"You know your driving makes me want to puke. Now you're sinking to blackmail?" She hit the steering wheel. "Do I need to remind you that

I do all the driving now? Why should I negotiate?"

"I know all about car sickness and hanging on for dear life." I didn't feel the need to admit that her driving had grown on me, and now I could go for miles without having to squeeze my eyes shut. "How does driving the speed limit make a person sick, anyway?"

Fab turned on the radio, searching the stations until she found one where the music blasted out the speakers.

Hoping to force her to answer, I turned it off and held my hand ready to smack hers if she dared touch it again.

"Oh all right," she grumbled. She made a hard right, jerking the wheel, and cut across a vacant property where there used to be a commercial building. It had burned down, and the lot was now a shortcut to the boulevard that ran along the beach. The impatient woman behind the wheel didn't want to drive the two extra blocks.

"Didn't I make you Director of Problems for The Cottages?" I asked.

"Security," she corrected. "Forget it. You mean you want me to take care of the problem— Joseph, I assume? You want me to shoot him and dispose of the body? Then call our crime-scene-cleaner friend?"

"Friend?" I shuddered. "'Friend' is a stretch. Just because we use his services more than the average homeowner… I call, he cleans, then sends the bill."

"Pity," Fab said, as if she'd really been looking forward to killing Joseph.

"What would you do with Svetlana if you knocked off her old man?" I asked. I had a fondness for Joseph, but he always pushed the boundaries; it made me wonder why I hadn't evicted him long ago.

"I'd put Svet and her clothes up for auction. What do you suppose I could get for a used rubber doll?"

"Eww. You'd make sure she went to a good home, wouldn't you?"

"I'd pay Mac. She'd find some old perv who'd salivate to get his... uh... hands on our girl Svet." Fab slowed before pulling into the driveway of The Cottages. "I'm checking for livestock. I don't want any dents in the Hummer."

"There's another happy ending. The stolen horse got sent to a ranch to enjoy his golden years. Not sure how long that is." I looked at Fab in question.

"Don't ask me," she said indignantly. "Returned to its owner?"

"No, the human parents were forced to relinquish custody in exchange for avoiding prosecution. They had previously housed it in their backyard. They did exercise it regularly, riding it up and down the street every day. Can you believe not a single neighbor called the cops?"

"Did you make that up?" Fab eyed me with suspicion.

I put my hand on my heart and replied, "It hurts me when you question my truthfulness."

Mac opened the office door and leaned against the frame, waiting for us to join her. She adjusted the straps on her bikini top. I blinked at her full skirt; from a distance, it looked like felt.

Surely not.

Up close, the shade of green reminded me of the color of felt that lined a pool table. She'd managed to find a pair of Birkenstock wannabes with boa feathers glued to the tops.

"Is Joseph still hiding in his cottage?" I asked her.

Mac nodded without taking her attention away from her chest, adjusting herself and giving her girls a final pat. As I headed down the driveway, she called, "Wait up," then said to Fab, "You better hustle; you can't hear squat from here."

"Open the damn door!" I yelled and administered my best cop knock.

Fab and Mac clustered behind me. One step backward, and I'd be in their collective faces.

I put my ear to the door—nothing. "Fine!" I yelled again. "I'm calling for a tow truck!"

A few seconds later, the door flew open, hitting the wall hard enough to embed the door knob in the drywall. "You can't do that," he wheezed.

"Show me *legal* paperwork." I held my hand out. "I'm betting you can't, since the tags expired last year."

"It's only for two nights. I owe Itsy. If I screw him again, he'll kill me for sure." He grasped the door frame, out of breath.

"I thought you shined up your act. Itsy's a thug. He tried to sneak out the back at Jake's, stiff us on his beer tab, and now he's banned."

Joseph's eyes pleaded.

"No." I shook my finger at him. "I'm not losing my property over your illegal activities. The court will say I knew and turned a blind eye. What happens when Kevin notices and runs the tags? He'll escort you to jail, and they'll squeeze you hard to rat on Itsy. Why do you owe him?"

"I told him where he could get a six-dollar blow job, and the chick bit him. He had to go to emergency care, says I owe him for the bill and that I should have warned him she was a nutcase."

"A what?" I asked. "Not the nutcase part, the other."

Fab banged her forehead against my back, making faint noises that I'd bet my last buck were laughter.

Joseph shifted from foot to foot, stammering, "I… uh… didn't want my regular girl, you know… uh… doing him. I swear I didn't know Fila would do that. Word will get around, and I think that would be bad for business."

You think?

"Who does that for six dollars?" I knew a couple of women who offered those services, but not for six dollars, and they were homeless.

"What exactly do you get for that piddly amount?" Mac asked.

I shot a glare over my shoulder, then turned back to Joseph. "This—" I pointed at the Escalade. "—is leaving now. Go park it at the boat launch ramp. Just know that once you pull out of the driveway, you run the risk of an arrest."

"I don't have the keys," he whined.

I gave him a look of disgust and turned my back, walking far enough away that he couldn't eavesdrop. Then I pulled out my phone and flipped through my contacts. The call I made was short and to the point.

"You're getting the slate wiped clean," I said as I turned back and closed the distance between Joseph and me. "A tow truck is on its way. I can guarantee that Itsy will never bother you again. Should you bump into the man, I suggest you ignore him or run."

"I'm going to go lie down." It surprised me that he took me at my word. He even looked relieved, a tinge of color coming back into his cheeks.

"There's one more thing. You owe Spoon. He asks, you deliver. Got it?" I knew Spoon would never ask Joseph for zip. The man had proven himself to be a flake, and Spoon's connections were far superior.

At the mention of Spoon's name, fear filled Joseph's eyes. His moment of peace evaporated, he mumbled, "Thanks," and disappeared inside, double-locking the door.

"Shooting him would have taken care of the problem much faster," Fab said.

Mac poufed up her bouffant, forgetting that she never had a hair out of place thanks to Aqua Net. "Who's Spoon sending?" she asked.

"Probably Billy. I think he's been assigned to all problems labeled Fab and me, since we have a rapport."

"Would you come to the office?" Mac motioned for me to follow her. "I have something to tell you." She crooked her finger at Fab. "You might as well come along too. Then Madison won't have to retell it."

"You better not be quitting," I said. I put my arm around her as we walked up the driveway. "I'll keep whatever it is a secret. We can send Fab to check on Miss January." I eyed the woman's empty chair. All seemed quiet, for the moment.

"Miss January got her drunk on early, and Score's still liquored up from last night. They're sleeping it off," Mac said.

"I'm not going into that cottage. There's a dead cat in there," Fab huffed.

"Trust me, sissy girl, Kitty will ignore you," I told her. "Take a pair of gloves in case Miss

January put her in the oven again."

Miss January's cat died years back and had since been stuffed and re-stuffed. It usually lounged at the end of the couch, except when Miss January sat outside, and then it lay in her lap. It was unclear to me if the woman remembered that the cat had passed on.

Fab grumbled and cut around me, and headed for the office.

Mac unlocked the door and swept her arm out in a gracious gesture to enter her domain. My aunt hadn't spent much time here, as she rented to year-round tenants. I'd spent a few hours here back in the beginning, and it had made me claustrophobic if I had to stay long.

The Cottages had needed a facelift to take it from drab to eye-catching. Along with painting each unit in fresh bright colors, I'd given the landscaping an overhaul. The trees were pruned, and I added my signature lighting at the base of the palm trees and around the trunks. Flowers had been added to all the planters to discourage smokers from using them as ashtrays and passersby as bathrooms.

The office went from a drab hole to an inviting place to sit and transact business. The walls got a new coat of green paint, and the old battered desk and ugly chairs were replaced with dark-colored bamboo pieces. The chairs and the couch in brown leather passed the comfort test.

Mac knew my priorities and kept a full snack

bowl, which she plopped down on the desk, then passed over our drinks of choice from the fully stocked refrigerator. She settled herself in her chair and kicked her feet up on the desk, wiggling the sandals off her feet.

I claimed a chair opposite her. Fab reclined against the back of the couch, opening and closing the shutters and keeping a watchful eye on any stray pedestrian or car that went by.

"I'm getting a divorce," Mac said matter-of-factly.

I stood up and walked around the desk, enveloping her in a hug. "I'm sorry," I whispered.

"What the hell happened?" Fab demanded.

"None of your business," I answered for Mac.

"It's okay." Mac sniffed, and tears leaked from the corners of her eyes.

I reached across to a shelf unit that ran along the side wall and handed her the Kleenex box.

"He proposed to someone else, someone half his age. Unless he wants to end up in jail for bigamy, he needs to divorce his inconvenient wife." Mac wiped her eyes.

"Ouch," I said. The whole cheating thing sucked. Why should they get to be happy when you just want them to fall in a ditch?

"You say the word, I'll take care of him, pay him a little visit in the middle of the night and pistol-whip his ass," Fab said with a disapproving edge to her voice.

I smiled at her, loving that she was the kind of friend who would beat up your boyfriend/husband for such a betrayal.

"The hell with him." Mac brushed her hands together. "I don't want him back, now that he's been dipping his wick somewhere else."

"Anything we can do?" I patted her hand. "Girl lunch? A nighttime shopping trip, perhaps to South Beach for something that blinks and flashes? Shoes perhaps?"

Fab made a retching noise. Tourist paraphernalia held no allure for the hot French woman.

Mac glared across the desk, arms across her chest. "I want to date. It will ease my pain. Find me a boyfriend that can give me the sex that I read about in my romance novels."

Fab closed her eyes, her signal that she had checked out of the conversation.

"Put together your wish list. If we can't introduce you to a nice man, I'll put Mother on it. You'll have to audition him yourself for the sex thing," I said.

"Forget nice. I want a bad boy."

Fab groaned and covered her face with her hands.

Chapter Twenty-Three

Fab flew down the interstate to Little Havana in record time. Mother had called in a frenzy; she'd forgotten to pick up the cigar order for one of her private parties at Jake's. It had been my idea to install the standing humidor, but I hadn't thought about having to drive into Miami to replenish supplies.

A parking space opened up in front of Patron's Cigar Bar, and a war of wills ensued, as an eastbound driver had every intention of hanging a U-turn and commandeering the space for himself.

I grabbed the armrest, just in case, as Fab hit the gas, cutting the other driver off, threw the shift into reverse, and backed into the tight space. My heart ceased its pounding as I yanked open the door, tossing Fab a glare before I jumped out.

Sylvia Patron met me at the door. An older woman, always elegant and casually dressed, she was the sweetest woman ever, and had helped me out on a couple of occasions, making suggestions when I was choosing gifts for Mother. Patron's cigars were the highest rated in the business and had the distinction of being hand-rolled on the premises.

"It surprised me when your mother called and informed my sister, Marta, that you would be picking up the order. I know Madeline enjoys her visits here. Marta wasn't happy; they've become fast friends, and when your mother comes in, they share a cup of coffee, enjoy a cigar, and gossip," she laughed.

"Do you join them?" I asked. Mother had impeccable manners, so I couldn't imagine she would exclude the woman.

"Can you believe it? I don't smoke and a cup of Cuban roast makes my heart flutter. I feel like I can fly." Sylvia smiled. "Then the aftermath— it's like a delicious drug."

The front door banged open, and Sylvia's gangly teenage son stumbled across the entrance with his arms full of boxes.

"The Hummer?" He motioned to it.

I nodded. My mouth almost fell open when I saw that Fab had moved to the passenger seat. I handed Sylvia the check and hugged her, then followed her son to the SUV, opening the back for the purchases.

I slid behind the wheel, wanting to savor the moment, a stupid smile on my face. Fab leaned her head against the window, phone resting on her shoulder. One of her patented evil smiles slid over her face as she continued the conversation in French.

A little love chat with the boyfriend, I thought. Since his arrest, their bond seemed tighter than ever.

Left to my own devices, I switched off the snooty GPS reminders and, with my backseat driver otherwise engaged, turned off the busy boulevard at the first opportunity to avoid the endless traffic lights. It took a couple of wrong turns before I found the little-used two-lane road that cut over to the freeway. I zoomed past empty fields and run-down commercial businesses that couldn't afford the rates of the heavily trafficked main streets.

It surprised me when I looked in the rearview mirror and noticed a black sedan with blacked out windows. It hadn't been there a moment ago, but now it rapidly approached and practically rested on my back bumper.

"A-hole," I murmured.

He probably would have gone around and left me in the dust, which I was used to, but a big rig took up several car lengths of the lane on my left. I had no room to maneuver. With one eye firmly glued to the rearview mirror, I sighed with relief when the sedan veered to the far left, attempting to blast around the truck into oncoming traffic, a terrible way to treat what appeared to be a new Chevrolet SS. My relief was short-lived when he turned the wheel hard back into my lane and began once again tailgating me. The driver played a game of speed up and slow down, each time getting closer to having a chat in the back seat.

Under pressure and already just over the speed limit, I stomped on the gas to try to clear the big rig, or at least give the car enough room to swing around me and be on its way. As I sped up, so did the other car. I knew that if I had to brake suddenly, it wouldn't be pretty. A moment later, fear swept through me as I wondered if it was someone Fab or I had pissed off, who was orchestrating the right time to run me off the road.

My hands sweaty on the steering wheel, I stayed steady on the gas but knew I couldn't keep up the high rate of speed. I lacked the nerve for fast driving. I reluctantly gave up on the hope that the SS would get bored with the game of intimidation and turn at one of the many signals we passed, make a U-turn…anything. I flung out my hand, slapping Fab on the arm.

Fab correctly diagnosed from my rigid posture and the fear on my face that I needed her help. She turned toward the back window, then ended her call on a seductive whisper. "What's going on?" She continued to stare at the road behind us.

"Hell if I know," I hissed, one eye on the rearview mirror, the other on the road.

"Wait until I tell you, then tap your brakes. Now!" she said. "Car's dropped back an inch."

"I have no room to maneuver. The shoulder's

too narrow, and it drops into a ditch."

"Okay, then just ease your foot off the gas. The other car will probably go around. If it doesn't, you can pull over." She glanced out the side window. "And stay out of the ditch. Option two, I hang out the window and shoot out the tires."

"Let's leave door number two as a last resort." I did as she instructed and sighed with relief when I felt the Hummer slowing, gradually getting back to the posted speed. I glanced in the rearview mirror and blinked. My mouth dropped open. Flashing lights inside the Chevy's grill and windshield went on signaling—law enforcement.

"What the hell?" I spit out at the top of my lungs. The last thing I wanted to do was pull over on the shoulder and park the SUV taking up half the traffic lane. Up farther, I spotted a sign hanging by a thread in the distance, so I continued. When I didn't immediately pull over, the driver began laying on the horn to accompany the siren.

I pulled into the driveway of what was once an old fast food restaurant. A half-dozen men loitered on the property, leaning against the boarded-up building. They looked up as I rumbled over the gravel and then scattered when the police car pulled in behind me. Every one of them disappeared before I even got the engine shut off.

"What did you do?" Fab asked as she handed me my wallet.

"No idea." I put the window down, license in hand before he could ask.

The police officer's face appeared in the window. He was in full uniform, and the patch on his shirt read Miami Police Department. I guessed him to be fortyish, but it was hard to tell with the reflector sunglasses covering most of his face. Instead of it being a comfort to find out he was law enforcement, it made me really mad. I sucked in a deep breath, struggling not to say anything stupid.

He took the license from my fingers. "Does this tank have registration and insurance?"

Fab had already retrieved them from the console box and handed them over.

"Do you know how fast you were going?"

I ground my teeth. "Fast enough to get away from you. You were speeding. You tailgated me. And you scared me witless."

"Scared you?" He huffed a half-laugh.

"Your car's not marked and looks like it belongs to a drug dealer." Calm down, I coached myself.

"Don't go anywhere." He paused for a second and started back to his pimped-out car.

I stuck my head out the window and said, "Your erratic driving forced me to speed up to get away from you."

He didn't miss a step, not acknowledging that I'd said anything.

Fab started laughing. "Miss Slowpoke is going

to get a ticket for speeding." She slapped the armrest.

I glared at her and flung my head back against the seat. I hoped he'd let me go when he checked my record and saw no tickets or accidents. I watched the clock, tapping the steering wheel in a steady beat as the minutes ticked by. Ten minutes later, we were joined by three more patrol cars, one a K-9 unit.

"Get out your carry permit," I said to Fab. I pulled my Glock from my waistband and dropped it in my purse. "I think we're in big trouble."

The original officer came back to the window. "Both of you need to get out and stand over there." He pointed to where two officers stood staring. I handed over our concealed carry permits and told him the guns were in our bags. "Both of you, hands in the air."

He walked us to the back of the Hummer, where we were joined by another officer, and they conducted a pat down. The officer in the K-9 car opened the door, and a German Shepherd jumped to the ground. He headed straight for the rear tire on the driver's side and lifted his leg.

Fab poked me in the side.

The dog continued to sniff around the outside of the SUV. The officer opened the passenger door, and the dog jumped in and sniffed the interior. The officer was joined by another, who opened the back door. From my vantage point, I couldn't see what they were doing.

An older officer, sixties and Cuban if I were to guess, stood less than a foot away. He flashed me a friendly smile.

"What's going on?" I asked the man.

"They should be done in a minute. As long as everything checks out, you'll be on your way."

Fab bristled. "You'd think we were drug dealers."

The original officer conferred with the K-9 officer, his jaw set with determination, then came over to us. "The dog scented on something. We're going to transfer you to the women's jail for a thorough pat down."

Before I could say anything, Fab pinched my arm. "What is it you want to see?" She lifted her top and did a three-sixty.

"Fabiana." I winced and exhaled a puff of air.

The officers were enjoying the show.

Fab motioned to me, so I followed her lead and said a thankful silent prayer that I'd outgrown my no-bra stage.

"That was cooperative of you." He gave us an oily smile.

I asked the older officer, "Was this necessary?"

"You'd be surprised the things we find inside bras and taped underneath."

The original officer, who'd disappeared for a moment after making a beeline for his car, was back, ticket book in hand. "For everyone's safety, it would be prudent to follow the posted speed limit. By my calculation, you flew by at least three signs posting the maximum speed, which you ignored." He shoved the annoying book at me. "Sign here." He pointed. "You can avoid a trial by sending three hundred dollars to this address."

"Three hundred dollars?" I gasped.

"I did you a favor and kept the miles per hour under the limit that would require a mandatory court appearance, more expense, and more points on your driver's record." Officer Watters, according to his name badge, acted like he wanted a thank you. He'd wait a damn long time.

"We'll be seeing one another again." I scribbled my name at the bottom. "I hope you'll remember me when I show up in court to contest this ticket."

"Go ahead. Boo hoo, you're innocent. Judges hear it all the time. Whose word do you think carries more weight? Mine and my fellow officers' or yours?"

"Officer Watters, is it?" I glanced again at his name tag. *That's a name I'll never forget,* I thought. "I'll be bringing my own character witness— Chief Harder. He knows exactly how I drive." I retrieved my license and handed back his book.

He shook his head and handed me a copy of the ticket. "This is what comes from being a nice guy. You're free to go."

Fab watched as the officers got back in their

cars, pulling out one by one. Watters finally turned off his flashing lights. "That was nervy."

"You're driving." I walked around to the passenger side. "What in the hell?" I shouted.

Poking my head inside, I saw that our bags had been turned upside down, the contents scattered on the floor. The change of clothing I'd insisted long ago that we both have was strewn across the entire back of the car, our changes of underwear on top.

My hands shook with the anger that rolled through me, and I tightened my grip until it subsided, willing myself to calm down.

"What did we do to piss him off? Are you calling the chief?"

"No, but he doesn't know that. I *will* be telling Creole all about Officer Watters." I gathered our belongings together and comingled them in one bag. We could sort it out on the living room floor at home. I unscrewed the top of my water bottle and downed it. "*I am* going to court. I'll have a talk with my hotshot lawyer. He'd never lower himself to go to traffic court, but he can give me pointers."

"I like this tough-girl side of you."

"I'm not paying a ticket I don't deserve," I seethed.

Fab sat behind the wheel, watching out her side mirror, until Officer Watters pulled back out onto the highway. Then she pulled out, turning onto the highway. Fab stayed under the speed limit and hooked a turn in the opposite direction at the first opportunity.

"In the future, you need to learn to have phone sex and drive at the same time. I suggest getting an earpiece."

Fab kept to the posted speed until we got to the freeway on-ramp. She broke the silence to say, "Let me know when the court date is. I'm coming to watch you in action. Your almost-lawyer bartender could give you tips."

"You know, I gave serious thought to going to law school. My problem was I lacked the discipline three more years of school would require. Instead, I went into business, found out that I was good at it, and never regretted my choice. I don't think I could sleep at night if a client I thought wasn't guilty went to jail. What were your career dreams?"

"I was raised to be an ornament: a wife, a mother, an asset on a man's arm. I'm well-educated and speak three languages, yet was expected to defer to my father or husband. Then I met my ex-husband, Gabriel, and he introduced me to pure excitement, the thrill of living on the edge, the rush… He was the complete package — wicked smart, breathtakingly handsome and, of course, a criminal." She half-laughed.

I knew a lot of her memories weren't pleasant.

"I didn't know what I wanted," she said. "At the time, I only wanted someone that my parents would hate. But now — I have more than I ever thought possible: a man that I love, a best friend, and a family that doesn't seem to care that I'm flawed."

Chapter Twenty-Four

Fab expertly parked the Hummer next to her Mercedes. We'd both seen Didier's car parked in front, and before she could run into the house, I hugged her. "Mother and I both love you," I whispered in her ear.

Fab silently hugged me back.

"We're home," I yelled as we came through the front door. I flew up the stairs and packed a bag in record time, then showered, lathering up with Creole's favorite body wash, and pulled on a wildly printed mid-thigh dress with a deep slit and a little surprise underneath. I came back down to find Fab and Didier snuggling on the couch.

Fab pointed to my bag on the floor. "Didier and I sorted everything out."

I smiled at her. "If Creole stops by and asks where I'm at, tell the detective to come find me."

Didier chuckled. "I bet he finds you at his first stop."

"I hope so. Tell him I *hate* to be kept waiting."

Before heading to Creole's hideaway, I stopped at the local market and bought a piece of fresh grouper and an array of fresh vegetables.

Since no dinner is complete without dessert, I grabbed some praline ice cream.

I seldom made the trip down the Keys by myself. Usually the big man swept me off my feet, tossed me in his truck, and drove me to his house.

It felt good to use my own door key, to slip inside, kick off my flip-flops, and spread the groceries out on the counter to prep for dinner. To go with the food, I picked out a bottle of cabernet from a California winery that Creole liked. I slid open the pocket doors to the patio, welcoming in the fresh air. After cleaning and cutting up the vegetables, I tossed a small salad and whisked up a marinade for the fish, then went out to the deck and set the small round table for two that overlooked the pool and the beach below. Long ago, I'd surprised him by putting together a set of dishes in the tropical colors he liked: green, tangerine, and yellow. I'd bypassed stores that sold complete sets and instead scoured the dishware outlets and flea markets.

Creole's job would be to get the barbeque fired up and grill the grouper.

A nagging voice asked, *What if he doesn't show? Then I'll wrap the food in foil and eat the ice cream.*

* * *

I curled up on one of the deck chaises and

watched the waves ripple onto the white sandy beach until I fell asleep. My eyes flew open when I felt hard lips on mine.

Creole's face hovered over mine, his blue eyes dark with amusement. "I found you," he whispered. He lowered his head and his mouth came down on top of mine again, hot and intense and every bit as good as I'd daydreamed on the drive to his house. Finally, he sat down next to me and pulled me into his arms. He had changed into shorts, but he wore no shirt and his shoulder-length dark hair was wet at the ends.

"Hungry?" I made little circles on his chest with my finger. "Dinner is prepped and waiting for you to fire up the barbeque."

"I'm starving." He gave me another long, thorough kiss.

I put my hand on his chest and shoved lightly. "Feed me first." If he needed convincing, my stomach grumbled at that moment.

He stood and pulled me to my feet. "I like coming home and finding you curled up here. We don't get enough time alone absent pending drama."

The details of the encounter with Officer Watters can wait until later, I decided. "I crave quiet time with you. My favorite is to lie in your arms and just talk, watch a movie, or read. I love my family, but when they all descend, it's loud and noisy and everyone watches what everyone else is doing. It's hard to even sneak a kiss. What is it

Mother calls us—lovebirds?"

"I have something planned for after dinner." He arched his eyebrows and grinned.

"I'm so sorry," I said in my most innocent voice, biting my lower lip.

His eyes filled with confusion. "Do you have something planned?"

"I do." I pulled away and walked into the house, where I opened the drawer on a side table and retrieved a deck of cards. I put them on the counter in front of him.

He studied them, turning the pack over.

"You're at the whim of your hostess." I teased his lips with my finger. "We're going to play strip poker, and the first person to lose all their clothes is sadly not the winner. The other person gets to decide what we're doing the rest of the evening. The loser doesn't get to complain."

"Good thing I've got the evening already planned." He winked.

"You're very sure of yourself."

"I'm a very good player."

"I'm not half-bad myself."

* * *

Creole pushed me down on the chaise, straddled the cushion in front of me, and shuffled. He fanned the deck, holding them out. "Best two out of three?"

"I'm willing to put it all on one game." I

leaned forward, puckering my lips. "Shall we smooch on the deal?"

His fingers wrapped around my chin and brought my face forward, sealing the stakes. "Are the cards marked or something?" He flicked the cards, giving them a cursory glance.

"Deal!" I poked the cushion.

"Did Fab find anything at Lauren's that I don't know about?" he asked after laying down the last card.

"Are you forgetting that I waited in the car?" Not waiting for an answer, I continued, "I'm not giving you Fab information — ask her."

"Is Fab going back to Lauren's?" He held his cards to his chest.

"Fab never tells me stuff like that. I have to catch her in a lie or sneaking back in the door. She's an insomniac, and it's worse when Didier's not home. She has a tendency to disappear in the middle of the night."

He smirked at his cards and winked. "Just so you know, I offered to cover her back."

"Yes, I heard about the offer of your services. Don't take it personally if she sneaks off without you."

"How many?" He snapped his finger, pointing to my cards.

I covered my face with my hand and stifled a groan — nothing but low-numbered cards, with the exception of the ace. I tossed the rest face down. "Four."

"Sorry, hon." He took three.

"No you're not. It's so ungentlemanly to gloat."

He turned his cards over, showing a pair of tens.

I flipped my cards over as well. Once again, the ace was the only decent card, and it meant nothing by itself.

"I'll show you what a gracious loser looks like." I stood and unzipped the back of my dress, sliding it slowly over my shoulders. I let it fall in a puddle on the ground and stepped out, standing before him in nothing but a smirk. "Surprise."

"Looks like we both came to play." He stood, unzipped his shorts, and kicked them on top of my dress. He had the same surprise for me—whichever way the game went, it was destined to be over in one hand.

He scooped me up and carried me inside to his big, king-size bed.

Chapter Twenty-Five

Two days later, Phil called early, asking to meet for breakfast at The Bakery Café. Her background check on Balcazar was complete, and she wanted to share her findings.

I shoved my foot into a tennis shoe to protect my toes and hobbled down the hall, stopping in front of Fab's door and giving it three stiff kicks. "Rise and shine, we're leaving in twenty," I yelled, then hustled, giggling, back to my bedroom and into the shower.

I dragged on a clean uniform, which meant a mid-thigh flirty skirt, and t-shirt and took a look in the mirror. I made a face. The skirt was too short for my thigh holster, so I switched holsters to the one that fit in the small of my back. If I didn't know better, I'd say Fab had slept through my wake-up call, since I didn't hear a sound as I headed to the stairs. "Don't think I won't leave without you!" I shouted.

If I stopped to make coffee, we'd be late; besides I'd already decided to hold out for a latte. On the way out, I rang the doorbell a half-dozen times and slammed the door. I slid into the passenger seat and shoved the keys in the ignition, lighting up the dash clock. Five minutes — then I'd start honking the horn.

The front door flew open with a bang. Fab blew across the driveway and around to the driver's side. "Could you be more annoying?" she complained as she squealed out of the driveway.

"Do I really need to answer?"

"Go ahead, smirk now. Wait until Didier has a talk with you. We were…it doesn't matter; you killed the moment."

"My defense will be that I learned that trick from you," I said haughtily.

"Where are we going?" Fab grouched.

"Our favorite café for breakfast. A double latte and a pecan roll, and I'll soon have you laughing about the start to the morning." I bounced in my seat. "The best part is, the background check is back on Balcazar."

"We need to know more about Lauren. Where's that report?" she asked in exasperation. "Didier is still the prime person of interest. The cops aren't scratching his name off the list because they don't have a replacement."

Fab cut across the highway and lucked out on the traffic signals, making it to the café in record time. She growled when she saw our favorite table for people-watching, at the end of the sidewalk, overflowing with teenagers.

"Stop grumbling and hurry up. Phil got us a

table over there." I pointed. "Beats sitting inside."

"Our table empties, grab it," she said, heading inside the bakery.

"I'm hungry," I called after her. She knew that was code for her to order actual food and not just a danish.

"Fab's cranky," I warned, slipping into a seat next to Phil. "Some good news would be an attitude-changer."

"Well, it's not a smoking gun with someone else's fingerprints on it." She grimaced.

I leaned back in my chair, scanning the faces around us for anyone familiar.

A few minutes later, Fab slipped into a chair, plunking a box down on the table, a tented number on top. "Food will be out in a minute; they're not very busy." She leaned across to Phil. "I don't want to hear about Balcazar; the hell with him. Anything new on Lauren?"

Phil and Fab glared at one another for a moment. Then Phil jammed the top back on her coffee cup and slid her chair back, making a loud scraping sound on the sidewalk.

"Sit down," I said to Phil and turned to Fab. "You say something nice to make her stay."

Fab looked at her in all innocence. "Would you like another cup of coffee?"

I bit down on my lip so I wouldn't laugh.

Phil dropped back down. "No, I would not."

The few heads that had turned our way lost

interest. Finally, the server delivering a tray of food broke the silence.

"This looks yum." I picked up the plate with the individual frittata on it and pushed the goat yogurt and fresh berries in Fab's direction.

"It's new on the menu. I did peruse the ingredients and noted there wasn't anything listed that would make you barf. Your pecan roll is inside," she said, pointing to the box, "along with Didier's cookies."

"I'm taking over the meeting," I told Phil. "We both want to hear your report, and we'll save our questions until the end." I gave Fab a nudge under the table with my toes.

"Balcazar is a criminal and a crook," Phil said before she took a sip of water.

I was pleased to see that her opening line got Fab's attention.

"Ten of his high-powered friends formed a corporation that appears, on further investigation, to be nothing more than a multimillion-dollar Ponzi scheme. The company specialized in the buying and selling of overbuilt condos. The deals were set-up with phony buyers and documents that appeared legit, but were complete fiction. When the collapse seemed imminent, the partners severed ties and disappeared. All but three, I should say. One was found murdered, one is presumed dead despite never being found, and the third vanished." She smirked at Fab.

"What are the chances of having two friends/business associates murdered and another go missing?" I asked.

"It's rumored that the FBI was in the process of squeezing the dead man, Harry Gant, for information. He'd supposedly just finished negotiations on a sweet deal that he wanted signed before spilling what he knew. A security camera at his office showed him leaving late one night and two unidentified men hitting him over the head and dragging him to a waiting van. He turned up several hours later, his body beaten and smoldering in a dumpster at a nearby construction site."

A shudder went through my body at the thought of that gruesome death.

"The second man, Robert Stark, was under investigation in Gant's death. His ex-wife reported him missing because she needed her alimony check. The cops went to his multimillion-dollar house, which was in foreclosure. They found signs of a struggle and his tongue on a serving tray in the kitchen, blood everywhere."

I gasped, covering my face and trying to block the image from taking hold. I put what was left of my breakfast on the empty table next to us.

"No other parts turned up?" Fab asked.

"Nothing, but the three of us know how easy it would be to make a body disappear with the right connections," Phil said.

"Anyone investigating the corporation?" I asked.

"An investigation was opened by the state's attorney and, as far I can tell, has gone nowhere. Even though some of the investors lost big money, no one is uttering a word." Phil pointed to the bakery box. "Can I have a cookie?"

I held my breath, crossing my fingers that Phil didn't get her head bitten off.

"Help yourself." Fab pushed the box in her direction. "Lauren have a part in this scheme?"

"Can't prove it, but it's hard to believe she was completely ignorant. Lauren banged the man, going from receptionist to a six-figure job and million-dollar condo in a matter of months. Besides having a wandering dick, who knows what he told her while sharing the same pillow."

"Get any dirt on his wife?" I asked.

"Not a blemish that I could find. Tina Balcazar is the other half of the power couple. She came into the marriage with family connections and money, neither of which Balcazar had. Her daddy can call politicians, who actually take his calls, and claims at least two ex-presidents as friends." Phil took out a small notepad and thumbed through the pages. "Almost forgot, about ten years ago, Stark was the prime suspect in two other grisly murders, bodies found in a condemned house up near Orlando. A neighbor snooped around after noticing a car come and go, found them, and called the cops."

"Do you think Didier is in any danger?" I asked.

"He shouldn't trust anyone but his lawyer. I know Cruz, and he never talks about his cases, not even in a casual way," Phil said.

"This was a great choice for breakfast. We can meet here anytime," I said.

Phil bent down and pulled two envelopes out of her pale-pink designer tote, handing them to me. "Here's a detailed summary and my bill. You know where to find me if you need anything else." She stood and waved, then walked to where her SUV was parked at the curb.

"Do you have to be prompted to say thank you?" I asked Fab.

"Thanks!" Fab yelled at Phil's retreating back.

Chapter Twenty-Six

Phil had scribbled the address for the elusive Ursula on a sticky note attached to the top of one of the envelopes she'd handed me. I passed it off to Fab, who perused it before pulling out of the parking space. She called Phil and asked several questions, but the conversation lasted only a few minutes, during which Fab used her business voice. I didn't hear yelling from the other end of the phone and sighed with relief.

Ursula Richards had landed in an upscale, gated condominium community in Duck Key. The unit was owned by a businessman out of the Miami area, and according to records, it was a second home. What was unknown was whether she was a renter or a guest.

Fab had her foot pressed down hard on the gas, flying down the Overseas Highway on this sunny, blustery day. I kept my eyes peeled out the window, watching the palm trees sway back and forth, the waves churning in the Gulf of Mexico.

"How was your night the other night?" Fab asked.

"I lost at strip poker." I smiled. "I couldn't have had a worse hand."

"How many pieces of clothing did you start with?"

"One."

She threw her hair back and laughed. "Excellent idea! I'm going to boost a deck of cards from Jake's. I know where the new ones are stored."

"Winner gets to decide how to spend the rest of the evening. You'll have to plan everything in advance and remember not to gloat, since you'll probably cheat."

"Ohh." She frowned. "I'm not that great at cards. I'll have to choose something else."

"You can't be gracious and let Didier have his way once in a while?" Her frustrated look amused me.

"Didier *always* gets his way," she blushed. "Not that I mind all that much."

"Miss Fabiana," I mimicked Mother, "get your mind back on the job. What are we doing exactly?"

"Thank goodness for Phil. I'll smooth over the waters somehow."

My eyebrows shot up. "Let's hope she never quits or, worse, retires."

"Phil uncovered that Ursula owns an interior design business and has office space in an upscale furniture store in South Miami. She called Ursula and scheduled an appointment regarding a job redoing the lobby of the Shores Hotel," Fab related. "Phil bought us time to slip into the condo and have a look-see without having to worry about jumping out the window."

"How is Phil going to pull off this meeting without Ursula catching on? It's ballsy." I could see this plan ending badly.

"Phil assured me when I asked the same question that she's got it handled. She's sending an associate who's going to pass himself off as an executive of the hotel—invite her into the bar and interview her. Phil has every confidence in her man candy, as she called him. He's played the part of an executive on more than one occasion."

"I'd feel more comfortable if one of us was involved, but let's face it," I stared over at her. "Neither of us have the skills for that scam."

Fab ignored me. "Phil's always come through so far. She promises, she delivers, and doesn't have one suck-ass excuse after another, like most of the people we've worked with in the past."

"Language," I tsked in Mother's voice and shook my finger.

"You know damn well that if she were here, Madeline would laugh."

"I think Mother had a bit of a hidden wild streak before we moved to Florida, and now we've thoroughly corrupted her." I sighed. "How do we know Mr. Ursula won't be home?"

"I highly doubt Mr. Preston Sinclair III, the

property owner and esteemed businessman out of Miami, would appreciate your sneering tone."

"Answer the damn question. Do we have that angle covered?"

Fab shook her head. "You know I excel at last-minute improvisation. You're staying in the car. I'll check out the parking lot, knock on the door, all the normal things, and if things go awry, I'll text you. If Urs shows up, you text me pronto."

Fab drove into the Miramar Beachfront Condominiums and up to the security panel in front of a set of ornate pink electric gates, egrets framed in each panel. I never stressed over the key card scanner, knowing that Fab kept her counterfeited card regularly updated. So far, it had never been rejected, allowing us to wander around exclusive areas at will.

Mother watched her use it once and demanded one of her own. She and her friend Jean used it to sightsee through private communities when they tired of shopping. They'd been stopped by security guards a couple of times but were well-dressed, so didn't raise an alarm. Their flimsy excuse of the gate having been left open and not realizing it was a private community was always accepted, and the guard would point them towards the exit.

The three-story buildings were set in an S-curve, giving each unit a waterfront view of the Gulf on its own private beach. The natural setting had the feel of a bird sanctuary, with egrets, geese, and a variety of ducks strolling the property.

Most of the action took place in the center of the property at the overly large lagoon pool that boasted a tiki bar in the center. Four barstools had been claimed, and a handful of people were swimming. Several tennis courts and both basketball courts were in use by sweaty, shirtless men. The playground was empty.

Fab parked in front of a three-story building and scrutinized the outside. "I'll be right back. Call me when you get the call from Phil that the meeting is over."

"What if something goes wrong?" I whined, feeling guilty that I was the slacker who always sat in the car.

"I can hear you worrying—stop it! Get in the driver's seat. If the cops roll up, be ready to take off as soon as I jump out the window. Wouldn't be the first time." She made a face.

"Except that the unit is on the third floor." I stared up. "Don't you need jumping stuff so you don't break something, or worse?"

"Stuff?" She raised her eyebrow.

"Caught me," I mocked. "I don't know the name of the equipment crazy people use to jump from anything. As much as I hate jail, it beats a mashed-in brain."

"Must I remind you of our pact? No getting arrested."

I grabbed her arm. "Promise me you won't do

anything stupid." So what if I sounded whiney and clingy; I didn't care.

She patted my head like I was a child.

"I'd rather pay your bail. And Brick will cover it, even if I have to hold a gun to his head."

"No wonder he thinks you don't like him. Don't worry, I'll be back, and in one piece." She slammed the door.

I climbed over into the driver's seat, just in case. Somewhere in the wannabe-PI manual, there must be tips for being prepared for a quick getaway, and I clearly needed to memorize them.

Now seemed like a good time to text Creole our location. He tended to be less surly if I didn't wait until after the GPS alarm went off. Though that wouldn't be a problem this time, as Fab had disabled the unit again. Still, he and I had come to an agreement that I'd keep him updated when out on a job, no matter our location.

My finger hovered over the send key for the "B&E in Duck Key" text with a smiley face, but I chickened out. If he found out about today, I could always tell him I'd forgotten to text him. We'd agreed not to lie to one another, but it was such a tiny one that it would be okay, wouldn't it? I sighed and texted the address to him.

Phil's report had noted that, according to county records, Preston had purchased two adjoining units on the top floor and remodeled them into one. I reclined the seat until I had a perfect view of the expansive wraparound patio with four sets of French doors, which appeared to be open. I recognized the patio furniture as high-end, with everything cushioned and a pile of extra pillows; a great place to kick back and enjoy the view of the beach.

I tapped the clock on the dash, trying to control my anxiety. From personal experience, I knew it took time to snoop through a three-bedroom residence and make it look like the place hadn't been tossed. Next time, I'd asked for a timeframe.

Tick, tick—forty minutes. *This job was supposed to be in and out.*

My gut screamed that something had gone wrong. I continuously turned in my seat to scan the property through the side and back windows. Only one car had driven in while I was there. It had parked a few spaces away, and a woman got out with a bag of groceries and disappeared into the next building over. I kept watch for a security guard headed in this direction on foot or in a golf cart. One had gone by a while ago in the opposite direction and parked at the pool. I cracked the window, listening for the blaring of sirens in the distance, coming closer until police cars blew through the gate… But nothing. I turned my attention back to the patio, reassuring myself that Fab wasn't leaning over the balcony and deciding how to get to the bottom in one piece.

My phone chirped, informing me of an incoming text. "Interview over." I tapped out a quick text to Fab to hurry the hell up, and my finger was hovering over the send button when I glanced up to see her exit the lobby doors as if she had all day.

As I turned, my eye caught a flutter of movement on the patio. A tall, dark-haired man stood there. He was only wearing shorts and appeared to have just rolled out of bed, his hair standing on end. He watched Fab's every move as she crossed the driveway. From this vantage point, there was no mistaking the fact that he was hot.

I clenched my hands together to contain my nervousness and crawled back into my assigned seat. Something had gone wrong, but the good news was that the Hummer hadn't been swarmed by law enforcement. Brick would kill us, but he'd have to wait in line behind two angry boyfriends.

"You okay?" I asked when she opened the door.

"Now that was weird." She rolled down the window and waved to the man, and he waved back.

"Is he as good-looking up close as he is from here?"

The man pushed his hair back in an unconscious gesture, showing off a muscled bicep. I kept my eyes glued to the side mirror. He waited on the patio until we'd disappeared through the security gates, never taking his eyes off the Hummer.

"Preston Sinclair's delicious, a gentleman with a great sense of humor. If I weren't with Didier, I'd dump Ursula in a swamp somewhere."

"You break into the man's, excuse me *Preston's*, condo and now you two share some kind of mutual admiration?" I knew it was a dumb question, but I couldn't stop myself from asking. Men loved Fab. "Details." I snapped my fingers.

She grinned at me, having clearly enjoyed her breaking-and-entering foray. "I knocked, no answer, rang the doorbell—nothing. So I broke in. Imagine my surprise when I walked into the master bedroom, and found Sinclair leaning up against the headboard, working on his laptop in a pair of well-fitting boxer-briefs."

"Did you just break in?" Sinclair demanded, incensed. His eyes darkened, and his lips quirked on the sides. "I'm calling the police."

Fab noticed that he hadn't reached for the phone sitting next to his muscular hip to back up his threat. "I have a good reason." She flashed the smile that she reserved for men. "I'm sure we can work something out."

"I'm sure we can." He leisurely ran his eyes over her from head to toe.

The bastard's not getting sex, *Fab thought.*

He slid his legs off the bed.

Fab pulled her Walther. "Stay right there while we negotiate."

His face turned crimson. "You need a very hard spanking, pulling a gun on me. Put it away," he demanded with the arrogance of a man who was used to being obeyed.

Fab half-laughed. "Look, you domineering alpha male, are we agreed — no police?"

He nodded.

"This is about Ursula," Fab said, sliding her gun back into her waistband. "I have information you might like to hear, unless you like your women psychotic and vindictive."

"Yes, the beautiful Ursula is high-strung, but...do you have anything to back up your claims?"

Fab snorted at the term high-strung. "You'll thank me when I'm done cluing you in to her dark side."

Fab stared intently at the road.

"What did you tell him?" I asked.

"I'm getting there. And you don't think I listen to your ramblings but I do, and what I'm about to say proves it." She grinned. "I recited what we knew about Ursula in bullet-point fashion. Gave him the address where she lived with Ian, ran down the litany of repairs the house needed. I challenged him to check it out for himself to see if my retelling didn't do the wreckage justice, and said he should talk to the neighbors, specifically the next-door neighbor."

"Why do I miss all the good stuff?"

Fab sighed. "I suggested that he get rid of Ursula — the sooner the better. No sex is worth the havoc she can cause. He smirked until I got up in his face and instructed him to change the locks, alert security and give them a picture so that they have her on their radar, and call the sheriff if she ever shows her face around here again."

"He must have believed you. I haven't spotted a single police car headed towards the condos." Not getting arrested was huge. If they cuffed Fab, it wouldn't take long before they found me.

"At first, he didn't want to believe a single accusation and laughed off my warnings. It didn't help that he was distracted; he and his lower friend were in discussion about how to get me on my back in that big bed of his. Then the words 'cement in the drains' clicked in his brain, and he started to listen."

"Did you happen to get any useful information in exchange for your dire warnings?" I asked, staring out the window and wishing my toes were dug into the sand.

"Preston knew nothing about a storage unit but agreed that it made sense, as she didn't have time to sell anything unless she made arrangements with a junker in advance. He uses the garage for his cars, knows nothing is stored in there, and wouldn't allow it anyway. He took me into another bedroom that she'd converted into an office, and made himself comfortable in her chair while I showed off my tossing skills. I inspected the drawers, pulling them out, flipped through her books, peered behind pictures, all the usual places, and managed to put everything back in its place. I even used one of your tricks and fingered the knick-knacks."

"And all the while, Preston was stripping you naked with his eyes, picturing you over his knee, hoping you'd turn your attentions his way."

"Sarcasm is so unbecoming, Madison Westin."

"Is that your imitation of a disgruntled nun from your school days? If you pop out a ruler, I'm snapping it in half."

"I daydreamed about breaking Sister Celia's ruler one day," she said. "Instead, I hid it. My big mistake? Telling my best friend, Bridget. She got caught smoking in the bathroom and bargained that tidbit for a 'get out of trouble free' card. I got summoned to the principal's office; you would've thought I'd burned the school down."

"Aww." I gave her a sad face.

With light traffic on the roads, she hit the Overseas in record time and headed north to the Cove. A mask settled over her face. "Ursula had taped two files under the desk blotter. Preston copied them for me. In one, he found a storage receipt." She reached under the back of her shirt and produced the photocopied pages.

I skimmed through several pages of handwritten notes in a chicken scratch that was barely decipherable, and others with columns of dates and dollar amounts. A cursory glance told me nothing.

"Preston invited me to dinner."

"Of course he did." I made an unintelligible noise. "And you said, 'Can my boyfriend come along?'"

"Smarty. I told him about the love of my life, Didier; the only man allowed to spank me."

"Oh please." I giggled.

"We exchanged phone numbers, strictly business, and I offered to do a background check on the next girlfriend *before* he gives the lucky lady a key. He extracted a promise to keep him updated on the case and wants a call when I learn the contents of the unit. Preston said he supposed I would get into the storage place the same way I got into his house, which was how? So I informed him in my uppity French accent, 'This woman never leaves home without her lock pick.'"

"Let me guess, after that, he clapped his hand over his heart and swore he couldn't live without you. Insistent that you were the one he'd been looking for."

"It's the accent."

"How did you leave it?"

"Warned Preston to be very careful, watch his back and, if he breaks up with her, don't for any reason leave her unattended inside his home."

Chapter Twenty-Seven

"This is a disgusting area," I mumbled as soon as we exited the interstate. "This is the kind of area that would trigger the GPS warning, if you hadn't been fooling around with it. I predict a loud, noisy fight in French when Didier finds out. Have I told you how much it annoys me that you don't bicker in English, so I can eavesdrop?"

"I've lost count." She grinned.

"See this?" I held up my foot. "I'm going to put it someplace unpleasant if you don't stop messing with the GPS. I should make you take me home and let you come back by yourself—in your car."

"Look, we're here, and not a single gunshot's come our way."

"We still have to get out of here. Did you see the attention the Hummer attracted?"

The Storage Box was surrounded by a twelve-foot chain-link fence topped with razor wire. The signs read "protected by mean dogs," and were possibly more effective than the video surveillance adopted by their more upscale competition. I had yet to locate camera one—that would work in our favor if we had to come back.

"How did Ursula find this place? And when she got here, why didn't she turn around?" I asked.

The office building was a cement square. The windows were covered with hand-painted advertising that was barely visible behind the iron bars that crisscrossed them.

"Ursula's a smart one. The location may have been the selling factor. She'd never run into anyone she knew around here." Fab drove down the miniscule driveway and into one of the two parking spaces in front of the office, which was protected by a barred security door. An electric gate was off to one side for easy access to the rest of the lot. "It's easy enough to get in and have a look around, providing they have available units. But how do we verify that Ursula has a unit here? If she does, we need the number."

"Something doesn't feel right. Miss Snooty coming here and renting anything…this may be a dead end. I'm tired, I want to go home," I added, sounding like a five-year old. "I want to stop for those little homemade tacos and eat them on the beach."

"Don't make me drag you out of this car." She glared.

"Go ahead, I dare you. Sure, you'll kick my ass, but you'll be looking a little bedraggled yourself." *At least I hoped so.*

"Are you done, Drama Queen?"

"Not quite yet." I took a deep breath. "Okay, now I am. Let's just go in and bribe the owner. Looks like a place that could use a few extra bucks."

The front door was locked, but there was a hand-drawn sign with an arrow pointing to the doorbell. The sound was loud enough to wake the dead. After a second ring, the door buzzed and swung open. Standing behind the counter was a pimply twenty-something. It was hard to tell if we'd woken him up or if he looked like this all the time. His eyes were fogged over, and his hair bunched in a roll on the top of his head. His shirt and shorts were a wrinkled mess and in desperate need of a wash.

"Is the owner in?" Fab stepped over the threshold, not waiting for an invitation.

"Pops got better things to do," he answered in a bored tone. "I can help you with *anything* ma'am," he sneered as he ran his eyes over Fab's body.

Fab turned to me and rubbed her thumb across her middle and forefinger. *Why did the woman never carry cash?* She preferred plastic, which mystified me. At times like these, plastic got you nowhere. I fished cash out of the pocket earmarked for bribe money.

"We've got a business proposition for you." Fab waved a fifty under his nose. "We want information on one of your units."

"You cops?" He squinted in my direction and

dismissed me, his eyes returning to Fab. "What do you want to know? Then I can let you know if you'll need to run to the ATM."

I gave him my newly perfected creepy smile. "Don't get greedy."

"I have to measure the risk. What if I lost my job?"

Greedy and crafty, I thought.

"Does Ursula Richards have a unit here?" Fab asked.

He plucked the money from Fab's fingers and made it disappear under the counter. "I'm here every day, and I'd remember a name like that." He pulled up a screen on his computer and double-checked, shaking his head, his finger running down the screen. "Nope."

I pulled my phone out of my pocket, flipped it open, and held it out to him. "Do you recognize her?"

"Yeah. She's a snot-ass with a better-than-everyone attitude." He scanned the list again. "She used another name...here it is—Pearl Gardner. Let me know she was too good for this place, yet here she was, standing at my little counter, doing her damnedest to negotiate the price down." His eyes on the computer, he added, "Rented one of our largest units, paid three months up front. Couple of days later, a big-ass moving truck unloaded her stuff, and I haven't seen her since. I remember because I thought it was weird that the van didn't have any advertising on the side. It had been painted over."

Fab rested her elbows on the counter and smiled at him. "How about letting us look around the inside of the unit?"

I refrained from making a retching noise.

"Yeah—no! I don't have a key." He held his hands out. "But if I did, that would cost you because I'd have to go along and make sure you didn't steal anything."

Fab leaned in and stage-whispered conspiratorially to him, "I'll get us in and out. Long enough for a look and a couple of pictures. Ursula will never know we got inside. It will be our little secret."

"How much?" I asked.

"Three more of these." He held up the money, fanning it in front of his nose. "As a bonus, you two can look all you want and this—" he took the additional money from my fingers. "—buys my silence. I won't ever tell anyone you were here. What's the story?" he asked as he grabbed the phone lying on the counter and unlocked a steel door. "Follow me, girlies."

"For what you were just paid, you don't get any details," I grouched as I fell in behind Fab, smacking her in the back.

"You don't have to worry about cameras recording anything; we don't have any. Never had a break-in. We've got three Dobermans that patrol the property at night and are better than any security guard we could hire. Even if they fall asleep, they wake up at the slightest noise." He pointed to the rolled razor wire fence. "Don't like a person's chances of climbing over, only to end up as a snack for the dogs." He threw his head back and laughed. "Unit's over here in the last aisle."

Ursula had chosen an end location in the farthest corner of the lot. Fab popped the lock with precision and shoved up the rolling door.

Nothing prepared me for the mess inside. My mouth dropped open in shock, and that rarely happened as not much surprised me. But this... A ten-foot mountain of trash: furniture broken into pieces, cushions and pillows slashed, men's clothing shredded, bits of glass everywhere. It didn't look as though a single item had escaped her wrath.

"What the hell?" the man exclaimed. "People leave trash behind all the time, but this is going to cost big to haul away. Bitch!" He banged his fist on the wall.

Fab walked the inside perimeter, taking picture after picture; outside, she took several long shots.

I stepped around the mess, but didn't see a single fixture, appliance, cabinet, or anything that had been attached to the house. I'd suspected all along that she'd hired workers to do the interior demolition, then found some disreputable outfit that wouldn't ask questions and would pay her for the second-hand items that could easily be sold.

"She's not coming back, and the deposit won't cover the cleanup." The man twitched from one foot to the other in barely controlled anger.

"Sorry about the mess." Fab handed him the lock. "Thanks for your help." She grabbed my arm and pulled me into the driveway. "Let's get out of here."

He shouted after us, "Wait up, you need me to get out the gate."

"Ursula is dangerous," I whispered to Fab. "You need to warn your new hottie friend. It's hard to imagine that she ripped apart Ian's personal belongings with her own talons, but if she did, she's damn scary."

Fab made a grunting noise and otherwise ignored me.

The young guy ran by us to open the gate.

Turning to our accomplice, I warned, "If for some reason Ursula comes back, pretend ignorance. She's obviously unhinged."

Chapter Twenty-Eight

I derailed Fab's plan to drive straight home, asking her in a whiny voice to stop at The Taco Stand for a cardboard tray of their homemade specialty. I'd stopped one day at the family-run place to check out the competition and fallen in love with their hottest selling item — mini-tacos.

We zipped through the drive-through and took our food home, spreading it out on the patio table. I changed into my bathing suit in record time, grabbed bottles of cold water, and slid into a chair next to Fab, who was already in her suit. Today was proof that she actually could perform a wardrobe change in record time.

Fab grabbed a pile of napkins, and on a cutting board in front of her, she sliced a lime and an orange for our waters.

"Next time, margaritas." I toasted Fab.

Fab's smile disappeared when her phone rang. She picked it up and answered, "What's up?"

I scowled at her when she didn't hit the speaker button. When she hung up, I'd definitely be reminding her that not sharing calls wasn't part of our agreement.

"Behave yourself," she said into the phone,

tapping her fingernail incessantly on the tabletop, making an annoying clicking sound.

I put my hand over hers and held it there. Her voice lacked the irritation level that she reserved for most everyone, which had me jumping to the conclusion that it was one of her slimy clients.

"Got it." She rolled her eyes. "I know— yesterday. Call you back." She banged her phone down on the table.

"What dirty little job do you have for us now?" I asked on a sigh, refilling our glasses.

"He's such an arrogant dick."

I shook my head. "There's too many choices for me to guess."

"Preston Sinclair! When we met and I relayed in great detail all about the deranged Ursula, his response was to laugh. After some time to think, he's not laughing now. He sounded agitated. Told me every time he looks at her, she creeps him out. He wanted to know if she attacked the last boyfriend and if she was prone to physical violence in any way."

"He's looking out for little Preston." I made kissy noises. My guess was that part of his anatomy had done all the thinking when he met the woman.

Fab gave me her best imitation of a "behave yourself" look.

"Oh stop that, you're so bad at it."

She tried again. "Your mother said it was perfect." She pouted.

I shook my head. "Mother hates to hurt your feelings. Get back to the convo." I stabbed at the phone. "What else?"

"Preston wants Ursula out of the condo—pronto. He did a drive-by on Ian's house, and now he's afraid of what Ursula will do to his place. Apparently, she cornered him last night about his sudden loss of affection."

"I suppose he can't tell her he has cramps." I sighed when I finished off the last taco, licking my lips. I stood and swept the trash into a paper bag, taking it to the trash can. I wished the recycle bin's lid was open so I could practice my slam dunk, but instead lifted the lid and dropped my water bottle inside.

"Preston told her he strained a muscle during a workout." Fab pointed downward and laughed. "He's going out of town next week and wants us to organize her eviction and stay at the condo until he gets back. The best part? Ursula is supportive of his injury. She's playing nursey. He's certain she has no idea it's the end of the romance."

"Old Pres doesn't get to keep his hands pristine." I wiped away a non-existent tear. "We can move her out, but someone has to tell her she doesn't live there anymore, and it won't be one of us. Once we've finalized a real plan, you'll call him back and tell him."

"That's one thing I appreciate about you, your attention to detail."

"You think on it, and I bet you can come up with several things," I said. "Let me guess, is this a freebie?" I'd eavesdropped closely enough, and I hadn't heard a word about an envelope full of cash.

Lightning flashed in the sky, one thousand one, one thousand two, and a long boom of thunder rolled across the area, signaling that the storm was close by.

"You rope me into gratis stuff all the time. Do I complain?" Fab waved me in the direction of the house.

"*Every* single time," I said in exasperation and followed as it began to sprinkle.

"You're spoiled, working for Brick and the freshly printed hundreds he hands out," she whined and flounced down on the couch, kicking her feet up.

I chuckled, piled up several pillows on the daybed, and lay down next to Jazz, then hit the remote, turning on the overhead ceiling fans. "When Brick handed me my first envelope of cash, I took it to the bank to find out if it was real."

"You did not," Fab gasped. "What did they say?"

"I have a favorite teller, who knows I own The Cottages and that I come in with the occasional bundle of money. I told her a tourist paid in cash, and I just wanted to be sure it was real. She laughed and informed me that most people, if they had a doubt, wouldn't say a word and instead spend it all around town."

"That's a good way to go to jail." Fab pulled a notepad out of one of the drawers in the coffee table, jabbing at it with a pen. "Have you come up with a plan for getting rid of Ms. Ursula yet?"

I eyed Jazz sleeping along my side and wished I could join him in a nap. If only I could figure out how to fall asleep in ten seconds. "I get that men hate messy breakups, but can't Preston toss Ursula to the curb himself?"

Fab snapped the beach-themed pen in half in irritation.

Now wasn't the time to tell her that it was one of my favorite purchases from the tourist paraphernalia store she loathed. "First off, tell Hottie that he's never, ever to mention our names to anyone. Ursula will get even, and it will be ugly. Next, you'll inform Pres that this whole plan is on hold until he gets his butt back to town. We need him to keep Ursula distracted and away from the condo for the entire day."

"Who packs her stuff?" Fab demanded. She'd found a different pen, since she destroyed the first one and was scribbling madly. "Just so you know, I'm not doing it."

"Look, Princess, the fewer people involved, the better. We pack, hire someone to do the heavy lifting, arrange for storage, and give Preston the key. "And," I cut Fab off, "I suggest your non-paying client change the locks for every key on his ring as well as all his security codes."

"Sometimes you amaze even me."

"Unfortunately, I have experience with less-than-stable people." I stared out the window as the rain came pouring down in buckets. Free plant-watering, but I wished it would stop so we could go back outside.

"I'll also tell him he needs to notify security at his other residence and business," Fab said.

"Here's a thought—it could neutralize Ursula for a few months. He rents her a place to live, prepaid for, say, six months? We arrange to have her boxes and car delivered, and at the end of the day, he drops her at her new digs and hands over the keys." I paused, thinking about what I already knew about the woman. "I'm thinking Preston should get her out of the car before unveiling his surprise. There's always a chance she could go crazy on him and possibly involve the police. He could get a restraining order based on her past acts, but you and I know that a person can go off the rails in the meantime and create havoc before they can be stopped."

"You take care of planning her move, and I'll coordinate the security issues."

"That's why we're the perfect team; you're the looker and I have the good ideas."

"I have good ideas," Fab growled.

"If we shoot everyone, we won't get any clients. And there will go my fun."

"It's all about you, isn't it?"

I hung my head and laughed. "Yes," I squeaked.

"In the future, I need to remind myself that the best jobs are in and out and collect our money."

"Hmm…when was the last time we had a job like that? I'm thinking never." I grabbed the notepad and pen and added to her notes. "Inform Preston we need a list of which rooms, closets, and drawers we'll find her stuff in. I'll get moving men from Spoon. His guys aren't slackers, and they won't blab any details."

"Ursula hasn't been in residence very long, so hopefully, she won't have much stuff there. Do you think she'll go away and we'll get lucky enough to never hear her name again?"

"Ha! Getting even will be foremost in her mind. Look at her track record. She humiliated Ian and left him with nothing except for what was in his suitcase, from a ski trip no less. Then spread scurrilous accusations all over town to anyone who would listen. Bet you she's left behind gruesome memories for other victims."

"I'm going to suggest he get a beefy male housesitter for when he's not in Duck Key, at least for a little while."

"I've got just the man for the job. He's not beefy, but he's mean as stink."

"Really, Madison," she said in her haughty voice. "Where do you meet these people?"

"When one of your white-collar criminal friends starts housesitting, have them send over a business card. Mine are more reliable and don't steal. Supply them with beer and greasy food, and they'll stay as long as you need."

Fab whooshed out a long breath. "I'll call Hottie and run down the plan, let him know you'll be emailing him a detailed checklist so this goes off with no guns being drawn."

"Amen, sister. You might mention to Mr. Freebie that if he has a legal job that needs to be done, he should us a call. You also might want to mention that this job isn't exactly legal. If he wants to keep his hands unsullied, inform him that to get Ursula out sooner, he'd have to pony up a huge bribe or get a court order, which could take three to four months, depending on how savvy she is around the legal system. She's the type to find out how to prolong the eviction process."

"Do you think we can pull this off without involving the law or getting into any trouble?" Fab looked hopeful.

"With you involved?" I arched my brow.

The front door flew open. "Fabiana Merceau!" Didier bellowed. My stomach sank; the man didn't sound happy. I'd never heard him yell like that.

Didier marched into the living room, Creole right behind him, both of them in bicycle attire, covered in sweat. Fab looked at him in surprise.

"Why isn't the GPS working—again?" Didier bit off, glaring down at her.

I narrowed my eyes at Creole and gave him a dirty look, knowing damn well this must be the "surprise" he mentioned a while back.

Fab made a few sounds in French.

Didier cut her off. "English! I'm sure your best friend would like to hear the answer."

I already knew but didn't think it prudent to mention it. If I were closer, I'd whisper, "Tell the truth," in her ear.

Fab stood. "Let's go upstairs."

"No!" he thundered. "Sit back down and answer the question."

"I didn't…" she started. "I don't…" She stared at her angry boyfriend.

I looked down and squeezed my eyes shut. Fab was going to lie. She had to know that Didier already knew the truth and she needed to cough it up, no matter how uncomfortable.

After a long pause, she blurted, "I disconnected it."

"Why? I know you don't give a damn about your safety since you think you're invincible, but what about Madison?" He was still angry but not yelling.

She reverted to French, as she always did when she spoke to Didier. He cut her off with a curt gesture.

"How many units have you dismantled? Driven over?" Didier demanded. "You still haven't offered a good reason for it."

Creole turned and went into the kitchen,

pulling up a stool.

"Would anyone..." I started and saw Creole shake his head. The hell with him; he started this mess. "How about a cold drink?" I offered, hoping to lighten up the awkward silence.

Didier smiled for the first time. "No, thank you."

Creole wiggled his finger at me, but I ignored him. If he wanted something, he was sitting in the kitchen; he could get it himself.

"I don't like that your ass...your friend over there is keeping tabs." Fab's words were tinged with bitterness. "As hard as this might be for you to believe, just today I thought about not doing it again."

Didier put one finger under her chin and lifted her head, forcing her to look him directly in the eyes. "I love you. I just want you to be safe."

Fab whispered back a response.

Didier held out his hand, helping Fab to her feet. "You—" he pointed at me. "—should also be mindful of your safety. I'm sure Creole will have plenty to say." He glanced over his shoulder at his friend.

"That will be difficult, since I'm not speaking to him," I said.

Fab smiled, and I winked back.

Chapter Twenty-Nine

A rustling noise from the top of the stairs made me crack open an eye to see if it was Fab or Didier who had the insomnia. Creole had gotten a phone call before we could discuss the drama that had unfolded in the living room. After he exchanged a few terse sentences with someone, he gave me a toe-curling kiss and whispered against my lips, "I'll make this up to you. All of it."

After he left, I lay on the daybed with Jazz's head on my chest, too tired to walk upstairs to my bedroom, and read until my eyes closed.

The nightlight illuminated a long, hairless leg as it came into view. I shook my head, thinking the woman couldn't stay out of trouble for five minutes. "Where do you think you're sneaking off to?"

Fab squealed, peering over the banister. "You scared the hell out of me."

I inwardly groaned. The blue jeans thrown over one arm and tennis shoes in her hand meant an unsanctioned night job. "Pretty underwear."

"Bought it special for Didier." She twirled

around, showing off the small piece of black lace and string.

"I bet you have the cleanest butt in town, since you floss every day."

"You're disgusting." She scowled, tossing her shoes on the floor and skinnying into her jeans.

"If I were standing, I'd curtsy. Does Didier know you're slinking out into the night? You think it's a good idea to go out by yourself after the safety talk?" I rolled onto my side, facing Fab exasperated with her and tired of wringing the details of her escapades out of her when she snuck back in.

"I'd like to know where you're going!" Didier barked from the top of the stairs, shirtless, his hair tousled.

"You two sleep like dead people and you're both awake?" Fab took a step towards Didier.

It shocked her when he held up his hand. "You want to sneak around, go ahead." He started back up the stairs.

"Stop!" she yelled. "Come back and let me explain."

"If this is about your insomnia, I don't want to hear it. I can't believe I was stupid enough to believe that story." He leaned against the banister, not taking a step in either direction.

I relocated Jazz and stood up. "I'll see you two in the morning."

"Sit back down." She motioned to me. "You might as well hear this. I have chronic insomnia, and that was never a lie," she insisted. "Once I wake up, I rarely go back to sleep. I lay in the dark and think about my cases and sometimes come up with a plan of action that I hadn't given thought to or one that is better executed during non-business hours."

"Which client?" Didier demanded.

"Will you please come down and sit?" She held out her hand.

The two engaged in a stare-down, then he moved slowly down the stairs and threw himself in a chair opposite the couch.

"It's not a client," she said in a soft voice. "It has to do with the man I love, and he needs my help whether he wants it or not."

Feeling like a third wheel, I was happy to see Didier's face relax as he exhaled his frustration. "So what's your plan?" I asked, having a good idea what it was and hoping Didier wouldn't flip.

"I've put off searching Balcazar's offices long enough. At some point, Lauren's office will get cleaned out, and I'll kick myself for the missed opportunity."

"Fabiana." Didier ran his hands through his hair.

"I swear to you," she held up her hand, "in and out, and I'll come straight home. Ask Madison, these jobs are uneventful."

Didn't you just walk in on a man in his bed in a supposedly vacant residence? I kept silent.

"The ass you referred to earlier mentioned he'd like a go at those offices. At the time, I figured Creole mentioned the idea so I wouldn't be surprised when you decided to sneak around and do it yourself," Didier said.

I sucked in my breath and glared at Fab. "I'm sure you didn't mean Creole. I never call your boyfriend names."

Didier snapped out a laugh. "Thank you, *chérie*," he said to me.

"I'll go as backup," I offered. "What the hell; I'm awake anyway."

Didier shot me a glare. Right after he moved in, he'd given Mother and me a shaking finger every time we uttered a "coarse" word.

"Hell's not so bad; it could've been worse," I teased.

"I'm going. Give me five minutes to change," Didier said. "Don't waste time arguing. You," he pointed at me, "need to change. I plan to learn from you how to be backup."

"The sweat shorts are fine. Don't forget a shirt and tennis shoes, in case you need to make a run for it," I said over my shoulder on my way upstairs.

Chapter Thirty

We parked down the street from Balcazar's beachfront headquarters. The building was dark, except for a few stray office lights that burned overhead. The bars had closed, and in addition to there being no cars on the road, there wasn't a single person wandering the sidewalk.

Fab drove with Didier by her side, and I rode in the backseat, stretched out, reading on my phone. The only sounds were the mumbling of the two in the front, who couldn't be bothered to speak louder so I could eavesdrop. I was quite certain that sticking my head between the seats would earn me glares from both of them.

"You know what to do." Fab looked at me over the headrest. "Text me if anyone shows up. I'll message you when I'm out, and you can pick me up around the corner." She leaned across, kissing Didier. "If you need to shoot someone, let her do it. She's a damn good shot."

"Are you sure I can't talk you out of this? It's not too late," Didier muttered.

"We can leave if you want, but I'll just come back when you're out of town."

It took a minute for him to reply. "Fine."

"Don't worry." Fab opened the door. "You two behave." She put on dark sunglasses that covered most of her face and pulled her baseball cap down.

Normally, I'd crawl over the seat, but with Didier in the front, I got out and slid back in behind the wheel. "First, hard as it is, try not to worry. Keep alert for anything unusual." I pulled my phone from my pocket. "What's really first is to text Creole our location."

"I wanted to go with her, but she politely pointed out that I didn't have the required skills to commit a felony and stay out of jail. What kind of man lets his girlfriend put herself at risk?" Didier stared out the windshield.

"I failed to mention that you look hot in your work clothes." I ran my eyes down his long legs to his designer tennis shoes. His finely sculpted arms showed from under his short-sleeved shirt. "To heck with those designer suits."

"Is that how you change the subject with Fabiana? Feed her ego with sweet comments?" he laughed.

"Usually I give her a double dose of sarcasm, and that snaps her right out of her funk." I kept my eyes peeled over the steering wheel at 100 Ocean Boulevard. "If you see any lights go on or off, let me know. That would mean Fab has company."

My phone rang, and I looked down and

grimaced at the screen before answering. "What's up?"

"What in the hell?" Creole's voice boomed through the phone.

I wished I'd remembered to hold it away from my ear. I pulled it away and glared at it as though that would help. Didier took it from my fingers and spoke in French.

"Oh no you don't!" I jerked it out of his hand. "On my phone, you speak English. What?" I barked at Creole.

"Hold on a minute," Creole said. I guessed from the lack of sound coming through the receiver that he was getting his anger under control. "Let me guess… Fab broke into Balcazar's offices, and you and Didier are lookouts?" Creole asked with fake calm.

"Yes, dear."

Didier tugged on my hair and shook his head.

"Don't think I won't pay you back for my near-heart attack," he grouched.

"If you forget, I'll remind you."

Creole cleared his throat. "How long has Fab been upstairs? Text her to take pictures. And you, text me as soon as she gets back in the car."

I sent the text to Fab and hunched over the wheel, staring up. No lone figure scaling down the side of the building—that was a good sign.

I felt like I'd forgotten something. There wasn't a checklist for this job, and I still needed to work on being patient while waiting. Surely

Fab would've been back by now if there had been any cars in the underground parking lot. I scanned the building, but nothing had changed. The lobby was still well-lit and empty. Headlights caught my attention, and in the side mirror, I saw what looked suspiciously like a cop car roll up behind the SUV.

"Hang up," I whispered, jerking my top over my head and leaning into Didier.

He quickly did so, then turned and looked out the back window. "What are you doing?"

"We're going to put on a show of smoochy face without actually doing it."

Didier put his arm around me, grabbing the back of my head. "Good thing you're wearing a bra, or this would be more awkward than it is."

I'd enjoyed my braless days, until someone sent a group photo and my girls were the only ones that looked droopy. The next day, I went to Mother's favorite lingerie store and got measured for one that fit correctly. To my satisfaction, they now sat in the right place.

A light flashed into the driver's side window, followed by knocking. A man's voice called, "Roll down the window."

I made a show of being startled, turned, and lowered the window. "Hi…" I did a double take. "Officer Watters. Nice to see you again." *What were the chances of running into the same cop twice?*

He shone his light in my face until I blinked, and then ran the beam down to my cleavage, where he lingered, and finally over to Didier.

"Miss Madison, aren't you two a little old to be making out on the street?" Not waiting for an answer, he directed, "License and insurance. Of course you know that."

"Nothing's changed since last time." I smiled sweetly as I handed him the documents.

"Don't go anywhere. I'd hate to have to shoot you," he chuckled.

His laugh unnerved me. While he returned to his car, several more police cars pulled up in front of Balcazar's building. The officers filed out and went in separate directions, surrounding the area.

"Police," I texted Fab, and lifted the top to the console glove box and hid it under a false bottom.

"I'm impressed," Didier whispered. "How do you know him?"

I filled him in on the unfortunate traffic stop.

"He looks familiar, as though I've met him and can't remember where…" Didier looked thoughtful.

"The last thing we want is for him to demand your identification. How would we explain being across from Balcazar's office?"

Officer Watters came back, handing me back my identification. "Do you believe in coincidence? I don't. And yet here we are once again." The shuttered look on his face was unsettling. It was hard to tell if he believed the make-out story.

"Is there a problem?" I inclined my head toward the opposite side of the street, where the cops still milled around.

He ignored my question. "Have you seen anyone lurking around? Cars? Anything?"

"It's been quiet, but then, we were mostly... um... engaged." I hoped I didn't sound as stupid as I felt.

"I'm going to be a nice guy and let you off with a warning. I could write you a ticket for parking in a time-restricted zone. You need to get over your bad habit of ignoring traffic signs. One fewer piece of clothing, and I could haul you in on a sex charge that would force you to register as a sex offender. Next time, get a hotel room. If you can afford a Hummer, a room shouldn't be a problem." He flashed his light one last time in Didier's face.

A chill ran up my spine. He seemed to be enjoying himself. "Thank you," I mumbled.

Once the window closed and the ignition caught, Didier said, "You need to careful of that man. He dislikes you with an intensity that surprises me, given you've only met him twice."

"Maybe Creole talked to him." I pulled out onto the deserted street. Well, deserted if you didn't count the police cars.

"We can't leave Fabiana here," Didier said angrily, hauling himself around to look at the building.

"We don't have any choice," I hissed at him. "Officer Watters is following us. We're going to the backup plan."

"Do you even have one?" he snorted.

"Have a little faith. Fab wouldn't want you to swoop in and do something chivalrous and get arrested. The last thing you need is for some cop to identify you and ask questions." I cut him off before he could speak. "Give me a minute. I excel at what-to-do-next plans."

With Watters on my bumper, I headed to the Z Hotel. I'd let him think I'd taken his suggestion. I'd never stayed at the five-star establishment, but I'd had lunch there a couple of times. I glanced quickly at Didier. "Call Creole and ask if it's a good idea to double back to the building on foot."

Watters made a U-turn right after I signaled that I was turning into the hotel parking lot. Not having the nerve to park, I bypassed the lot and pulled over on a side street.

I fished out my phone and texted Fab, "You okay?" I turned on the GPS, asking it to find the closest grocery store, and smiled when one popped up within a few blocks. We could park there, and no one would ask questions.

"He's not answering." Didier threw his phone on the dashboard. The back popped off and the battery fell out.

My phone beeped, and I handed it to Didier.

"It says, 'Tell Didier not to do anything stupid.

This might take a while but don't worry — well hidden.'" Didier wrapped his fingers around it, holding tight. "What now?"

"We need to hang out where we won't be noticed and wait for Fab's call. A fast food joint would be ideal, but most aren't twenty-four hours anymore, so I located a market."

"How do you know this stuff?" he asked, seeming impressed.

"Your girlfriend taught me. Fab will call and tell us where to pick her up." I turned onto the main boulevard and headed toward the big illuminated Food Barn sign.

My phone rang between Didier's fingers — Creole's ringtone. "You might as well answer it. Creole can calm your nerves."

One thing about grocery shopping: whatever time you chose to do it, day or night, there were always other people pushing a cart. I slid backwards into a space from which it would easy to keep an eye on the entire lot. Out of good manners, and stressed over the creepy Officer Watters, I climbed over the seat while Didier and Creole conversed in English and French. I lay on my side and closed my eyes, willing Fab to call.

* * *

The ringing of my phone woke me from an uncomfortable snooze in a fetal position. The screen lit up, and Fab's face beamed back at me. I sat up and glanced outside, and was surprised to see the beginnings of daylight streaming in the SUV windows. "How much is the bail?" I asked.

"I need a damn ride. Where are you?"

I could almost hear her foot tapping. "Your taxi awaits, if you don't mind sharing with the annoying French guy I can't get rid of." I winked at him.

"Go north on Ocean. I'm on the beach side in front of The Shrimpery. Hurry the hell up. I'm calling Didier now." She hung up.

Didier scowled at me. "I wanted to talk to her."

I held up my index finger, my middle finger, and then his phone rang. For some reason, I'd thought I'd get to three. I got out, stood and stretched, then slid in behind the wheel. Glancing at the clock, I realized that it had been daylight for a half-hour and Fab had been trapped inside the building for hours.

I half-listened to the one-sided conversation going on next to me. Not that I could understand a word, but it was amusing listening to Didier's voice change from sweet and sexy to grouchy and back. I waited for the conversation to heat back up and made kissy noises when it did. Didier glared at me, and I giggled.

When we turned onto Ocean Boulevard, Didier rolled down the window and stuck his head out. Never having picked Fab up from a job, he didn't know she'd probably be jumping up and down in the street. This early, she wouldn't have to worry about getting flattened by another car.

Reaching over, I tugged on the back of his shirt. He ducked back in, glowering at me, and his arched eyebrows seemed to yell, "What?"

"Fabiana doesn't like it when passengers hang their heads out the window like oversized animals," I managed to say with a straight face.

He stared at me and leaned forward, a loud barking growl erupting from his lips, then shoved his head back out into the wind.

No laugh? I knitted my brows, chuckling slightly to myself. *Too early in the morning? Couldn't be that I was too annoying... Could it?*

"Who's that?" Didier demanded, pointing up ahead.

He had to know that Fab, the man magnet, could attract anyone, from the oldsters to the twenty-year-old with the surfboard who stared hopefully at her now, just like all her conquests.

"I guess you have to be reminded that your girlfriend is a hot, sexy French woman and men can hope. But I happen to know there's only one man she gets horizontal with," I said with feigned innocence.

Didier clearly had a retort on the tip of his tongue and wrestled with whatever it was.

"Is horizontal unclear? I know more descriptive adjectives."

He threw his head back and laughed. "The

next time Fabiana complains about your attitude, I'm going to be more sympathetic."

I clutched my heart and winked at him. Mission accomplished, he'd finally laughed. I pulled over to the curb. Fab said something to her new friend, who waved and sauntered down the sand.

Fab rushed to the passenger-side window, leaning in to kiss Didier. I pretended I didn't notice and jumped out, giving them privacy. Fab came around the front, and I enveloped her in a hug. "You're so amazing," I whispered in her ear.

"I'm only allowing this display because if things were different, we both know there would be no touching during a jail visitation."

"Don't speed. That cop from the other day was outside the building earlier, giving us trouble." I filled her in on the details.

That surprised her. "Hmmm... I don't like that, not one bit. We'll talk about this later."

Chapter Thirty-One

Happy to be home, I grabbed Jazz and escaped upstairs to my comfortable bed. Looking in the mirror, I could see worry wreaking havoc on my face. I looked like I hadn't had a good night's sleep in a week.

The three of us had rocketed down the interstate to the Keys, making excellent time before rush-hour traffic started. The only thing Fab said was that Balcazar was doing a little late-night office cleaning, and she'd almost been discovered. Balcazar had snapped at the Miami police when they came up empty-handed, failing to capture the uninvited guest, and suggested they were slacking off on their jobs. Didier said the rest of the details could wait for Creole's arrival.

I slipped between the cool cotton sheets and my eyes drifted closed, succumbing to sleep as soon as my head the pillow. It seemed like only a few minutes later that the bed dipped. Creole shifted next to me, and his arms tightened. I cocked one eye to make certain.

"Nap time," he said, sleepily rubbing his face against my cheek.

"Hmm," I cooed, wiggling against him.

* * *

The afternoon sun was beating through the bedroom window when my eyes fluttered open. Against my back, Creole radiated heat, and I felt the little puffs of his rhythmic breathing against my neck.

I arched into a stretch, trying not to disturb Creole's sleep. His arm, curved around my waist, tightened. "Where do you think you're going?" he murmured, flipping me onto his chest and wrapping his legs around mine.

I pressed my lips against his. "Let's sneak out the back, go to your house, and turn off our phones."

He raised his head and kissed me. He coaxed, seduced with his lips, his tongue, the murmur of his breath, his taste. His hand lightly slapped my bottom. "I need to debrief Fab. That stupid ribbon was on their door when I got here." He chuckled in my ear.

I wriggled against him. "Five minutes," I said throatily.

He rolled me onto my back. "I aim to please."

* * *

An hour later, having heard Fab and Didier down at the pool through our bedroom window, we walked downstairs hand in hand in our bathing suits.

"About time," Fab called from the kitchen island.

Creole sniffed the air. "I take it you're not cooking." He laughed at the dirty look she gave him.

I picked up Fab's glass and took a taste. "I'll have one of these."

Didier nodded at his friend, handing him a beer, then retrieved a glass and poured me a sparkling water with a lime wedge.

Creole took a couple of steps into the living room to make a call. He turned back after a few minutes, "Food's on its way."

"Wait...you didn't ask us what we wanted," Fab griped.

"Fabiana!" Didier gave her the evil eye.

"You probably won't like it." Creole made a sad face. "But I happen to know there's frozen waffles."

I wanted to jump in front of Creole and protect him from the searing look Fab sent his way. I managed to remain neutral and reached for a tray, handing it to Fab. She and Didier filled it with assorted snack food; munchies should keep an argument from sparking.

Creole wrestled the tray from Fab and carried it outside. Didier filled an enamel tub with ice and stuffed it with beers and a large bottle of mineral water and followed him.

Outside, Fab walked up behind Didier, wrapping her arms around his waist. He turned and lifted her into his arms, and she began shouting threats once she realized where she was headed. Four steps later, he jumped with her into the pool. They surfaced together, and before she could continue her tirade, his mouth covered hers and his legs wrapped around her.

Creole dove in, coming up next to a beach ball, which he bounced off Didier's head. The testosterone shot up as Didier grabbed the ball and slam-dunked it in the hoop that was anchored on the side of the pool.

I took a safe seat on the steps, and Fab swam to my side.

"I appreciate it that your lug kept Didier from losing it while waiting for me to make my escape. Didier said it was a good thing you were there, or he'd have marched into the building," Fab said.

"I did my part," I half-laughed. "I fell asleep in the back."

"Look at those two." Fab pointed. "Everything is a competition."

They were splashing around, jumping, shooting, trading mild insults.

"It's fun to watch them having such a good time." I lunged for the ball when it landed in front of me, cutting off Fab, and tossed it to Creole.

Fab shot her arms in the air. "Madison's not

playing fair."

I splashed her with water and hustled up the steps. Fab treaded water and retrieved balls, tossing them to Didier.

"Unfair advantage," Creole yelled.

A few shots later, Didier claimed victory.

As Creole swam to the side, hoisting himself over the side of the pool, Fab's phone began ringing. A moment later, it stopped and mine started. I rolled over on the chaise and handed him my phone. "Here," I thrust it at him. I knew who it was without looking.

Creole glanced at the screen and glared. "What do you want?" he answered. "If you don't say something, I'm hanging up." He bared his teeth at the phone. Like Fab, he never used the speaker button which disappointed me. King Brick only called for something he labeled an emergency, but then, that was how he classified all his jobs.

"I'm sorry," Creole drawled. "She's *tied* up at the moment." He winked at me. "Can I give her a message?"

I shook my head at *tied up.*

"I'll pass it along. Just so we're clear, I found out recently that I can get a twofer rate on making sure a body is never found—that rate could include your brother."

Creole held the phone away from his ear.

"Interesting choice of words," he snorted. "I'm just setting the record straight so there are no misunderstandings." He hung up. "Brick wants you two in his office first thing in the morning."

"Did he give you a clue as to what he wanted?" I tossed him a towel.

Fab climbed out of the pool. "Thanks for having my back. Maybe someday, I'll do the same for you," she said to Creole.

"How do you do it? Work for that man?" Creole asked.

"Brick gave me my first job and has been loyal since day one. There are times, though, when I entertain the idea of serving him up as an alligator appetizer."

Didier wrapped a towel around her, his arms strong and steady. His hug lifted her off the ground, and then he pulled her down on the chaise in front of him.

"Do alligators eat everything, or are they sloppy and leave telltale DNA?" I asked.

Creole looked at his buzzing phone. "Food's here." He jumped up and ran inside the house.

"Thank goodness, these healthy crackers taste like paste, and they stink." I scrunched my nose.

"I fixed those myself," Fab said.

"You spent hours slaving in the kitchen, opening the box and pouring them in a bowl?" I bit my lip.

Didier laughed and got an elbow to his mid-section.

Creole came back through the patio doors holding four bags with Roscoe's logo blazoned on them. The drive-thru boasted the best burgers in the Keys.

"What the hell?" Fab sputtered when she saw the bags.

Didier scowled at her and whispered in her ear.

She jerked away. "I suppose there are greasy fries in there too? You're so cheap, you should've called Jake's and got free food."

"Fabiana," Didier scolded.

I covered my face with my hands, peeking through my fingers and laughing.

Creole handed out the bags and tossed down a roll of paper towels. "Look, Princess." He leaned in her direction. "You don't want it, I'll eat it. You can go make yourself a bowl of cereal."

Fab glanced over her shoulder, and Didier glared back at her. She jerked the bag out of Creole's fingers, and instead of a thank-you, she gave him the stink eye. I held up a packet of ketchup, and Fab rolled her eyes, but took it. All conversation stopped as we ripped into our bags. Fab made a show of pulling the bun apart and sniffing.

"Balcazar called me earlier," Didier said between bites.

"Did he suspect Fab of being the one he wanted ferreted out of his building and carted off in cuffs?" Creole asked. "He called downtown and attempted to throw his weight around."

"At first, his call unnerved me, had me

thinking he knew about Fab. He mentioned the break-in, and I told him I hadn't heard about it and was surprised it hadn't made the news, then changed the subject. The social call stunned me, since he's ignored my attempts to get in touch. He hasn't made a secret of the fact that he thinks I'm guilty," Didier said.

"Crappy friend," Creole hissed.

"He had the nerve to ask why I hadn't called, when he knows that I have, and left several messages too. I'd already written off the relationship, but I was curious and pressed him about why he thought I was guilty. He said he was sorry if he gave that impression; he hadn't recovered from Lauren's death. He went on about how she was like family and her passing was painful."

"That's laying it on thick." Creole rolled his eyes. "I'd love to have a little one-on-one chat with him. See what he knows and if he's withholding anything."

"Right before we hung up, he blurted out that he thought someone had gone through his files. He didn't say whether from his office or otherwise. Having learned this trick from my beautiful girlfriend, I answered with a question, 'Why in the hell would I do that?'"

I shook my finger at Didier, imitating him in a pseudo-French accent, "First damn, now hell," I tsked.

He laughed. "Thank you, feels good to laugh."

"That was the worst French accent," Creole whispered in my ear. "But oddly a turn-on." He brushed my hair aside and kissed the back of my neck.

"Did he happen to mention whether anything was missing, files or otherwise?" Creole asked.

"I did ask and got a vague response, that it was 'just a feeling.' Once he heard my snort of disbelief, he added that he was trying to prove my innocence."

"There must be something aside from his shady business practices he doesn't want anyone to find out," Creole said.

"Before realizing I wasn't alone, I tried to place a couple of bugs in his offices so you could get your answers from the man himself," Fab said. "Sorry."

Oh great. She'll never be content with just snooping through Balcazar's offices now. Next stop will be his house, I thought. Creole exchanged some kind of secret-code look with Fab. Translated: He had her back if she was going to commit another felony.

"How did the conversation end?" he asked, hanging on Didier's every word, taking in the information.

"He wanted me to know that if he did discover anything in the files that would prove my innocence, he would turn it over to the district attorney. I informed him that I had nothing to prove because I wasn't guilty. And if he thought me capable of murder, then we were never really friends. The call ended, and we both knew the friendship was over."

Fab stood, stretched, and leaned down, kissing Didier's cheek. She picked up the dinner trash and tossed it in the bin. Miss Picky had wolfed down her burger and fries like the rest of us.

"Were you able to get a look at any files?" I asked when she sat back down.

"Balcazar should worry about his computers having no passwords. I can give him a recommendation for a reclusive, nerdy geek from one of my more nefarious contacts. Isn't that how you refer to them?" Fab looked at me.

I shook my head. "If this is a contest as to whose friends are more badass, you win hands down." I cracked a phony smile.

"Balcazar left his computer on, so I connected with Big Al, and he remotely installed a bug that would track Balcazar's every keystroke and copy his files. Interestingly, the filing cabinets didn't contain file one. They were primarily used for the storage of office supplies. I'd just finished snapping pics and was about to place the bugs when I heard a man's voice coming down the hall. Since I didn't hear any response, I assumed he was on the phone." Fab stabbed her finger in Creole's direction, and said, "I forwarded you all the pictures."

"Call me the second you hear from your information person." Creole raised his eyebrow, wanting her to confirm that she would call and he wouldn't have to wait until he stumbled on some tidbit.

"Haven't I shared everything so far?" she asked.

Didier kissed the back of her neck.

"One more thing, not sure if it's important. In an armoire, he had an impressive stash of condoms, sex toys, and some kinky looking outfits. It appears he favors a little game of dress-up," Fab revealed, looking at Didier.

The last revelation clearly caught him by surprise.

Creole stood, lifted the bucket of cold drinks, and moved it to a small table in front of us.

I reached for a bottle of water. "I have my own contribution. The boys got us a copy of the coroner's report. I'm picking it up tomorrow."

"You mean those two weirdos at the funeral home?" Creole asked, plopping down behind me on the chaise.

I glared at him. "At least my weirdo friends don't ask for cash."

"Some of them do," Fab reminded me with disgust.

Creole wrapped his arms around me, pulling me back against his chest. "If my friend in the police lab hadn't been on vacation, I could've gotten a copy. But there's a lock-down on the files, and no one's talking; word has it Balcazar has high-placed friends. Anything we didn't already know in the report?"

"Not really. According to Dickie, the opinion of the Miami coroner is that it's someone she knew. Whoever murdered her looked her in the eye and took the shot up close. Makes me think a lover or a good friend. We've got our info broker working on it." I tried to stand and was held firmly in place.

"Where are you going?" Creole whispered.

I pushed against his embrace, and he tightened his hold. "Nowhere, I guess."

Didier appeared thoughtful. "Lauren never talked about her personal life. If she had a boyfriend, she never mentioned him. No reason she would, really. We were friendly, but it was all business. Everyone knows about Fab." He leaned in and kissed her. "Sweetheart." Didier turned her face to his. "I don't want you involved anymore. You hate jail, and I can't bear to visit you there."

We both hate jail, I thought. I tried to think of one positive thing about the experience—there were none.

"Fab," Creole started, "If Balcazar does have something to hide, the last thing you want is to get caught snooping. Who knows what he'd do."

Fab jerked on Didier's arm and shifted in his lap until they were face to face, then said, "If you think I'm going to sit and do nothing while you're railroaded, you've got the wrong girlfriend."

"Didier, was it on the first date—after the hot sex, of course—that she disclosed her interesting career choice?" I asked. I jumped and restrained myself from rubbing my bottom where Creole had just pinched me. Instead, I rammed my elbow back, but he moved before I could make contact with his ribs and I hit the chaise cushion instead.

Didier laughed. "She told me she was a licensed private investigator; made it sound sexy and glamorous. The first morning at your house, when I watched you both accessorize with guns, I knew I'd gotten a glossy version of the job description."

I remembered that morning, walking into the kitchen for a cup of my morning addiction and finding a shirtless Didier, sporting a serious case of bedhead and eyes as blue as the ocean, pouring himself a cup of coffee. With the first word he uttered in that delicious accent, "Bonjour," I was completely charmed.

Fab hadn't bothered asking Didier whether he wanted to move in or not. She just went to his hotel, packed his suitcases, and checked him out. He found out when his key didn't work in the door.

Fab cut in, "I finally fessed up, and in excruciating detail. Now I tell you everything." She beamed at him.

"After the fact," Didier muttered.

I grasped Creole's hands in mine before

asking, "Did you tie her up to get the details?"

Didier and Fab glared at me. Creole snickered.

"Really, Madison!" Fab scowled, letting me know she'd get me back.

"Since we're all in the spirit of sharing," I said, "what about Officer Watters?"

"It seems we're all in agreement that it wasn't a coincidence he stopped you a second time." Creole narrowed his eyes. "I did a little checking. He's a loner, no friends and a rep as a major a-hole. Unblemished personnel file. I'll keep on it."

Our heads snapped around to the patio doors at the sound of the front door slamming.

Creole jumped up. Halfway off the chaise, he set me on my feet on the patio. "Who's got a gun, just in case?" he demanded.

Fab slid her Walther out from under her towel and handed it over.

It wouldn't have been the first time that, minding our own business, indulging in a leisurely swim, we were caught without firepower.

Creole and Brad met in the doorway. Julie peeked around his side.

"What were you going to do—shoot me?" Brad pointed at the gun.

Creole whisked it behind his back. "I didn't figure anyone making as much noise as you did was here to rob the place, but it pays to have a ready weapon in this house."

Liam came through the door and announced, "We brought dinner."

Fab went up behind Creole, took the gun out of his hand, and put it in the bottom of her beach bag, which was hanging over the back of a chair.

"We've eaten. Did you bring dessert?" I hugged Liam.

"Heck yes," he said. "Brad said we didn't need it, but I reminded him that everyone in the family was dessert-addicted."

"You should make everyone thank you or no dessert. Here's my thank you." I kissed his cheek.

The women in this family were spoiled when it came to food preparation—the men took over. Creole and Didier headed for the kitchen, Brad and I hugged, and he followed. The men enjoyed flexing their culinary muscle or just serving up takeout food. Fab and I sat and watched. Most of the time, we even got out of dish duty.

Brad walked past Julie, kissing her cheek. She turned to me and shook her head before slipping inside behind him. I interpreted that to mean she hadn't told Brad about her loathsome ex.

Just great, I thought.

Before she left tonight, I'd give her the time's-up talk: "Don't dick my brother around. Tell him or I will." Brad was already going to flip out on both of us because it had taken so long.

Fab hooked her arm in mine and pulled me over to the pool steps, where we sat with our feet in the water. Fab flashed a smile. "What do you suppose Brick wanted? Maybe we should call him."

"Let's wait until tomorrow and be surprised." I flashed her hair-tingling smile back at her. "Earlier, I drew straws for us, and you won. You get to update Brad on Didier's case when no one's around to listen. You two need brother-sister bonding time."

"What straw?" She kicked water on me and got it all over herself. "You know I'm not good at these kinds of things. Besides, I don't think he's all that comfortable with a second sister."

"I threw the straws out because I knew you'd take my word for it," I said with a straight face. "Just hit the highlights. If it comes from me, he'll grill me, but he'd never do that to you."

"Remember when you were going to fix us up?"

"Good thing I didn't follow through on *that* bad idea. It turned out good; he's happy, and you're ecstatic."

"And how's your relationship with the big guy?" Fab asked.

"Romantic that I am, I hit pay dirt. He passed the obstacle course: fits into the family, tolerates you, and has never suggested you move out. Have you noticed that you and Creole are working together on Didier's case? He's a keeper."

"You two look happy together." She eyed me closely.

"As long as I don't follow your bad example, we rarely fight, and when we do, there's make-up sex to look forward to."

Chapter Thirty-Two

"Where's your big-boobed receptionist?" I asked Brick, opening the refrigerator and helping myself. I passed a water to Fab and picked through the snack bowl before making myself comfortable in one of his oversized leather chairs.

Brick had glared when I started picking through the candy and cookies, snagging my favorites. He got surly when I pointed out that they were made to eat, not save, and he should be more gracious to valuable contractors.

Bitsy's chair in the showroom had been empty again. The frowning receptionist wasn't on guard duty when we filed in and up the stairs to Brick's office. I'd looked over the counter as we passed to see if she was hiding there. If she was, I'd have snapped pictures to torment her with later.

"This is the second time we've missed seeing her." I stuck out my lower lip. "Sadly, she hasn't been hanging out at her desk. She didn't screw someone—again—and have to disappear?"

Fab laughed. "I can get you a good rate on a funeral if Bitsy turns up dead."

"Bitsy's on vacation," he grunted, "if you two have to know every damn thing. She's good for business; the men love her. When there's a delay in paperwork and a client has to cool his heels, she keeps him entertained. No one's perfect; get over her petty transgression."

I rose out of my chair, but Fab jerked me back down and saved Brick from an in-his-face tongue lashing. *Transgression! I could've been shot.* "I didn't know your cars required paperwork. I thought all it took was a large bag of crisp hundreds."

"Don't be a smartass," he growled.

"That wouldn't be any fun."

Brick pushed two envelopes across the desk. "Good job on the Ursula case, although it didn't turn out like Ian hoped."

Before I could reach out, Fab snagged them both, handing me one.

Brick cleared his throat. "You two are going to work at the Gentleman's Club for a couple of nights or whatever it takes, get friendly with the girls. I need information."

"Club" was misleading; it was a strip joint located in an unpopulated area of Alligator Alley. Men didn't seem to mind going to the middle of nowhere for their entertainment. Brick advertised various entertainments with beautiful girls, and he delivered.

"What the hell kind of job?" I snapped. "I'm telling you right now that I'm not swinging on one of your poles."

"Don't look at me." Fab stood up. "I quit," she

said and started for the door.

He yelled, "Get the hell back here and sit down! You two make my ass hurt."

"That's so ungentlemanly," I tsked. "What's the job?" I ripped the wrapper off a mini snickers and shoved it in my mouth. I needed a sugar rush just to listen to the job description. I balled up the wrapper and handed it across the desk, a simpering look on my face.

He scowled and, with a dirty look, threw the wrapper in the trashcan. "Two of my girls are being harassed by a pimp. Find out who he is, and I'll take care of the rest."

Great, I thought, *I've never known a pimp that wasn't trouble.* "Why don't you call the girls into your office and just ask?" I demanded.

"Would you be here if that tactic had worked? They're denying there's a problem, but the bruises they show up with tell another story. I got wind of it from the manager, but she didn't know the sleazeball's name."

"Could be a boyfriend. Women have a tendency to stay in abusive relationships way too long." Fab hit me on the shoulder and pointed to the snack bowl.

I fished out a bag of peanut butter cookies and handed them over. "I thought you had this daddy relationship with your girls; they sit on your lap and spill their troubles." I didn't bother to disguise my sarcasm.

Brick hunched his large frame across the desk

until we were eye to eye. "Mock me all you want, but you know I take care of my girls," he spit out.

"What do you have in mind?" Fab broke the tension. She ripped open the small bag and dumped the contents on the corner of Brick's desk. She bent and sniffed, popping one in her mouth.

I struggled not to laugh. I expected Brick to clutch his chest and keel over, but he managed to contain his rising temper. "You'll come in as new hires, start training, and get to know everyone. Ask questions. Snoop around. You're certainly good at that."

"Training for what?" Fab's eyes narrowed.

"Decide between the two of you. One of you works the dressing room, helping the girls into their costumes, the other trains as a hostess. You'd have free run of the place. As a trainee, both positions require you to follow a regular employee and be pleasant."

I arched my eyebrows at Fab. "Well?"

Fab nodded slightly.

"Let's talk terms. The usual?" I asked. "Quadruple if guns get drawn?"

"You two are thieves," he barked.

"Don't quibble, it's so unbecoming," I forced my lips into a half-smile. "We have another job of yours to finish up, so we need a few days."

"You'll start next week. Both girls work on Monday, which is typically our slowest day. Hopefully, anything you screw up can be fixed."

He leveled a glare at me. "You'll need to go in ahead of time and get fitted for your costumes."

"Just so we're clear, since I've never stepped foot in your establishment and have no idea what these *uniforms* look like, mine better cover my ass. I don't object to a little cleavage." I looked at Fab, wanting backup on this issue, but she didn't say anything.

"Think of it as dress-up." Brick rummaged in his desk drawer. "You women like that kind of stuff. No granny drawers." He pulled out a business card, scribbled on the back, and held it out. "Call Tilly and let her know you're coming in for your fitting. She'll be expecting you."

I whisked the card from his fingers and shoved it in my pocket, knowing that the mundane tasks always fell to me.

"Let's go." Fab stood up. "Call Tilly and tell her we're on our way. We're going to get this over with." She grabbed my arm. "Don't think we're going to parade around half-naked. If you double-cross us, we'll walk."

He threw up his hands. "Everyone says I'm the best boss except you two."

For once, we actually walked down the stairs as Brick commanded us to on every visit.

"Who's going to tell the guys about our new job?" I asked. "We could flip a coin."

"Since we're not going to be swinging naked, I don't think they'll have too big a fit." Fab used the key fob to unlock the car doors.

I hopped in and said, "I was thinking that we should tell them both at the same time."

"If I'm doing it, expect the announcement to be as we're walking out the door," She humphed. "You realize this job will probably last a few days if we're lucky. The hours will suck; we'll have to arrive before the girls and be the last to leave."

"Maybe we should suggest to Brick that one of us work inside while the other covers the parking lot."

"Forget that idea, especially the part about sitting in a parking lot at night alone. We're sticking together." Fab waved to one of the salesman as she blew past him out of the driveway.

Chapter Thirty-Three

The morning didn't go as planned. I had already penciled in hanging by the pool, reading, and generally doing diddly. Fab's ringing phone interrupted the peace. The conversation was short. I paddled my raft around so that I couldn't make eye contact. My toes itched to be on their way down to the blue-green gulf water.

Fab used the leaf scoop to haul me back to the steps while informing me that Hottie was back in town. He'd carved out time in his all-important schedule and wanted Ursula gone. I had no energy for doing free work, but swallowed my gripey retorts. I'd mark this down in my black book of favors and remind her of it when I needed help.

I emailed Preston a list of the tasks that he needed to complete, and to my annoyance, he pushed the details back on us. I was pissed when Fab didn't put her foot down. He pitched a 'tude over paying for a new place for Ursula to live, and it took some discussion to convince him a homeless Ursula would spin out of control—fast. When we both refused to go house hunting, he foisted the chore off on a realtor friend. The woman came through in record time, finding a condo in an upscale neighborhood. She sealed the deal, forwarding pictures, and Preston signed the six-month contract, paying upfront.

* * *

After a rocky start, moving day came and went like clockwork.

Fab and I arrived early and sat vigil in the Hummer until Preston's white Porsche Carrera rolled out of the garage and through the security gates, Ursula in the passenger seat.

We got a head start on the movers and had all of Ursula's belongings boxed and ready to be dollied out by the time they arrived. Fab started off by throwing things haphazardly in a box until I barked, "Don't break anything. It will be more fuel to her wounded ego."

She sniffed, "I hate manual labor."

"I should have left you at home and brought Mother."

She flounced down on the king-size bed and crossed her arms. "I'm tired."

"You get your ass up now," I growled, hands on my hips. "This is *your* freebie client."

"Why do you have to be so mean?" She sulked.

"Go ahead, sit there and relax and watch how manual labor is done." My words dripped with sarcasm, "I insist."

Fab eyed me suspiciously. "What are you up to?"

"I can't wait for… hmm… Didier, or perhaps Mother, to ask how the day went."

She jumped off the bed, twisting her hair in a knot. "You would, wouldn't you? Fine. How can I help?" she said sweetly.

I turned away and bit my lip to keep from laughing. "You clean out the drawers and closets. Toss everything on the bed, and I'll fill the boxes, tape and mark them up."

Preston had left Ursula's car keys on the table, and when we were done with the rest, her BMW was quickly loaded onto the car hauler.

* * *

Fab revved the engine of the Hummer while I gave the address of Ursula's new residence to the driver of the moving truck. Both men looked amused at Fab's antics as she stuck her head out the window and waved. She drove the speed limit to the Overseas and then took off like a rocket, only slowing for the well-known speed traps.

I kept my eyes on the side mirror and, to my surprise, the truck managed to keep up. "Please—" I knocked Fab on the shoulder. "— slow down. If that trailer jackknifes and sends Ursula's car hurtling into the air, you're to blame. Don't forget to signal when you're getting ready to exit. Give the guys behind us time to get over and not have to double back."

"Yes, Mother."

"One of these times, you'll be so annoying, I'll make you walk home," I said through gritted teeth.

She didn't brake, but eased off the gas, and we slowed down some. I felt my heart rate returning to normal.

"Remember Creole's advice. If the police show up, plead ignorance and toss Preston under the bus."

Creole didn't like this job because what we were doing was technically illegal. He felt some empathy for Preston but thought he should handle his own problems. But he didn't complain about this job because he was tired of hearing about Ursula. "Women like her are the reason I don't let my dick do the thinking," he said.

* * *

Fab pulled into a visitor's space at Ursula's temporary home, a nondescript, multi-story, all-white building that boasted a good address. As soon as we stepped over the threshold of the one—bedroom unit, I knew Ursula wouldn't be happy. The dark space had the feel of an over-sized closet, and the patio was the size of a postage stamp, with a sliver of a water view if you leaned precariously over the balcony and craned your neck. There was no disguising that this unit was a rental. The furniture was worn and sad-looking, and had several gross stains. I'd seen the realtor pictures and decided they'd been photoshopped.

The movers showed up at the door, both pushing dollies filled with boxes. They'd loaded the truck in less than half an hour, and hopefully this would go even quicker and we could all go home. I directed them to stack the marked boxes against the wall in the living/dining room. Ursula could unpack her own crap.

One man dropped the keys to Ursula's BMW in my hand. They'd off-loaded it into her assigned parking space in the underground garage.

Fab entered behind the movers, turning up her nose. "Next time I move, I'm hiring you."

"Aren't you the one who showed up at my house with two suitcases and a handful of boxes?" I smiled as I said, "I can be rid of you in an hour."

Arriving home late one afternoon, I'd found Fab parked on the couch, Jazz stretched out across her chest. Her suitcases on the floor and boxes in the garage, she'd announced that she'd moved in. We'd come a long way from when she didn't want to be friends, mostly because I badgered her until she caved.

* * *

Fab's phone rang on the way back to the Cove. My antenna went up when her vocabulary dropped to four words: yes, no, maybe, and okay.

When she disconnected the call, I pressed my forehead to the passenger window, waiting for her to convince me that she needed my help for one of her smarmy clients.

"The break-up with Ursula didn't go well." Fab sighed. "This is a job that doesn't want to go away."

"What happened?" I didn't want to know, but since it seemed like it was about to affect me, now would be a good time to listen.

"Instead of having a quick lunch and severing the relationship, he spent the day with her, even bought her a bracelet that she admired in a jewelry store window. On the way to her new address, he made the mistake of giving her the 'let's be friends' speech. He should have waited until he got her out of the car."

"Is he still alive?"

Fab glared at my tone of voice. "Barely. He said the words scarcely passed his lips before she flipped out. In an instant, she started screaming and reached across the car, jerking the steering wheel. He managed to avoid a multi-car crash, wrestled the wheel back and ran his Porsche into a tree, crunching the front end up to the windshield."

I shook my head. "Ursula okay?"

"They're both lucky; neither of them has a scratch. Apparently that made her even angrier. She launched herself at him, clawing his face bloody, all the while cursing his ancestors. She jumped out of the car, spewing a litany of four letter words. Her parting shot was, "I hope you die," as he lay dazed, head against the steering wheel, the sound of sirens coming up the street."

I covered my eyes and said, "Ursula cannot find out about our part in this whole mess. First Ian, now Preston. She might kill us. I'm happy this case is over and we have a few days before we start our stripper careers."

"Not exactly," Fab said.

I stuck my fingers in my ears. "Keep it to yourself and take me home."

Fab waited until we pulled into the driveway and cornered me before I could make it through the front door. "Preston has to go out of town on business, one night only, and wants me to stay overnight. Please don't make me do it by myself."

I didn't blame her for not wanting to be by herself in that condo with Ursula on the loose. "I'll go."

Chapter Thirty-Four

"Knowing Creole's aversion to this job, I'm surprised he hasn't called," I said over my shoulder from where I was hanging over Preston's balcony, looking down at the patio below.

Preston had freaked out when an unidentified woman called his office and his assistant told the caller he'd be out of town. The woman had hung up without giving a name. He was a man used to snapping his fingers and getting results. Fab knew just how to handle those kinds of men, but all they did was give me a headache.

It was a good thing Fab had only shared the entire story of the drop off with me, but it also made me queasy. If Creole and Didier found out, they'd never let us leave the house again. I didn't waste any time in informing Brick. I hit the highlights regarding Preston and told him to warn his friend. He informed me that Ian and his daughter had found a new house in a different part of the Keys, had already moved, and would put the old one on the market as soon as the repairs were finished.

My backup plan, if all else failed, was to call

Spoon. He excelled at getting rid of bothersome people, but I wasn't sure how he would feel about relocating a woman, even if she was a psycho pain. Fab and I had breathed a sigh of relief that we hadn't been implicated in this mess yet and, fingers crossed, it would stay that way.

In the week since the break-up, Ursula had called Preston's office frequently; he'd had his cell phone number changed. When her calls went unanswered, she snuck past security and was waiting for him in his office when he returned from a meeting. Realizing they'd never rekindle the relationship, she faced him down and attempted blackmail. After a litany of complaints, including that she hated her new residence, needed money, and had lost expensive pieces of jewelry in the move, she threatened to call the police if she didn't get a blank check. Preston, to his credit, called her bluff and reminded her that the condo was temporary. As for the police, he told her to file a report, and if she ever stepped foot in his office building again, he'd have her arrested and thrown in jail.

"Didier was a grouch this morning, wanting to know why we couldn't specialize in lost animals and dead people. You need to have a talk with Creole and mention that he needs to keep our business private."

"They're best friends," I reminded Fab. I wondered why I should be the one to initiate that talk. "We share everything; why shouldn't they?"

"What are we supposed to do all night?" Fab paced the living room.

"Check out the security." My plan had been to curl up in a chair and read.

"The front gate code's been changed — I checked both the old and new. All the locks are new. I can't see Ursula scaling the wall to the third floor."

I replied, "A security gate without a guard isn't a deterrent. Anyone with a little patience can get in; just wait for another car and follow it. She could do the same with the lobby doors."

"A letter went out, warning the residents to beware of anyone using that trick and telling them not to let anyone through the lobby doors who didn't have a key." Fab stood up, moving to stand inside the patio doors. "Preston's paranoid about this trip. He's certain that it was Ursula on the phone, inquiring about his schedule."

"If Ursula shows up, what do we do? Shoot her on sight?" I asked.

"For once, I hate that idea. If we so much as get a whiff of her, we call the police. That might take care of the problem for good. You can deal with law enforcement; you're better at it than me."

I made a face. *Great…the police!* "Let's make it appealing for Ursula, in case she does show up. We won't turn on any lights; make her think no one's home. You can watch television in the bedroom. I'll lie on a chaise and read until I get tired."

* * *

I put some muscle into moving the oversized wicker chaise and pushed it over to the corner, where I'd have the best view of the driveway. I nestled back and listened to the chirping of the crickets, random barking from a dog in the distance, and a few other unidentifiable sounds. The occasional car drove into the complex, but none came towards us. Our section remained quiet. I craned my neck, but didn't see any lights reflecting off the bushes below, so I assumed the people below were not at home or were in another part of their condo. After reading a couple of paragraphs of my new book, I nodded off.

A hand clamped over my mouth, jerking me awake.

"There's someone in the bushes," Fab whispered in my ear. She crouched down beside me.

"Ouch," followed by a groan, could be heard from directly below us. It was hard to tell whether it was a man's or woman's voice. But there wasn't an innocent reason for someone to be lurking in the bushes.

I rolled over the side of the chaise and onto the ground next to Fab. We stayed hidden behind the patio furniture.

A bright object flew over the balcony, landing on the cushion where I had been sitting and exploding into flames. The heavy chaise caught fire instantly. The burning chair sat close to the hurricane shutters; it would be a short jump through the patio doors, and from there, the fire would leapfrog through the interior.

Fab grabbed my hand and tugged me up. "We need to get off this balcony before we get trapped."

We had done our recon on the place earlier, inside and out, and there was no way to go over the balcony without ending up severely hurt. It was two floors straight down, with nothing to cushion the landing.

I ran and grabbed the handle of the sliding door. I had the door halfway open when we heard the sound of an engine starting. Fab darted back to the railing to look. "Fab?" I hissed.

"Just great. The bushes are on fire. Do you remember seeing a fire extinguisher?" Fab yelled, racing through the sliding door.

I slid the door behind her with a bang, hoping it would slow the flames from getting inside. Fab sprinted out the front door. I was two steps behind her, hitting the fire alarm button on the security pad as I followed her down the corridor.

A blast filled the air.

What the heck was in that bottle?

"Elevator or stairs?" I ran into Fab's back

when she stopped suddenly.

"Stairs. But we need to make sure the stairwell door doesn't lock, in case we need to come back up." Fab held the door open. "This has to be Ursula's doing. And if she somehow managed to get into the building, then either escape route is a poor choice."

I had no intention of sacrificing my new workout tee, so I pulled it over my head, my sports bra next. I rolled up the bra and stuck it in the doorjamb.

"I always wondered, since your boobs are bigger than mine, if they hung to your waist. Guess not."

"You're loathsome." I looked down, giving them an admiring glance before pulling my shirt back on. Fab jumped down the steps, and I kept up, running behind her. "Should we stop on each floor and bang on the doors?" I asked.

"Keep moving. That alarm would wake the dead."

When we escaped the building, it surprised me to see that the gates to the complex stood open.

A man walking his dog yelled, "I called 911." He held up his cell phone. "I never leave home without this baby."

Fab made a beeline across the parking lot toward him, but came to a halt when the wiener dog growled at her. "Did you see anything?" she called.

"Don't worry about Poochy. I've got her on a leash," he said.

I'm sure Fab noticed that he didn't say a word about the dog not biting, which was a completely different issue.

"You know," he said slowly, "I watched a person set the fire but honestly didn't know what I was seeing until the flames licked up. What caught my attention was the person walking up and down, squirting something on the bushes."

"Male? Female?" Fab asked impatiently.

"I couldn't say for sure—dressed in dark clothing with a baseball cap pulled low." He cupped his chin, pausing for a moment. "I'd guess, from the slight build, a woman. I can't swear to it."

Sirens sounded in the distance, rapidly approaching.

Fab asked our eyewitness a question that I didn't hear; I was busy, staring at the entrance, hoping the fire department got here before the building burned down.

"I'm not good with makes of cars," he said. "A car is a car."

In my car-oriented family, that statement would draw some incredulous stares, I thought.

"Look around." Fab waved her arm. "Do you see anything comparable?"

"It was a sedan." He looked proud of himself. "Dark in color."

Fab looked ready to choke him, so I cut in.

"Everything you can remember will be helpful to the police."

"Damn." He smacked his head. "I almost forgot. I got the last three numbers of the license plate."

"What are they?" Fab asked.

"Not sure I should be telling you. You're not a cop, are you?"

Before Fab could give him a hard slap, I said, "We're friends of Preston's. Maybe we could text him and see if recognizes it. You wouldn't want the arsonist to come back, would you?"

"You're a thinker." He smiled at me and scrolled through his phone. "E-R-W."

The fire trucks arrived first, followed by the local police, both of them turning off their sirens as they entered the front gates.

The fire fighters had the fire out in record time. The bottom unit had sustained the most damage; thankfully, those people were not at home. And the neighbors on the second level had gotten out right after us.

An older man in a fire uniform approached us and introduced himself as the chief. I supposed this wasn't the appropriate time to notice that he was every bit as good-looking as the rest of his team: bushy grey hair, dark eyes, and of course, the man-in-uniform appeal.

"I understand you two were staying on the third floor. Can you tell me what happened?" he asked.

Fab poked me in the back.

Why did I always have to be the front woman?

I related what had happened, reorganizing the details a bit—we were talking on the opposite end of the balcony when the bottle flew over the railing. It was the first time we'd stayed here, and we knew nothing about the owner's personal life.

"Phone," I said to Fab and held out my hand. After she slapped it into my palm, I scrolled through it and gave the chief Preston's contact information.

The police questioned us and the residents of the building. No one had any useful information, and they shifted their attention to the eyewitness.

After we spent two hours standing around doing nothing, a different police officer took our contact information, and we were free to go.

I snapped my fingers at Fab and motioned her over. "Go get our stuff. The only thing I brought was the giant tote bag."

"Why me?" She looked at me, suspicion on her face.

"Because one of us can charm the pants off a man in a hot second, and it takes longer for the other—wastes precious time. See the hottie blond who can't take his eyes off you? If you bat those beautiful blue eyes of yours, I bet we get our stuff back before we leave."

"I'll sneak in."

I grabbed the back of her shirt. "No, you won't," I said in exasperation. "That will cast suspicion on us, and for a change, we haven't done anything."

"You're no fun."

"I'm tired of hearing that," I said to her retreating back.

Chapter Thirty-Five

It was one of those rare days that I had the house to myself, and I wasn't going to waste a minute of the warm sunshiny day. Fab and Didier had taken a drive down the Keys for some alone time. When I returned from the beach, my bucket was filled to the brim with sand dollars; the waves washed them ashore for a few days once a year.

As I climbed the steps that led up from the beach, my phone buzzed in my pocket. I looked at the screen and smiled. "Hey you."

"My mom's in trouble. Can you come to The Cottages?" Liam sounded frenzied.

I leaped up the rest of the stairs, slipping through the fence into my backyard. Setting down the shells, I raced into the house, grabbed my keys off the bench in the entryway, and headed out the door. "What's going on?"

"Striker showed up; he wants my mom to marry him. They got into a screaming fight when she told him no for, like, the third time." He sounded out of breath, as though he'd been running. "I didn't know who to call. It's Kevin's day off, and he turned off his phone."

"Don't hang up, I'm on my way. Stay on the phone and talk to me until I get there. Where are you?" I slammed the SUV door, started it up, and skidded to the corner, remembering to make a full stop, in case it was speed-trap day.

"I'm out by the pool." A chair scraped across the concrete. "He can't get in—doesn't have the code for the gate."

I mimicked a few of Fab's antics, cutting around cars, but instead of a one-finger greeting, I waved, and I stopped short of tailgating. "Where's Mac?"

"I went to the office first, then noticed her car's not here. I gotta get back to our cottage; Striker might do something stupid."

"That's not a good idea. If Striker got the chance, he'd use either you or your mother to manipulate the other. Don't hang up; I'm going to put you on hold." I thought for a moment. "Go sit behind the tiki bar. You'll be able to see Striker if he heads in your direction; if he does, then duck down behind it." I didn't wait for a response before I put him on hold.

I hit the speed dial for Mac. "Where are you?" I asked when she answered.

"I'm just headed back to the office; I'm not far. What's up?"

"Julie's ex is back, and I'm going to need backup. Do you have your gun on you?"

"Do cherries have pits?" Mac snorted.

"Step on it and don't pull into the driveway.

299

We'll meet at the corner." I skated through a yellow light.

"Where's your usual backup?" Mac asked.

"Licking on her boyfriend…somewhere."

Mac sighed. "If she needs any help with that, tell her I'm available."

I laughed. "I'm five minutes away, don't dawdle," I said, then clicked over to Liam. "You okay?"

"I'm probably overreacting. Everything's quiet. I'd like to know why Striker hasn't left yet. Mom told him she's not interested. She doesn't even like him."

"Stay by the pool; I'm just a couple of blocks away." Having learned from the master, I took a shortcut across a vacant commercial parking lot.

"I warned Mom he was piece of…and that she shouldn't let him in the door. Told her to creep up to the peephole and, if it's him, ignore his knocking. She thinks he's harmless and will get the message and go away. Not sure why she thinks that. I don't."

Mac and I rounded the corner at the same time from different directions. I hung a U-turn and parked in back of her pickup truck.

"Mac and I are here. Cut through to the side street and give me your keys," I told Liam.

I met Mac in the street. "We are not going to shoot him unless he makes a move on one of us. Apparently, Julie and Striker were fighting earlier. We'll assess what's going on and try to defuse the situation and send him on his way. Then I'll be calling Spoon and letting him know I have a relocation job. That way, he won't be back." I motioned for her to follow me.

"Your mother is lucky. Spoon is a bad boy without the criminal tendencies; in fact, a decent citizen, as far as I can tell," Mac said. Spoon had a checkered past, but he'd overcome it and made something out of his life, and now gave back by helping others. He still had connections, but he kept his hands clean.

Liam ran across the street. "I want to come along," he said when he handed me his keys.

"No, you will not!" My eyebrows went straight up. The thought of something happening to him had me rattled. "What happened to your eye?" It was red, with faint bruising around the corner.

"Striker elbowed me, claimed it was an accident."

Mac retrieved her Beretta from a thigh holster and shoved it in the waistband of her skirt. "Any of your friends ask, tell them the other guy is in the hospital. You'll get a rep for being a tough guy." She smiled at Liam.

I winked at Liam and shook my head slightly, letting him know that was a bad idea. "You can sit in the Hummer and fiddle with the electronics. Figure out how Fab renders the GPS useless."

"I accidently got Fab in trouble for that." Liam frowned. "Creole came around the corner just as I asked her how she did it. They exchanged threats, and she stomped off while he was still talking. Creole said, 'I'd like to strangle her.' I told him that she was your best friend and you'd be angry. He thanked me for reminding him."

I ruffled his hair. "You're more mature than some of the adults around you. We'll be back." I turned to Mac. "Sneak attack — we unlock the door and surprise them."

We cut diagonally across the street and skirted along the path through the banana trees that ended at the back of Cottage Two. From that vantage point, we had a good view of the front door and the rest of the driveway before making our final run.

"What if we're wrong and they're all lovey dovey?" Mac pulled off her mid-calf, full jean skirt and dumped it on a chair next to the office door as we passed. Her electric-yellow spandex shorts were quite a contrast to her white, ruffled cotton blouse.

"Then you apologize for us, and we leave."

"Yeah, great," Mac groaned. "How about 'Striker, if you weren't such an a-hole, we wouldn't be here.'"

"Nice apology."

Mac scoped out both sides of the cottage. She shook her head, which meant Striker wasn't crawling out the bathroom window. He'd only get stuck, but that hadn't stopped previous tenants from seeing it as a way to flee.

I pressed my ear to the front door. Even with the air conditioner on, I could hear a loud male voice. Looking at Mac over my shoulder, I knew that she could also hear it. I pulled my Glock, inserted the key in the lock, held up my fingers up, 1-2-3, and kicked the door open.

Julie and Striker had their backs to me. Both jumped and turned around with looks of shock, and the color drained from Julie's cheeks.

"What the hell?" Striker yelled, taking a step forward.

I brandished my Glock. "Take another step, and I'll shoot you. Do you want him to stay or go?" I asked Julie.

Striker grabbed a handful of her hair, dragging her to his chest and wrapping his arm around her neck. "We're leaving together, and there's not a damn thing you can do about it."

"A records check shows that you're on probation. Looking for a trip back to prison to finish your original sentence? Maybe even get some extra time?" I asked.

Julie gasped. "I thought that was all behind you."

"You're standing in the way of us being a family," Striker insisted. He clearly believed his own delusions.

"Let go of my mom!" Liam yelled from the doorway.

"Liam, go back outside," Julie said frantically.

Liam launched himself on Striker's back, effectively breaking his hold on Julie. She jerked away. Striker rolled to one side, heaving Liam to the floor. The thud made me flinch.

"How could you?" Julie screamed at Striker, rushing past him, only slowing to kick him in the shin, which left him hopping as she scurried to her son's side.

Mac waved her Beretta at Striker. "Julie's brother is a sheriff. Want me to call him?"

"Do not call anyone, especially not Kevin." Julie helped her son to his feet.

I made eye contact with Striker and aimed my Glock at his crotch. "Mac, you see this guy on my property again, shoot him."

Julie moved in front of Striker, making herself a human shield. "It's over." She patted his shoulder. "I've moved on, and I'm in a relationship. You need to do the same. Please don't come back here. I don't want any dead bodies."

Mac opened the door, keeping him in her sights.

Striker brushed by me. "This isn't over, bitch," he said to the room in general, grinding his teeth.

"Get moving." Mac stepped away from the door and kept her distance. Once he cleared the outside steps, she followed him.

I shoved my gun back in the holster at the small of my back. "Are you okay?" I hugged

Liam and whispered, "What happened to staying in the SUV?"

"It was cowardly, and I wanted to help," he said, straightening up to his almost-six feet.

He had grown up in general and looked more like a young man than a teenager. He took after his Uncle Kevin, his brown hair bleached out by the sun, but Liam was a good inch taller and better-looking.

I looked over Liam's shoulder and asked Julie, "You okay?"

Julie had clearly been crying, her eyes red-rimmed and swollen. "Thank you." She looked ready to burst into tears again.

I felt sympathy for her, having made a few poor man-choices in my past. But the last thing I wanted was Striker lurking around and anyone getting hurt. "Striker ignored my first warning and came back. It's not going to happen again. I have a problem-solver for these kinds of issues— Spoon." When I first met Spoon, he'd offered me his "problem-solving services" for anything, big or small, and he'd never let me down.

Julie said, "But—"

"Mom, it's better for someone else to send him packing; that way, he won't blame you." Liam put his arm around her. I caught his eye and inclined my head towards the door. "I'm going outside," he said abruptly, and headed out.

I cleared my throat rather than saying something inappropriate to get Julie's attention.

"This way, by the time Brad finds out, Striker will be long gone, and my brother won't end up in jail for killing his useless ass. You know my brother's protective when it comes to you and your son, don't you?"

"Brad doesn't—"

I held up my hand and struggled not to yell. "Oh yes, he does need to know." My words still came out louder than I wanted. "Take it from someone who's had to deliver less-than-positive news in the past. He might flip, but not as bad as he will if he hears it from someone else. You can't hide this. This is a small town, and even smaller when it comes to gossip. If anyone saw Mac escorting him off the property with her gun drawn, that tidbit will have raced down the block already and soon to be hot news on the dock."

"If you hadn't barged in," she bristled, "I could've handled Striker, talked sense into him, convinced him that we'd both moved on."

How many women believed that right up until something bad happened?

"Sometimes a person needs help," I said in exasperation. "You can ask any of us at any time. I would never say no and neither would Fab or Mother."

Her shoulders sagged. "If I don't leave now, I'll be late for my booking."

"I can take Liam to my house, and you can pick him up when you're done with your voiceover."

Julie hesitated. "Are you going straight home?"

What was she asking?

She noticed my questioning stare. "I just don't want him to go on a job with you."

"I would *never* do that." I tried not to sound offended, but I was. "I'm only stopping at the Farmer's Market. If you think it's better for him to stay here by himself, then I rescind the offer."

"I just worry and will probably do so even after he's married with kids of his own." She grabbed a large tote bag that was stuffed full. "I need to apologize to him before I leave and reassure him it won't happen again."

"Liam loves you. He called me because he was worried Striker would hurt you. If it weren't for him, you could also be sporting a black eye. Or worse."

"That was an accident," she said emphatically.

"Are you sure? Liam doesn't think so." I couldn't tell what the woman was thinking. She maintained a neutral expression, having gotten her emotions under control.

Julie flew out the door and across the driveway to where Liam stood. He met her in the middle, and they shared a few words. They laughed, and he picked her up and twirled her around, setting her back on her feet.

I closed up the cottage and double-checked the locks.

Mac beelined in my direction, holstering her

gun. She'd retrieved her skirt and pulled it back on as she moved to join me, concealing that she carried.

"Where did Striker go?" I whispered to her.

"Loser got into a junker a few houses down; had to crank the engine several times before it kicked. Then he used Corker's driveway to turn around, damn near hitting a parked car, and disappeared in a cloud of black smoke." Mac craned her head and scanned the street.

"You're the best. But don't expect a raise," I warned.

"In lieu of money, I'd consider us even if you'd let me shoot the next loser."

"Who'd deal with the sheriff and the paperwork?" I asked.

"Killjoy."

Julie continued to laugh as she climbed in to her RAV, honking and waving as she exited the driveway.

I handed Liam back his keys. "Let's go have fun."

"Is Granny coming over?" he asked with a smirk.

I started laughing. "I dare you to call Mother that to her face."

Chapter Thirty-Six

The non-stripping female employees at the Gentleman's Club all wore the same costume—a black bustier with a full skirt that didn't quite brush the bottom of their butt cheeks. Tilly had informed us that we had to purchase our own G-strings. I had to pinch myself to keep from making a retching noise as I wondered how I would withstand ten-hour shifts with floss in my crack. I compromised on a pair of lacy boy shorts that I knew would be wedged there before the night was over.

Twirling in front of the mirror, I admired my elevated cleavage, admitting that it looked damn impressive. Maybe I could borrow this outfit for a sexy dinner at Creole's. I fished out a pair of black onyx earrings from my jewelry box and a matching bracelet watch, a gift from Mother. When I bent at the waist, the round part of my cheeks flashed me in the mirror. My legs were tan, so I ditched the stocking idea and shoved my feet into low, chunky-heeled pumps with a strap. I twisted my curls into a loose bun and used a big clip to hold it all in place.

The plan to tell the guys at the last minute had

fight potential written all over it, so I fessed up to Creole the night we accepted the job. It took him so long to respond, I got nervous, wondering if this would be the job where he'd draw the line and demand I bail on Brick. He grilled me on the details and extracted a promise that Fab and I would work the same shifts and leave the club together. If there was a hint of trouble, he'd better be my first call and not be told after the fact.

Creole and I had spent the day together, walking on the beach and tossing a Frisbee. We ended up on the deck overlooking the water at Bart's waterfront dive, sharing a grilled seafood platter. Then I enticed him into his big bed, telling him I was in desperate need of a nap so I wouldn't fall asleep on the job. We arrived back at my house in time for me to change my clothes and get to my first day on the job early.

After one last look in the mirror, I grabbed a sweatshirt jacket that would cover my backside for a just-in-case moment and crept to the stairs to survey the room before being seen.

The element of surprise eluded me. Creole's and Didier's heads immediately snapped up from where they sat opposite each other across the coffee table, commandeered for a game of poker. I contemplated a sexy entrance, slinging my leg over the banister, à la saloon girl from the old west, and sliding down. A flash of me tumbling over the railing headfirst made me reconsider. I descended the stairs, holding eye contact with Creole and adding just enough wiggle to my step to give him something to think about.

Creole wolf-whistled and cheered. Standing, he met me at the bottom of the steps, hand out.

I slipped my hand in his.

"You look really hot," he rumbled into my ear, nibbling on the lobe. "Now go upstairs and put some clothes on. I'm thinking sweatpants and a long-sleeve shirt."

"Very nice, *chérie*." Didier checked me out from head to toe.

"Close your eyes," Creole barked at him.

"Ta da." Fab stood at the top of the stairs, arms spread wide over her head, making her entrance like an exotic dancer. Not a stumble.

Creole kept me glued to his side as Fab breezed by into Didier's outstretched arms.

"You two are not to be separated." Creole looked down at me, then over at Fab. "Didier and I are in agreement about how much danger you will place yourselves in, and it's a very low bar. Right, Fab?"

Fab glared back at him.

Didier tightened his hold on his girlfriend. "Fab reassured both Creole and I that this job was about gathering information and handing it over to Brick for him to take action, and that the two of you won't be involved with that part. Correct?" Didier scrutinized us, one dark brow arched. "I'd like to hear a verbal confirmation that there will be no misunderstandings."

I wanted to laugh at the frustration on Fab's face. She'd never outright lie to him.

"You have my word," I reassured both men. "No playing the hero, even if I have to put a bullet in your girlfriend's a...backside to stop her."

"You need backup for *any* reason—" Creole raised his voice slightly to reinforce his order. "Call or text the first number on your speed dial. I've arranged for a friend who lives out there in a shack he's named 'The Palace' to show up. He assured me he can be there in five minutes. You'll recognize him straight-off; he dresses in camo and smells rank."

I smiled up at him. "You know the most interesting people."

"This is a pot/kettle situation, considering the people you know. It amazes me—*you* can call the most unlikely people, and they never say no."

Fab snorted. "That comes from her folksy, 'How's the family?' crap. Ouch." She stepped away from Didier, hands on her hips, and glared. "It's true," she huffed.

"Come on, sister." I held out my arm. "Nice boobs," I said with admiration as I looked at them neatly on display.

Fab ran a finger across her cleavage. "They came out good, didn't they?" She smiled down at them.

Creole and Didier laughed.

"Only girls can get away with those kinds of compliments," Creole sighed. "You two look hot." He shook his finger. "Stay out of trouble."

Didier took Fab in his arms, murmured something in French, and kissed her.

Creole laughed again.

Fab turned. "Eavesdropper."

"You've got a lot of nerve, eavesdropper extraordinaire," Creole grinned at her.

Chapter Thirty-Seven

One hour into my shift working the dressing room at The Gentleman's Club, and I loathed it. My toes felt swollen, trapped in tight leather. I'd do anything to wear a pair of flip-flops. The dancers would probably laugh at me; not a single one complained about strutting around in killer stilettos. I worried about Fab serving drinks to the drunks but knew she could handle men of any age.

My preconceptions about strippers were blown to bits after meeting the girls. A couple of them I'd met before, but by silent agreement, nothing slipped out indicating that we had met previously at Brick's. Not after they were warned by the boss himself to keep quiet or else.

"Or else" had me wondering what action he would take, but I didn't ask.

Most of the women had families to support and, in a couple of cases, children's private-school education to pay for. There were a few working their way through college, who knew it couldn't be done on minimum wage. Others were looking for a daddy. Few saw it as a long-term option, with the exception of a couple looking to get into management.

Brick had hired almost all female staff, except for a half-dozen burly men that guarded the exits; however, a woman was in charge of security. He'd given us the name of the two girls we had to befriend and snoop into their private lives—Octavia and Delight. I noticed a third girl, Nala, who showed up for her shift with a shiner, claiming to have run into a kitchen cabinet door. She spent quite a bit of time in front of the mirror, slathering on makeup to hide it.

The manager, Tilly, informed us on our arrival that the edict from Brick was that Fab work the floor as a trainee cocktail waitress and I the dressing room. We arrived early. The music was blaring and not all the tables were filled, but they were at half-capacity.

Given the choice, I'd rather be the cigar girl. I had a minute to chat with her while helping to fasten the tray across her shoulders, which she insisted didn't hurt. She laughed, saying the harness she used forced her to have perfect posture. The tips were excellent, and due to her costume, the touchy-feely by over-amorous customers was kept to a minimum.

I helped the girls with their costume changes, fetched accessories, and refilled cold drinks, all the while asking questions under non-stop, frenzied activity. Fab had whispered a reminder to skim through the girl's belongings when I got a chance. I balked at that idea, knowing I'd be tempted to shoot anyone *I* caught doing that. There wasn't any reasonable explanation; they'd be convinced I was stealing.

I was in the changing room, going through Octavia's bag without finding anything useful, when I saw movement out of the corner of my eye. My heart pounding, I looked furtively in the mirror. My breath whooshed out of me when I saw that it was Fab who stood in the doorway, waving me over.

"I hate this job," she grumbled. "My feet hurt."

"Stop your whining. Good thing I threw your ugliest pair of shoes in the back of the SUV. Go change," I ordered.

"They have a smooshy heel, and they make me look dumpy."

If she hadn't had such a woeful look on her face, I'd have laughed at her. "You can rock those shoes, and your feet will thank you. The girls will be envious." *Okay, they wouldn't, but it sounded good.* I gave her a shove into the hall.

Tilly burst into the room thirty minutes later, ready to explode. "Anyone seen Fab? The new girl." She glared at me.

I shrugged and shook my head. The clock said we'd been here for three hours.

A thorough search of the club was ordered, but Fab couldn't be found anywhere. The dancers paraded in and out between changes, but tongues wagged and gossip ran rampant. "Fing the owner was how she got the job," I heard whispered. I hoped that Fab was just pulling one of her stunts and wasn't in real trouble.

An hour later, Fab returned with a swagger and an unrepentant look on her face, picking up a tray as though she hadn't gone missing. I timed my break just right and had a ringside view from the bar area. One of the bouncers ordered her to the manager's office, but she'd only made it to within a few steps of where I stood when Tilly intercepted her. The short, blistering lecture the manager served up about her unprofessional conduct burned even my ears. Tilly signaled for a bouncer, and two showed up to escort Fab to the door, one on either side of her. "You're fired and don't come back," was Tilly's parting shot.

Tilly waylaid me before I could take a step, and said, with derision in her voice, "You can get your things and leave. If your friend left anything, get it now." Her hands twisted into fists as she barely controlled her fury. "This is what happens when men let their dicks do the hiring."

* * *

"Why? Why? Why?" My voice got louder with each word.

Fab slunk down in the driver's seat, head hunched over the wheel, and remained silent.

"One night!" I exploded.

"Oh, calm down. It's not like we need this job to climb the ladder of success," she snipped.

"Don't you mean *pole*?" I snapped. "I've never been told to leave on my first day on the job. At least I wasn't sacked like you."

"You're mean."

"Aww." I wiped the non-existent tear from my eye.

"Once you hear what happened, you'll feel guilty about your bad attitude towards your best friend."

I kicked off my shoes and tossed them in the back, ignoring her completely.

Fab let out a melodramatic sigh, "I came out to change my shoes and couldn't force myself to go back in. Then I got sidetracked, using a handi-wipe to get the beer stink off me." She shuddered. "I hadn't been there an hour, one I'll never get back, when another girl bumped into me. Beer mugs tumbled off her tray, and the liquid spilled down my legs. Can you believe she blamed me?"

I looked at her, letting her know she'd lost her mind.

Fab put her hand down her top, removing cash. "This goes in the change holder. I'm saving it to get drunk as soon as feasible, so I can forget this night. More than once, an anonymous hand stuffed money in my cleavage while I was supposed to be cleaning tables."

I smiled at the visual of Fab bussing a table,

then lowered my seatback, reclining it as far as it would go. "I want to go home," I said, and closed my eyes.

"Can I go fast?"

Chapter Thirty-Eight

The next morning, I woke up before anyone else and took my cup of coffee out to the pool, flinging my feet over the side and into the water. I had texted Creole the second we arrived home, and instead of calling back, he showed up, informing me before the first kiss that he couldn't stay long.

"We were tossed off the property," I murmured.

He gave a deep, throaty laugh. "I've got the cure for a crummy day," he said and kissed me. He disappeared through the opening in the fence.

Lost in thought, I brushed my chin, reveling in the whisker burn, hoping it wouldn't go away anytime soon.

Fab plopped down next to me. "How are we going to finish up this job?"

"We're not. And you can be the one to tell Brick. I'm sure he's heard about last night, and I'm sure he's not happy."

My phone rang, giving her a reprieve from answering. Seeing Brick's name, I groaned. Fab had no intention of dealing with this mess—she'd obviously turned her phone off. *Might as well get it over with.*

"What the hell happened last night?" he screamed, loud enough that I didn't need to hit the speaker button.

He cut off my attempt at a hastily edited version of events. "Can you finish this job on your own? If I override Tilly and send Fab back, she might quit."

"I'm in a relationship and very happy. If I go back there alone, my boyfriend might take his anger out on you and follow through on his threat to make you disappear." I tossed out a hastily conceived plan about staking out the parking lot, ignoring Fab's gesturing at me to put the call on speaker.

"This is all your fault," I informed him. "You've known Fab long enough to know this idea was frankly, a bad idea."

"Let's go with Plan B. If you don't get anything new tonight, I'll think about a Plan C," he grunted. "The girls really liked you."

"Then you won't mind if I keep my uniform?"

"The boyfriend likes it, does he? Can't say I'm not a romantic."

His dirty laugh made me scrunch up my nose as I ended the call.

* * *

Fab spit out frustrated noises, swerving onto Tamiami Trail in the direction of the club. "I hate this job."

"Oh, stop your whining. If you hate it so much, call your friend Brick and tell him we quit. You should thank me for convincing the man to let us confront Octavia and Delight outside the club. Otherwise, you'd have no choice but to bail on the case."

"What have we got so far?" Fab asked testily.

"You know we don't have zip," I frowned at her. "I thought the idea that someone would show up inside the club to harass the girls was stupid with a bodyguard at every door."

"Which means the harassment must be happening at home."

"And we don't know where that is," I said. The addresses Brick had on file were a dead end; Octavia used a mail drop and Delight an empty lot.

She heaved a sigh. "What do you think about installing a pole in the living room?"

"Absolutely not. Mother would fall and hurt herself."

Fab started laughing. "You've got the coolest mother. Unless she's lecturing you over your bad behavior, that is. Did you know she talked to me about having a nicer attitude towards Didier? We'd gotten into a fight, and your mother didn't bother to hide the fact that she was listening in. She not only interjected her two cents into the argument but took his side. I stuck my tongue out at her."

The corners of my mouth turned up. "What did she do?"

"She pointed towards the stairs and said, 'You go to your room.' And I went."

"You know you're an adult now and don't have to go, don't you?"

"I couldn't get away fast enough. I should have told her she hurt my feelings by taking his side, even if I was in the wrong. I did later and even apologized."

"Oh…" I made a sad face.

"She hugged me and said she wouldn't do it again—to either of us. I assured her that Didier wasn't going anywhere, and we'd already made up. Then she got this dreamy look in her eye and said, 'That's fun, isn't it?'"

"That's a story we don't need to share with Brad."

Fab pulled into the parking lot and headed for the middle row. It was early, and there were only about a dozen non-employee automobiles. She parked between two of them in a space that afforded a direct view of the entrance.

"Look!" Fab pointed to Tilly's assistant, who came out a side exit, shoving something in the jamb to keep the door open. She had a liquor box in her hands, and from the way she carried it, it appeared to be heavy. She juggled it while unlocking the trunk, then stored it inside.

"I've forgotten her name," I said, not taking my eyes off her.

"Don't ask *me*."

The woman looked in both directions before going back in the same door.

"We can't be one-hundred percent certain she's stealing, and we're not here to investigate employee theft anyway," I said.

The door opened again. The woman came back out with a smaller box and two Styrofoam takeout containers, which she put in the trunk as well before going back inside.

"Before we leave, I'll pop the trunk and check. If she is stealing, I'll inform her that I'm telling Brick he has a problem and should investigate. She can quit or take her chances."

I didn't bother to respond to that. I frankly didn't care if Brick's employees were stealing him blind. We were just there to find out what was happening with the girls. Delight's shift would end soon and Octavia's would start. According to Brick, they were both dropped off by their boyfriends, and we were there to get the license numbers so we could have Phil run a check on them. At least then, we'd know where the girls spend their free time.

Fab tapped my arm, motioning to the windshield. We were getting close to shift change, and dancers would be coming and going. A navy blue BMW sedan pulled up to the dancer's entrance and sat idling.

Octavia stepped out of the car and started towards the door. The driver honked, and she held up her middle finger in response. The driver-side door flew open, and a scrawny, six-foot man in a wife beater that displayed his tattoos got out and waved his arms wildly.

Fab stuck her head out the window. "I can't hear a damn thing, just a bunch of garbled, loud words."

Octavia shouted back, shot him the double bird, and disappeared inside. The man beat his fist on the roof of the Beemer and slid back behind the wheel. He squealed the tires as he started up, but instead of heading for the exit, he zig-zagged to the far side of the lot, making his own parking space.

An older model tan Impala pulled in next. It was in immaculate condition, with dark-tinted windows and lowered suspension. The driver circled the lot and parked alongside the BMW, their driver's doors facing one another.

"I can't see what's going on from here." Fab opened her door.

I grabbed her arm before she could get out. "We don't care," I snapped. "Delight's leaving." I cocked my head towards the dancer's entrance.

Delight surveyed the parking lot, eyeing the two cars parked side by side, then turned and went back inside.

"That's interesting," Fab murmured.

The Impala pulled away and began to circle

back around toward the entrance. Suddenly, automatic gunfire tore through both cars.

I bent over, arms over my head, not sure what to do. Fab slid down and over across the passenger seat.

The gunfire seemed endless, but at last it was quiet. Fab and I rose up just enough to peek over the dashboard. The Impala had veered off and embedded its front end in the back fence. The BMW hadn't moved. No one got out of either car.

"I'd say Octavia no longer has a problem with her boyfriend. We need to get out of here." The words had barely escaped my lips when a number of unmarked police cars blew into the driveway.

"Get your boyfriend on the phone," Fab ordered. "They're going to find us. We'll say we stayed crouched down because we were scared."

"At least your story is the truth." I pulled my phone from my pocket and pressed speed dial. "Wait until Creole finds out that calling him was *your* idea."

Cars doors flew open and plainclothes cops wearing bulletproof vests spilled out. Several officers checked each car. The blood-splattered windows told their own story. One cop signaled to the others, and a couple of them reholstered their weapons.

"They look like friends of Creole's. He'll know how we can get out of here." Fab pulled out her phone. "Calling Brick," she said, answering my unspoken question.

"No answer," I grumped and sent a text. Then I called the number Creole had added in case of emergency.

"Yeah," a male voice answered.

"Creole said to call if we needed help, and this situation qualifies." I hit the highlights of what had just unfolded in front of us.

Help listened in silence until I was done, then said, "Which car is yours?" It was then I recognized his voice—I was talking to Creole's undercover partner."

Confused, I said and looked around, "The Hummer."

"Stay inside and don't go anywhere. Someone will be over to talk to you."

"Thanks," I mumbled, but he'd already hung up.

Chapter Thirty-Nine

I threw myself down on the daybed. "I don't want to work for Brick ever again," I complained as I squinted over at Fab to make sure she was listening.

Creole burst through the French doors. "I'm here." He gave a bow.

Didier and I laughed.

Creole rushed to my side and put his hand on my forehead. "You okay?" He sat down, lifting my head into his lap.

"She's not sick, you weirdo," Fab sniffed at him.

"Thanks for sending Help. It was nice to see a friendly face. Well, a familiar face anyway," I grimaced.

Creole's undercover partner, Help, had banged on the driver's side window. "Tell me exactly what you saw," he ordered after he climbed in the back seat.

"Don't look at me." Fab closed her eyes. "She's the master at storytelling."

"Just facts," Help spit out.

"I've never seen you so chatty." I smiled at him. Two, three words of out him were the usual. But a

whole sentence? Never. Unless "mind your own business" counted.

I recounted the details in living color from the time the BMW pulled into the parking lot until the gunfire broke out, careful to only include what we actually saw from our vantage point.

After he left, a local police officer took our statement. We sat for several hours before being given the go ahead to leave.

Creole had called around that time. "It's only a matter of waiting. They have video tape, which is better than an eyewitness account." He hung up after promising to see me later at my house.

Brick had burned up Fab's phone with one question after another. He seemed more annoyed about the club being closed for a few days than the two dead bodies that had yet to be carted away.

"What are you thinking?" Creole asked.

"Octavia showed up for work; Fab and I saw her get out of the car and go inside. Her boyfriend gets murdered, and now Brick says she was a no-show and didn't call in."

"And the other dead guy was Delight's boyfriend," Fab said. "Neither of them are having boyfriend problems any longer, which closes our case." She brushed her hands together.

"When do we get our quad-pay?" I asked.

"We didn't actually do anything…"

I rolled on my side in a fit. "I worked. I wasn't the one who got fired the first day. I stood in those stinkin' heels until my toes almost fell off."

"*Chérie…*" The frown on Didier's face let everyone know that this was the first time he had heard this story, which was no surprise to me.

"You misunderstood." Fab flashed the "cover for me" look.

"You're right, I guess I did," I said, heavy on the sarcasm. Creole pinched me lightly. I'd already served up the details to him, and he'd had me laughing over the situation. "'Your fired and don't come back' wasn't very clear." I looked at her.

"I hated that job," Fab sulked. "I came home smelling like the bottom of an ashtray."

"Me too," I commiserated. "But at least you got tips. Judging by the cash you put in the drink fund, if you'd turned on your sparkly personality, you would've had enough stuffed in your cleavage to take the four of us out to a nice dinner."

Creole's phone rang; he glanced at the screen and answered. "Yeah, okay, good, thanks." He hung up. "Octavia got picked up on the northbound turnpike south of Orlando. She'll be charged as an accessory."

"By the way, why were the cops there so quickly in the first place?" I asked. It had been bothering me ever since they squealed in before the echoes of the gunfire had even faded.

"The police got wind that the heads of two drug gangs were getting together to hammer out whose was bigger. Turns out neither one. Law enforcement didn't expect it to take place in the parking lot of a stripper joint. I'm surprised that backup from the rival gangs didn't hop out of the bushes when the first bullet flew. It was over for the both of them in the first few shots, but still…"

"What happens to the gangs now?" Didier asked.

"They'll both name new leaders and go to war. Depending on who they choose to lead, they might work out a truce, but I doubt it," Creole said.

"Did you mention to Brick that he might have a thieving employee?" I eyed Fab.

"She's fired. He's calling her into his office to share some security footage with her. Apparently, she's been doing it for a while and got confident, then sloppy. He says he has her on camera on at least three separate occasions," Fab related.

"I haven't met this man. Would I like him?" Didier asked.

Didier had directed his question towards me, which surprised me. Creole was already shaking his head. "No!"

"Probably not," I said. "But you'd certainly never say anything mean about him."

Fab shook her head.

"You're his girl," I told her. "I just get to come along because he doesn't know how to shake me."

Creole stood, scooping me up. "I need to get my beauty sleep," he said as we headed upstairs.

Fab laughed, "Good luck."

Chapter Forty

As Fab and I sat at the kitchen island, movement in front of the garden window caught our attention, and we both stared at the twenty-something guy that passed by.

The doorbell rang.

Fab made a pair of scissors with her hand.

Rock, paper... I rolled my eyes. "We're not six. Besides, it's not my job to answer the door."

"It's your house," Fab said, hands on her hips.

"Yes, but you already have your Walther out. If there's a problem, give a shout; I've got a backup bullet." I pulled my Glock from my thigh holster.

As she went to get to the door, I sucked down my last sip of coffee, momentarily feeling sorry for whoever stood there. We had zero appreciation for strangers showing up unannounced and uninvited.

Fab cracked open the door, sticking her head in the opening, "What do you want?"

I decided to move closer to listen, as Fab tended to leave out pertinent details in the retelling of stories. I knew I wouldn't be able to hear a word he said from where I was, so I hopped from my stool and sidled up behind Fab, peering over her shoulder as she jerked open the door.

As soon as the guy spotted the Walther, he jumped back, the color draining from his cheeks. I almost laughed. Really, he had more to fear from me, and I'd reholstered my gun.

"Delivery," he stuttered, "for Fabiana Mercer and Madison Weston."

"It's Merceau," she snarked as she shoved her gun in her waistband.

"Hi, I'm Madison." I gave him a friendly smile in the hopes that he wouldn't call the sheriff.

"Get him a tip." I nudged Fab. "I'll sign for the envelope and the pretty box."

Although I preferred colorful gift wrap, the black box with the silver satin ribbon made a statement, and that statement was "expensive."

"The tip has been taken care of by the sender," the delivery guy said in a shaky voice, then turned and bolted down the driveway. Another delivery person we'd scared the hell out of — pretty soon no one would come a-knocking.

I looked at the tag on the box and sighed, handing it to Fab. The envelope had my name on it. Tired of watching Fab inspect the outside of the box, shaking and sniffing at it, I slid onto a bar stool and ripped open the business envelope. No special wrap for me.

Looking up, I said, "If it was going to blow up, it would have by now."

I turned the envelope upside down, and a business card and cash fell onto the counter. Printed neatly on the back of the business card was: "Thank you for a job well done." The signature was indecipherable. I flipped it over: Trenton Preston III. "Your boyfriend-in-waiting sent me money. What did you get?"

Fab removed the lid, revealing the silky lining inside the black velvet box. She stared and smiled, running a finger over her gift, then pulled out a diamond bracelet, holding her arm out and wrapping it around her wrist. "Help me with the clasp."

I secured the toggle and squinted at the gemstones. "I bet these are real. I got one of these once. Well, not quite as big, but still my favorite piece of jewelry."

"Preston and I are just friends," Fab whispered.

"In your mind, he's a friend. But that—" I pointed at the gift. "—is an invitation to call if you ditch Didier."

Selfishly, I hoped that never happened. Preston was cute in that tall, dark and handsome way that we were both attracted to, but he wouldn't fit into our foursome.

Chapter Forty-One

Creole sat in a chair across from Didier and tugged me down onto his lap as we waited for Fab to make her entrance. Didier looked at his watch for the fifth time. Wouldn't she be surprised when she saw that neither Creole nor I were dressed to go to dinner. The common theme of late was dressing up for these couples get-togethers, but I was in the mood for greasy tacos and a margarita. Creole had licked his lips when I mentioned a change of plans, his thoughts going directly to tamales. Our dining choice didn't require anything more than shoes and a shirt, or so the sign said.

Fab emerged on the landing and flounced down the stairs in a short black A-line dress and heels that showed off her long tan legs, her hair tumbling in waves down her back. She absentmindedly played with the bracelet on her right wrist.

Didier whistled in appreciation. The man had on a black silk shirt and slacks, and had the best taste in shoes as he favored Italian loafers.

Creole whispered in my ear, "You look pretty delicious in your shorts, which I know would come off with one yank."

I wiggled in his lap.

Fab turned her attention to Creole and me. "Why the hell aren't you two dressed?" Her hands flew to her hips.

Didier leaned back and smiled, not the least bit concerned that we were on the hot seat. He'd warned us earlier that she would throw a fit.

"We—" I pointed to myself and Creole. "—aren't going, but thank you for inviting us." She started to speak and I held up my hand. "I should've told you sooner but chickened out. If you wait on us to get ready, you'll be late for your reservations, which I already changed to two people." I smiled.

"If we invited you to greasy hot dogs instead of a five-star restaurant, you'd be ready to go," she huffed.

"Sadly, yes." I winked at her.

"Now that that's settled," Creole said. "Call us if a gunfight breaks out."

Didier reached out and took Fab's wrist in his hand. "That's a nice bracelet. I don't think I've seen that one before."

I tensed in Creole's arms.

"What?" he whispered.

I shook my head. Fab had a way of letting the truth trickle out; I had no idea what she would say about this one. I hadn't said anything yet either, but then, the delivery had only happened this morning.

"Remember Ursula?" Fab said.

"You steal that from her?" Creole hit the arm of the chair in amusement.

Fab turned and glared. "I did not."

Didier wiped the smile off his face before she turned back around.

"Mr. Preston sent it as a thank-you gift for a job well done." Fab fingered the stones.

Didier eyed the bracelet and pulled her into his lap. "So you have an admirer. Should I worry?"

"I told him from the beginning that I had a boyfriend."

I spoke up. "Actually, she said, 'I'm with the love of my life.'"

Fab blushed, and Didier tightened his hold on her. "I feel the same way," he smiled. "But don't think I won't call him and threaten him with a painful disappearance. I have my own connections."

Creole ran his fingers up and down my arm. "What did you get?"

"Cash. Just once, I'd like to be the hot one." I stuck out my lower lip.

He turned my face to his. "You're my hot one." He kissed me.

"Stop with the kissy face," Fab grouched. "We're going to be eating soon."

Chapter Forty-Two

Fab and I lay by the pool, but we'd moved our chaises under the tree in the far corner, giving us shade from the sweltering sun. She checked her phone frequently, worried that she hadn't heard from Didier. He'd had an appointment with his lawyer, and both of them hoped to hear that the police no longer considered him a person of interest.

"I'll take a lemonade while you're up," I grinned. "Not too much ice."

"I guess you didn't notice I was sitting." She stood. "But please, let me." She slunk her way across the patio in her black string bikini.

"Thank you," I called to her retreating back.

I closed my eyes and breathed in the salty air, relishing the do-nothing day. After ten minutes had passed, I said to myself, "Where's Fab?" I looked at the French doors. If we were out of our drink of choice, she'd improvise; she knew everyone's favorites. I tapped my foot on the chaise, noticing that she'd left her phone behind. Changing my mind about a quick swim, I headed for the house.

From the doorway, I could see that the kitchen was empty. To make sure, I poked my head around the corner, in case she had the refrigerator open. No Fab. I stood at the sink, looking out, and saw both our vehicles parked in the driveway. The silence enveloped me. Not seeing a glass or anything on the counter, I realized that Fab hadn't even started on the drinks. A little chill ran up the back of my neck.

I'm overreacting, I thought. *Just call out her name.*

I slid open the junk drawer and reached for the Berretta. I could hardly stuff it in my bathing suit, so opted to hold it at my side, just behind my thigh. I stayed within arm's distance of the kitchen and yelled, "Fab!"

I waited, hearing nothing, then yelled again. "Fab!" It came out more like a screech. Jazz lifted his head off the pillow on the daybed.

Having no choice, I crept up the stairs, gun held out in front of me, finger on the trigger. Fab's door was open, and her room was empty. I peered in my bedroom, but nothing was out of place.

"Fabiana Merceau, are you up here?" I yelled, my throat not happy with me. Remembering that she'd left her phone on the chaise by the pool, I ran back downstairs.

"I'm right here." She came in through the doors from the pool, her gun poking the back of the wiry man stumbling in front of her. She'd cuffed his hands behind him and taken the time to get out her shiny, stainless steel professional cuffs instead of using the zip ties we kept in the kitchen.

"Have a seat." She shoved him down into a chair. "Caught him lurking around the front with this in his hand." She pulled out a Luger handgun and set it on the counter. "And lookie! Cuffs of his own." She placed those next to the gun.

"How can we help you?" I asked the man.

"Fuck you," he snapped.

I shook my finger. "Vulgar words are no longer allowed in this house."

He let out a chilling laugh. "You're a dead bitch."

I backed up into the entry and exchanged the Beretta for my Glock, which was in my bag sitting on the bench. "He's not very talkative." I arched a brow at Fab. This couldn't be good. Surely if he had the wrong house, he'd have tossed out that excuse already.

Fab clocked him across the back of his head with the butt of her Walther. He slumped over. "We need to go through his pockets. Hopefully, we'll find out who he is and what he wants. The Lexus he rode up in is what caught my eye."

"We? This is your find."

"His jeans are tight." She wrinkled her nose.

"I noticed that. It's not like we have to take them off; just check the pockets."

"If he's naked, he probably won't get any ideas about running off before we're done with him," she said.

"I suggest we get this over with and tie him to a chair." I dropped to the floor on his left side. "You do the other side. Then I'll call a pickup service, and get rid of him." I hesitated, then stuck my hand in his pocket and pulled out a cell phone.

Fab searched the other pocket and came up with keys and cash.

I grabbed the key ring off her finger. "You tie him up, and I'll toss the Lexus." I turned to go. "I only know one man who can get rid of him and the car at the same time."

"Take your gun," Fab instructed.

"Don't worry. I'll check both ways before making a move. I learned from the best." I smiled at her and grabbed my phone and fit it down the front of my bathing suit top. I found a pair of latex gloves in a kitchen drawer and snapped them on, then went out through the patio doors and into the passageway that wound around to the beach or the front of the house, depending on your direction. I huddled in the corner for a moment, scanning the property before setting foot in the courtyard. Passing the Hummer and Mercedes, I peeked in the windows—nothing. The street was clear in both directions, neither a person nor a car that I hadn't seen in the neighborhood before, aside from the Lexus parked at the curb. I texted Creole "911" and hit send. No answer. I called him without waiting for an answer, a thousand questions running through my mind. "What's going on today?" I yelled at the phone when it went straight to voicemail.

Before hitting the key fob, I looked in the windows of the Lexus, front and back. All clear. I gave a thought to opening the trunk and rejected it. I didn't want another surprise—a dead body, for example. I slid in and slammed the door, locking myself in. A piece of letter-size paper on the passenger seat listed my address, Fab's and my names, and the license number of the Hummer.

The car was clean, nothing under the seats or in the glove box, not a single piece of trash. That left the trunk. *Fab would have opened it by now,* I thought. *I'm not her,* I whined back.

Taking a deep breath, I found the trunk lever, bent down, Glock in hand, and pulled it up. The lid clicked open and I got out, and jumped behind the open door and waited. After what seemed like an hour, I went around to the passenger side and sent the truck lid flying up.

The contents made me nauseated, but I felt fairly certain I wouldn't retch in the street. Rope, rags, a golf putter; I didn't want to think what that might be used for. I used the muzzle of my Glock to poke at two folded plastic items, which turned out to be body bags. I slammed the trunk, locked up the car, and ran back inside.

"Les Nado." Fab pointed to the man. She'd left him lying on the floor, secured to an overturned dining room chair. Good luck standing up when anchored to one of those. He was coming around, mumbling and trying to move without success.

"Car's clean. Only this." I held up the piece of paper. "Our names and address. What's weird is the Hummer's license plate number." *Why?* I wondered.

"He's got our ugly driver's license photos on his phone. He's definitely here for us. What does he want?" she asked, as though I had an answer.

"He's here to kidnap us." I listed the items I'd found in the trunk.

"Who did we piss off now?"

"You figure that out while I go change. Will you be okay for a few minutes?" She nodded and I ran upstairs. I tossed my bathing suit on a nearby chair, pulled on crop sweatpants, tugged a sports bra over my head followed by a T-shirt, and smooshed my feet into tennis shoes, with the laces already tied. My sweat-soaked hair looked like a giant bush. I twisted it around and held it together with a clip. Finally, I strapped on a waist holster, slipped the Glock in it, and shoved my phone in my pocket.

"Everything okay?" I asked, coming downstairs.

Fab had her cell phone to her ear. "Voicemail

again," she huffed.

"That seems to be epidemic today. Same thing with Creole."

She scrolled through her phone. "Didier texted hours ago, that he'd gotten a call from Balcazar and planned to stop by his office. I've called him several times, but it goes to voicemail. Why would he agree to meet with that man?"

What started out as a great day had rapidly gone downhill. "We need help. I want this cretin out of my house." I called Creole, but his phone was still turned off. I scrolled through my phone, looking for a Plan B. My finger hovered over the name, 'Help.' Twice in one week was getting to be a nuisance, and I could hear the man grumbling already.

"What?" the ever-friendly man answered his phone.

"Can you find Creole?" I asked.

"No. Hi, how are you?" he chuckled.

Now he wants to do friendly instead of his usual get-to-the-point conversational style. I opted to stay silent instead of screaming my frustration in his ear.

"He's up in Miami," he said after a moment. "I can be at your house in a few." His tone was now all business.

Creole had once assured me that Help could be trusted without reservation. I told him about our unwanted houseguest and that we didn't know what to do. "Can you get a message to

Creole?" I asked, declining his offer of handholding.

"You need answers before you turn his ass over to the cops. I'll make some calls. You need anything, call back." He hung up.

"Look at this." Fab held up a business card. She had the contents of the man's wallet spread out on the floor, making it look like she'd ripped it apart.

"And it says?"

"Balcazar's business card, with a couple of Miami numbers scribbled on the back. Also, Les here has the man's office number and another number for him in his phone."

I leaned across the counter, taking the card from her fingers, and dialed both numbers. "No answer," I said. "Voicemail—pre-recorded."

"It's rare that Didier doesn't answer his phone, and when he misses my call, he returns it right away. Has he really been with Balcazar all this time?" she arched a brow. "There's some connection here. What are we missing?"

I hit speed dial. "I need a favor," I said when Brad answered. "Don't flip out." I put a finger to my lips and pressed the speaker button.

He groaned, "Anything. You need bail?"

"Do you think you can pull off covert and sneaky?" I smiled, knowing he'd be all in.

"It's in my genes," he snorted. "I've got just as much of Madeline's DNA as you do. I'm your man."

"Just make sure Mother doesn't hear you using her first name again. Don't think she can't send you to your room like when you were a kid," I chuckled. "Do you have Balcazar's personal phone number?" I moved to the garden window, staring out at the driveway.

I jumped when our unwanted guest let out a loud groan. The last thing I needed was for Brad to ask about the unfamiliar noise.

"Yeah, I've got it. He turned out to be a slimy piece. Thanks for letting me read the report and keeping me in the loop. What do you want me to do with it?"

"Call Balcazar, work Didier's name into the conversation, and hopefully he'll put him on the phone." I went on to explain what had happened, letting him think the prowler had run off. If he knew the man was lying on the living room floor, he'd race over here.

"That bastard comes back, you shoot him, and I mean dead. You know this is probably some weird coincidence and Didier will be calling any minute. We tease him, calling him 'pretty boy,' but I promise you, he can hold his own in a fight. He's a survivor. Okay, I'm on it and will call you back."

"You're the best brother," I said softly.

"Forget that," Brad barked. "Hopefully by the time I call back, Didier will have walked in the front door." He hung up.

Les Nado began a fight with the chair he was

secured to: rocking and rolling, grunting noises and the F-word flying out of his mouth. He had his back to us, unaware he had company.

I glared at Fab and pointed in his direction. "Do something," I mouthed.

She threw her arms in the air. "Fine," she shouted. "Shut up over there!"

The second the word "bitch" came out of his mouth, I smirked, knowing Fab would take care of the problem. It was my friend's least favorite word.

Fab jerked opened a kitchen drawer and grabbed a towel. Marching over to him, she shoved one end in his mouth.

"Do you hear that?" I smiled. "It's quiet again."

With Fab right behind me, I moved to the far side of the kitchen, out of the hearing of our bound intruder, and hit another number on my speed dial. "Are you on Spoonee's boat?" I asked Mother as soon as she answered. The big man had forbidden her to call him any term of endearment in public after he took a lot of ribbing for that one.

Without a word, she put him on, and the next thing I heard was, "Yesss, stepdaughter?"

I loved his growly laugh. "I need some of those 'I can do anything skills' you brag about." I explained about our intruder and that we were worried about Didier. "I promise you, we haven't pissed anyone off lately — too many anyway," I said as I struggled to keep my emotions at bay. "What am I going to do with Mr. Nado and his Lexus? I don't want him dead; we need answers out of him. Do you think you could persuade him to talk? Most people's knees shake at the mention of your name."

"What was that about Didier?" Mother exclaimed. "What happened to him?"

"I'll grab my toolbox; we're on our way," he said and hung up.

"Spoon's bringing a *toolbox*," I whispered to Fab.

Fab shuddered. "He wouldn't…not in front of your mother."

I laid my head on her shoulder. "Can we start the day over?" My phone rang again.

"That was a weird call," Brad said.

"Did you talk to Didier?" I tried not to sound impatient.

"Told Balcazar that Didier and I had talked earlier about setting up a meeting and I wanted to follow through with him. He told me that not only hadn't he talked to Didier today, but he hasn't in the last couple of weeks. He said that, in light of recent events, the deal was cancelled. He also claimed that he was so devastated over Lauren, and other unspecified issues, that he needed downtime."

"Why would Didier say he was meeting Balcazar if he wasn't? Didier would never lie to Fab or mislead her for her own good, like she does him," I said.

She slugged me in the shoulder.

"I'm in Lauderdale; just finished cleaning the boat. I'll leave the rest to my guys and go scope out Balcazar's office. If I spot Didier's car, I'll muscle my way in the door," Brad offered. "What's going on?" he said, more to himself than me.

I rubbed my forehead, refraining from banging it on the counter. Before he hung up, I told him about my conversation with Spoon, that he was on his way. I hoped Nado would be long gone so I wouldn't have to explain how I failed to mention that *small* detail.

"You two keep calm; don't go off half-cocked," he said. "Call me if you need another location checked."

"You call as soon as you get there. Be careful." I hung up and paced the kitchen.

Spoon's truck flew by, made a U-turn and parked across the street. Mother ran up the driveway, waving at me through the window. Spoon, several steps behind her, said something, and from the look on his face, he wasn't happy.

Mother beat on the front door, and Fab unlocked the deadbolt. "Good, you're still here. We can stop you from doing something stupid."

Fab glared at both of them. From where I stood, I wasn't sure which one annoyed her more.

Chapter Forty-Three

Apparently, Les Nado and Spoon were acquainted and required no introduction. Spoon uprighted the chair and dragged him out to the patio, tossing the towel gag on the floor. "Throw this away."

Fab followed and peeked out the door. "They're talking. So far, nothing violent."

"Spoon has a way of getting people to open up," Mother cooed.

Fab stood behind her, rolling her eyes, and I tried not to laugh. Spoon wasn't known as a badass for nothing.

My phone rang, and I pounced on it, thankful for the break in tension in the room. "Well?"

"Hey sis, Balcazar's offices are locked. The woman in the property management place said he and the wife took a couple of days off," Brad related. "I checked the underground parking, but didn't see Didier's Mercedes or Balcazar's Porsche."

"I appreciate the drive-by. I guess there's nothing to do but wait." I had no intention of verbalizing my plans while Mother was keeping an eagle eye on me. I made about as much small talk as I could muster, even though I was about to scream. The events of the day had taken their toll on the always-cool-under-fire Fab, who looked ready to explode in frustration.

"You're a little too calm. What are you up to?" Brad asked.

"Mother and Spoon got here a little while ago." I ignored Mother's inquiring look.

"Aww, she driving you nuts? I'm headed back to the Cove, so I'll stop by the house. Call if anything changes. Don't worry, Didier will turn up." He hung up.

I flashed the phone a dirty look, sick of the "don't worry" sentiments. "Balcazar's offices were a dead end," I told Mother and Fab.

Mother reached across the island and patted Fab's hand. "Any minute, Didier will come walking through the door."

Spoon, done with his poolside chat, came back inside. "Balcazar's got Didier at his mansion. Nado and Balcazar confronted Didier in the underground parking lot at the office building, and it was Nado that threw him into the trunk of his own car. After he dropped Didier off at Balcazar's, his new instructions were to pick up the two of you and take you back to Miami Beach, dead or alive didn't seem to matter. Something about a business deal gone south. Les wasn't interested in the whys, only the cash."

Fab jumped up with a growl, hurling herself

toward the patio, but Spoon grabbed her arm and swung her back around. "You'll only end up in jail if you shoot him. If you're worried he's not telling the truth—he is."

She jerked free and ran up the stairs.

"Now would be a good time to use your connections," Spoon said. "Give Creole's boss a call. He'll help you."

"I'll try Creole again." I turned away, saying a silent prayer that he'd answer. He would know what to do. I didn't want to go straight to his boss. What if the cops surrounded Balcazar's mansion, and Didier got killed? Once again, I got voicemail. I stalled, letting them think the phone was ringing.

Fab raced down the stairs. In record time, she'd changed into her work uniform, which she wore even when the humidity was off the charts: blue jeans, long-sleeve t-shirt, and tennis shoes. It was a telltale sign she wanted to be prepared for trouble.

"I'll call you later," she said in a frenzied tone.

"Hold on." I grabbed her shirt in my fist. "You can't go by yourself."

"Good thing Spoon and I showed up when we did. You two aren't going anywhere." Mother moved in front of Fab, arms crossed. "Sit down." She pointed to the stools. "We don't need three dead people."

"You're not going to stop me." Fab squared off with Mother.

"You're right. I can't stop you, but Spoon can." She waved her hand in her boyfriend's direction.

"I'd hate to have to shoot you both," Fab snarled.

"Ratchet down the noise," Spoon boomed. "I got connections in Miami. They can get to Didier before either of you. Didier and Creole would both want you to stay here, and you know it."

I reached for Fab's hand under the counter and squeezed. This was a battle we wouldn't win without causing a lot of bad feelings. I interrupted, saying, "I've got a headache," and shoved my stool back. "I need some aspirin." I grabbed my water and phone, clutching Fab's sleeve and hauling her along with me. "I'll talk some sense into her," I said over my shoulder.

"Some sense?" Fab hissed.

I walked calmly upstairs, dragging my reluctant friend into my bedroom and banging the door closed. "Quiet." I put my finger across her lips. "You can't shoot Mother. The guilt would kill you."

Fab bent at the waist, gulping in air. "I need to get out of here."

"I should slap you silly for thinking about leaving without me," I scolded, slipping my purse over my shoulder and patting my Glock. "Need a sweatshirt, in case there's a skyscraper to scale." I held one up. "No talking." I opened the door, peeked out into the hallway, and motioned Fab to follow. We crept over to the balcony, letting out a collective sigh when we saw that they'd gone out to the pool, and slunk down the stairs. It was cowardly not to stand our ground and inform Mother and Spoon that we were leaving, but the likelihood of them wishing us a good trip was nil, and this way, no guns were drawn.

I passed off the car keys to Fab. Thank goodness Spoon hadn't blocked in the Hummer, or Fab would be trying to get his truck hotwired fast.

From the passenger seat, I waved to Mother, who stood at the sink glaring, her lips moving as we backed out of the driveway. Spoon hadn't flown out the door. He wasn't stupid; he knew we'd break out sooner or later. I'd banked on neither of them following us upstairs since I pulled off appearing reasonable.

My phone rang. I looked at Fab, and she grimaced. Without looking, we both knew it was Mother. I pushed "ignore" and instead texted her, "We'll keep in touch."

Phil was my next call. "What's up boss?" she asked.

"Do you have Balcazar's home address? I don't have the file with me." Fab pulled into a gas station we'd never use except in an emergency and hopped out to fill the tank.

"He and the wife have a house on Hibiscus Island," Phil said. "I'll look in my notes. I know I have it written down. What are you two up to?"

I told her about the mysterious events of the day.

"Les Nado is a low-level criminal," Phil informed me as Fab climbed back in. "Balcazar didn't hire a professional. Must be short on cash. If Nado got arrested, he'd turn states evidence in a heartbeat to save his ass."

Fab gripped the steering wheel tightly, turning onto the main highway and heading north to Miami Beach. "Hibiscus," I whispered. We didn't need GPS to get to MacArthur Causeway, the highway that linked several manmade islands with the mainland.

"You be damn careful. Do I need to remind you that some people associated with Balcazar have disappeared or never been seen again?" Phil cautioned. "I did some more checking, and another of his business associates and his family of four haven't been seen in months."

"One murdered or missing friend is one thing, but several?" I grimaced. "Has Balcazar ever been a suspect?"

"Sources tell me the police tried to invite him in to chat a few times, but he lawyered up and blocked any meet-and-greets. Gotta say, the man is well-connected. An order came down from the top to 'look elsewhere.'"

"Harder?" I'd had several encounters, good and bad, with Creole's boss, but I found what Phil said difficult to believe. I couldn't imagine that Harder would cover for a murderer.

"Got the address; I'll text it to you. What's your plan? Knock on the door? Then what?"

"I can always use the missing cat/dog story. Are you trying to tell me you think this a wild goose chase?"

The mention of our oft-used missing pet story made Fab smile.

"Maybe, but what else do you have?" Phil asked. "You be careful—Balcazar's slimy. If he thought you knew about his illegal business dealings, who knows what he'd do. Where's that boyfriend of yours? You could use some official help."

My phone beeped and I glanced at the screen. "He's on the phone now. Thank you for your help." I switched over to the incoming call.

"Why are you sitting on the turnpike?" Creole growled before I could utter a greeting.

Traffic had come to a grinding halt on the three lanes of asphalt. Fab tapped her foot incessantly, frustration pouring out of her. We were caught between exits, and with the cars stacked up, getting over was unlikely.

"A better question is where in the hell are *you*? You track my every move, and I can't get ahold of you when we need you." I was hot and tired from sitting on the road waiting for what was probably an accident to clear, consumed with thoughts of Didier and praying for a happy ending.

"We had a bust today, and they're never in-

and-out. They unfold slowly, hopefully with no surprises."

"Just great!" I yelled. "You harp on my safety, yet when you walk out the door, I don't know if you're ever coming back." I couldn't imagine opening the door to an officer informing me Creole was dead. Most likely, Harder would do it because of our friendship, but that wouldn't do anything for the pain.

"Calm down, babe, I'm fine," he said softly. "Help was impressed at the efficiency with which you detailed your problem. That's high praise. Update me."

I gave him a rundown of what I knew, which wasn't much. Told him about Brad's stop off at Balcazar's offices and what Spoon had learned from Les.

"So where are you headed? The restaurant?"

"We're headed to the Balcazar mansion, have a look around. Nothing may come of it, but at least we'll feel like we're doing something," I said.

"How did you get the address so fast?" he humphed. "How's Fab holding up?"

"It's all in who you know," I sighed as we rolled by a fender bender pulled off to one side. We'd been doing one mile an hour, thanks to the drivers in front of us that had to slow and gawk. "She's a tough one and has shed a layer of frustration now that we can get back to the speed limit."

"Talked to your mother. Madeline is frantic, wanting me to convince you to go home. I can handle it from here. I'll call as soon as I get to Balcazar's."

"Will you?" My words dripped with sarcasm. "That's so accommodating. What are the chances Fab would agree to that, even if I did?"

His heavy sigh rolled through the phone.

"Then what?" I demanded. "Give the little girlfriend a call when you learn something?"

"I didn't mean it that way."

"I'll talk to you later." I hung up and tossed the phone on the console.

"Thanks for understanding." Fab gripped the wheel, her knuckles white, holding our speed at just above the limit, not wanting to attract attention.

I flashed her deranged smile at her.

She cocked her head. "Is that my smile? I like it!"

Chapter Forty-Four

Hibiscus Island was manmade, and had been dredged up and completed almost a hundred years ago. History had it that these small islands were developed for gangsters and celebrities, who built large mansions with views of the Intracoastal Waterway to have a place to party with their friends. Now some of the priciest real estate in Miami Beach, it held the distinction of being one of the first places to be evacuated in advance of a hurricane.

A Mercedes SUV had pulled up to the security gate ahead of us. The gates opened on its approach, and we followed right behind. If we'd been in a beat-up sedan, I imagine the driver would have called security, but so far, it seemed he hadn't.

"We looking for a cat?" I asked. "Balcazar has never met me and hopefully I look better than my driver's license photo. I can keep them distracted at the front while you sneak around the back."

"I thought we'd try a more subtle approach— I'll kick the door in."

"You mean after you shoot the locks off and

set off the security alarm?" I gave her a lopsided smile.

"Answer your phone," Fab said as it began ringing.

Picking it up, I noticed several missed calls from Brad. Mother had most likely roped him in to shovel more guilt on, and I knew he'd be worried.

"You two okay?" Phil asked. "I've got an update."

I hit the speaker button. "We're on Hibiscus now. The rich really know how to live. If something happens to either of us or we disappear, you make sure Balcazar doesn't get away with it."

The first house was a modern monstrosity, all chrome and glass, set back on two lots. Each successive house was bigger than the last.

"My money's on you two. Dirtball has to be desperate; the state attorney general is finally looking into his business practices. His office could no longer ignore the complaints—too many of them, no matter who Balcazar knows. Any support he had in the past has gone silent. No one's willing to speak up or offer help and end up implicated in something that would put their neck on the chopping block," Phil said.

"Do you think Lauren was offed by one of his associates as a warning or by someone wanting payback?" Fab asked.

"According to Didier, he didn't leave his

jacket in her condo, so how did it get there?" Phil asked. "Did he happen to mention where he last saw the jacket? If we're believing Didier's version, which I assume we are, then someone deliberately framed him. Anyone with a grudge that you know about?"

"Everyone likes Didier." Fab snorted. "Men, women, and it's genuine too, from what I can tell. He's one of those men that just fits in, no matter who he talks to. Unlike you-know-who," she said, pointing to herself. "He doesn't seem to mind that people find me off-putting and that I don't give a damn."

"You need to have a friendly chat with Balcazar. A gun to the face works effectively for getting someone to talk," Phil suggested. "Course, you can never be sure if it's a pack of lies to save their skin. Where are you now?"

"Driving by a garish, yellow Mediterranean monstrosity. U-shaped, two three-car garages on each side of the driveway, a call box at the gate. The front has more windows than I care to clean." I wrinkled my nose.

"County records show the property as just shy of twelve thousand square feet. How much *staff* would it take to run that place? Remember, Balcazar's probably not going to be home alone."

"If you stand at one end of the house and scream, can you hear it on the other end?" I asked.

"There's something wrong with you," Fab

said, pulling into the lot of a community park. We didn't dare pull over to the curb; that would garner unwanted attention.

"If anything goes wrong, call or text and I'll call the police," Phil offered.

"That's a good idea," Fab nodded.

We got out of the SUV for a quick look around. The fish pond in the middle of the park was the focal point, surrounded by lush green grass. Not being a connoisseur, I could only say that the pond appeared occupied by oversized goldfish of different varieties. A white bridge linked the two parts of the walking path that wandered into an overgrowth of trees. It didn't appear that the park ever got used, and why would it, when every home had its own manicured lawn?

Standing out in the open here didn't seem like a good idea, and I turned to tell Fab that.

A hand shot around me from behind, clamping over my mouth. I screamed, the sound muffled, and went into fight mode, struggling and kicking, determined not to be dragged from the park to who-knew-where.

"Oww, that hurt," a male voice growled in my ear. "Calm down before I strangle you."

I turned my head and lifted my eyes to see Creole's angry face. "You scared me," I whimpered, wanting to kick Fab's butt for not warning me. She stood a few feet away, arms crossed, enjoying the show.

"What the fuck do you think you're doing? This—" he swept his arm out. "does not look like your neighborhood."

"Such bad language." I scrunched up my nose, taking small breaths to control my pounding heart.

He jerked me to his chest and gave me a hard hug before pushing me back. "What are you doing here?"

"Looking for my lost cat." I tried to make it sound like a great idea, but his face turned almost purple, and I knew I'd failed.

He shook my shoulders. "It's bad enough you used that lame excuse once, but you trot it out over and over."

"I never said we'd go home."

Fab laughed, which elevated his coloring a notch. "Hey Neanderthal, we're here and not going anywhere. You got a plan? If not, I'll make one up while scaling the wall to that ugly-ass house. Oh excuse me, mansion."

"We've already wasted enough time having to wait on you two, knowing that you never do what you're told and then we have to do damage control," Creole seethed.

"We?" I looked at Fab as a familiar figure stepped out of the bushes.

"Nice to see you again." The man winked, putting his arm around Fab's shoulders.

Fab turned and elbowed him with a half-sneer; she didn't get the allure that was Help.

My heart had gradually slowed back to its normal pace. "We're here. We can be useful. You'll never keep Fab out of whatever you have planned, so you might as well figure out a way to include her."

"Found Didier's car," Help said.

Fab jumped. "Where is it? What about Didier?"

"Quiet." Creole pointed his finger first at me, then Fab. "The only reason you're still standing here and not back in the SUV is that I know damn well that, once out of sight, you'd double back around."

I made a key-locking gesture in front of my lips.

"If only…" He cleared his throat. "This job hasn't been sanctioned by the boss, so we have to make sure there's no unnecessary carnage."

Help spoke up, "Didier's car is in the garage, along with three others. He's inside the house, tied to a dining room chair, a maid, judging by the uniform, pacing around the room. Balcazar is with an unidentified gun-toting woman, and she appears to be calling at least some of the shots."

"Balcazar armed?" Creole asked.

"Balcazar's armed but doesn't appear to have the stomach for what's going down. He's up and down, nervous and jumpy; cracking under the stress, perhaps. The maid tried to get a call out, but the woman caught her, tossed her phone on the floor, and riddled it with bullets." Help flashed a frigid smile.

Creole's phone buzzed. He withdrew it from his pocket and read the screen. "The boss says we're on our own. We better have the goods; Balcazar's got well-placed friends." He turned to me. "Can I trust you to stay here until we get back?"

Help laughed in a gravelly tone. It sounded as though he didn't do it often. "Have Fab ring the bell, ask some asinine question, and create a diversion while we go over the wall. Oh, and girlie," he directed the remark towards me. "Don't step outside this park."

"Fab can't! Balcazar sent some low-life to kidnap them. Too bad for Les Nado that Fab caught up to him first. Balcazar's waiting for the delivery of these two, and Nado's trussed up, waiting for us to give him a ride into Miami," Creole related. "I told Spoon to get as much detail out of him as he could without leaving marks."

"Fab doesn't do asinine. I'll do it," I said.

"Absolutely not. You might get shot on sight when they realize you're free." Creole tightened his hold.

"I need to breathe." I squirmed. "You forget I'm an excellent shot, almost as good as you, and I never leave home without my Glock. Not anymore, anyway." I lifted my top to show my holster.

"You're not going to be bait," Creole growled.

"Boss." Help motioned to Creole.

"You two stay right here. Move and I'll tie you both to the same tree," Creole threatened.

"Okay," I muttered, hanging my head.

Fab moved to my side and patted my back.

"You made her cry?" Help sounded shocked.

"No I didn't." Creole snorted. "She's laughing at me. Laugh now, sweetheart," he said into my ear, "there's always later."

"You make having a girlfriend look fun, Boss."

Creole and Help conferred off to one side, both watching us to make sure we didn't disappear.

I grabbed Fab's hand and squeezed, making sure I had a good grip. "Don't you think you should hear their plan before running off? This situation is bad enough; I couldn't bear it if you got hurt."

She jerked out of my hold. "I'm out of patience," she said, then announced, "I gotta pee; I'm using that bush over there." She pointed to a row of hedges.

Before I could recover from the thought of Fab squatting in the bushes of a ritzy neighborhood, she was halfway there.

"Get back here," Creole yelled to her retreating back.

"She'll be right back; she's using the bush for a bathroom," I said.

Help chuckled. "I love a woman who's resourceful."

"Damn her." Creole pointed after Fab, who was running across the street, already disappearing from view down the side of the house.

"I'm on it." Help took off in a sprint.

"Are you going to do exactly what I tell you?" Creole squashed me to his chest. "No ad libbing?" He looked down into my face. "I don't trust you enough to leave you behind. No telling where you'll show up."

His lack of trust burned my heart. If I thought about it too much, I might cry. I focused on his instructions, repeating them a couple of times when he asked me to.

Chapter Forty-Five

Once the text "Now" popped up from Creole, I knew Help had located Fab and they were in place and ready to go. I edged the Hummer up to the gates, noting the video surveillance sign. I was to be the decoy at the gate, but once they opened, I wasn't to set one foot on the property.

The silence that followed after ringing the bell was nerve-racking. It was impossible to know if the button even worked. "This isn't the time for manners," I said to myself. I pushed it several more times. If it did work, the incessant ringing would be hard to ignore. Someone would answer, if out of nothing more than curiosity.

Finally, a woman's voice came over the loudspeaker. "How can I help you?"

Instead of answering, I rang the bell again; hopefully, she'd think she couldn't be heard. An older woman peered out of one of the floor-to-ceiling windows that framed the massive front door. I guessed her to be the maid. The gates rolled open, and she opened the door, shaking her head, making a shooing motion with the back of her hand.

"Is Balcazar home?" I got out, and yelled,

standing on the front driver's side of the car.

He appeared in the doorway, disheveled like he'd been on a drug bender, his clothes wrinkled and looking slept-in. He danced down the wrap-around steps in my direction, a gun appearing from behind his back, and motioned me forward with the hand that held it.

I threw myself to the ground, rolled, and came back up with my Glock in hand.

Balcazar suddenly lost interest in me, his attention drawn to the side of the property where I'd last seen Creole. He leveled his gun with two hands, finger on the trigger, steady for a second, but then the muzzle of the gun began to wave erratically, as if he was trying to follow a moving target.

I shot first. Balcazar whirled and returned fire, his shot going wild, shattering a flowerpot. The gun clattered to the ground along with him. He held his right shoulder, rolling back and forth and screaming, "I'm dying!"

Everything happened at once. Two more shots rang out from inside the house, and an assortment of dark sedans pulled around the corner, lights flashing.

I gauged my chances of being able to sneak into the house, wrestling momentarily between wanting to help, wanting to keep my promise to Creole, and the clincher, *not* wanting to take a bullet from law enforcement. I slowly walked to the back of the SUV, Glock in one hand, bent down, and laid it on the ground. I stood back up, palms out shoulder-high, thinking that now wasn't the time to make any sudden moves and happy that I hadn't done anything stupid.

The first uniformed cop was out of his car, gun drawn, yelling, "Hands on your head! Step away from the gun!"

My hands shot up while I wished I could text Creole to get his butt out here to vouch for me and assure them I wasn't some hardened criminal.

"On the ground," he barked, coming up the driveway.

"Can't we do this while I'm standing?" I whined, holding my breath at the sight of his finger on the trigger and the fierce look on his face. "I have a carry permit in the Hummer."

He spun me around, pushing against my back. My head hit the SUV with a thud.

"Ohhh," I gasped as my arms were jerked back and the metal cuffs clamped around my wrists and closed tight. "That was my head, damn you."

He pushed me into a sitting position on the grass. "Don't move," he warned, and took a position to the left of me, turning away.

Two ambulances rounded the corner followed by a fire truck and another, unmarked red truck. I had a good seat. From my vantage point, I could watch everything happening in the driveway. One of those ambulances would be for

Balcazar, but the other one?

I tipped precariously to one side and barely caught myself, visions of grass bugs crawling on my face freaking me out. I was certain I wouldn't be able to right myself without the use of my hands.

Next to arrive was a line of police vehicles. The officers hustled out of their cars and scattered in different directions, several disappearing up the driveway and inside the house. One uniformed officer caught my eye and an icy chill ran up my spine. *What was Officer Watters doing here?"*

It wasn't lost on me that he'd showed up several times these last couple of weeks. I made eye contact with him, and he had the gall to wave.

The last sedan to arrive had deeply tinted windows and edged past the other parked cars, managing to finagle a prime spot. The newest arrival took their sweet time in making an appearance. A ridiculously wide smile broke out on my face when, at last, the door opened and out stepped Creole's boss—Chief Harder. He'd been working out lately, more than his customary game of golf. Gone was his usual rumpled look, and he'd traded in his mom jeans for a pair of Levis.

"Chief!" I yelled, bobbing my head, frustrated I couldn't wave my arms. "Over here!"

The cop guarding me stared down at me.

Chief Harder cut across the grass. "You going to need bail money again?" His mouth twitched.

"You're not funny. And this officer was mean to me." I fidgeted in his direction. "My head hurts."

Harder hadn't actually had to pony up cash in the past, but he did once rescue me from the weeds and drove me back to civilization after a misunderstanding with a sheriff's deputy out in the boonies.

"He took my Glock. When you're done with your investigation, I'd like it back. It was a gift from my brother."

Harder inclined his head toward the cop guarding me. "Uncuff her. She's a pain but not a criminal." He narrowed his eyes, and added, "Not yet."

The officer had watched our exchange with his eyebrows permanently arched up, but didn't say anything. He just silently removed the cuffs.

"Chief, sir, I… uh…" I stammered, squeezing my eyes shut, "shot Balcazar."

"I've heard he's going to live." He looked disappointed.

"Fab? Didier? They okay?" I asked.

He nodded. "Yes, your pain-in-the-ass friend is going to be around to torment me in the future."

I felt weak as the adrenaline rush left my body. "You know she likes you a little better now."

Harder laughed. "Don't you dare cry on me, or I'll make sure that boyfriend of yours never gets a day off," he said gruffly and patted my shoulder.

We shared the same lack of enthusiasm for touchy-feely stuff.

"Don't go anywhere." He shook his finger. "Make yourself comfortable. This is going to take a while, and an officer will need to get your statement before you can leave. Your friend will be out as soon as they're done with her."

Officer Watters came up from behind the chief and stood next to him, listening to the exchange. The fierce way he studied me made me uncomfortable.

"Can I sit in the back of my car?" I pointed to where it had been moved into the street. "I'll keep the back open and stay in plain sight."

Harder nodded, then turned away. "She's all yours."

A bolt of fear shot through me, thinking he meant that Watters would question me. I breathed a big sigh of relief when I realized he was talking to yet another detective who'd just showed up.

"We've met before." I grimaced in recognition. "You rousted one of my drunk tenants, making him pee himself, and he hid inside his cottage for a week." He'd had a partner with him then, and I'd named the duo good cop/bad cop. Maybe his interrogation technique would remind me which one he was.

He smirked. "We'll sit in your vehicle, in case you feel the need to follow your tenant's unfortunate example."

He followed me to the car and waited while I opened the back. Before he could begin the questioning, however, his phone rang. He took a few steps away and answered it. I quickly walked to the front of the car and retrieved my phone from the console, returning to the back and texting Mother that everyone was unhurt.

I knew she was mad, because she didn't bother to text back. Spoon called instead, wanting to know if I was okay. I told him it would be a while and I'd text when we were on the way home.

The officer sauntered over and sat next to me. "Start at the beginning; don't leave anything out. I'll decide what's important."

Chapter Forty-Six

A paramedic wheeled Balcazar, strapped to a gurney, to the back of the ambulance. The woman who'd peered out the window followed, yelling, "I've worked for you all these years, and you treat me like this!" She hocked spit down the front of him. "Pendejo!" she screamed. An older officer grabbed her by the arm, turning her away. She exchanged words with him before calming down.

The ambulance left, with no flashing lights or blaring sirens. I took that to mean that Harder had been right and Balcazar wasn't in danger of dying.

Another gurney followed, flanked by two paramedics. Their attention was on the dark-haired woman strapped down on it and not moving, unlike Balcazar, who'd shouted a few obscenities. They loaded her in the back of the remaining ambulance and sped off, this time with sirens.

My bottom ached from sitting on the back ledge of the Hummer, and I was bored with sitting. The only exciting action had just pulled off down the street. I entertained thoughts of how to sneak past the two bookends on guard at the gate and get answers to the hundred or so questions on the growing list in my mind. But after being somewhat well-behaved, I'd be in so much trouble if Creole had to pick me up at the jail.

There he is again, I thought. Watters had joined the guards at the entrance, his arms crossed in an intimidating stance as he stared me down.

A shadow appeared in my peripheral vision, and I squealed.

"The investigation is winding down," Help informed me and held up his hand when I tried to talk. "Don't ask. You'll have to get your answers from Creole."

"Just one." I held up my index finger. "Who was the woman?"

"Tina Balcazar. Heir to a billion-dollar fortune and headed to jail if she survives. At least she'll have spending money."

Damn! I wished I'd gotten a better look. I'd seen society photos, but that didn't compare to up close and personal.

"Thank you for tracking Creole down for me earlier. I owe you one."

"No, you don't. I appreciate it that you kept your mouth shut about my identity and didn't broadcast it all over town."

"I'm good at keeping secrets," I said.

"Creole assured me that was the case."

"Shirl—you remember, my tenant?" I tried to maintain eye contact under his glare but ended up glancing away for a moment. "We never mention your name except in an abstract way. She can also keep a secret." They'd met while he was pretending to be an insurance agent named Steve, and she always looked ridiculously satisfied after he'd left her bed.

"It's hard, in my line of work, to have a relationship. Especially one I don't fuck up." He looked down, running his hands through his dark hair.

"It's none of my business, but whatever happens, just don't be a total dick to her." When he didn't respond, I said, "Stop by Jake's and give the bartender the secret code: 'free meal.'" Before he left, I wanted to point out Watters and ask Help what he knew. But when I glanced over to where I'd last seen him, he was gone.

"Thanks. They'll be out soon." Help waved and disappeared down the street in the direction of the park.

Every time I ran into Help, he evaporated into thin air like a ghost when it was time to leave. I'd like to ask him to teach me that trick.

* * *

It surprised me that there were no lookie-loos from the neighborhood. I craned my neck up and down the street, but not one single person was curious enough to investigate the sirens coming and going, not to mention the police and emergency vehicles. Lurking around a crime scene might tarnish their image.

"Madison!" a voice shrieked.

I jerked to an upright position from where I'd been lying in the back of the SUV. I squealed and sprang out, running to meet Fab and Didier, who were walking hand in hand in my direction. I skidded to a stop and flung my arms around them. "Love you both so much." I smiled at Didier. "You're so rumpled," I teased.

"*Chérie*." He scooped me up into a bear hug. "Honestly, I didn't think I'd ever see the two of you again."

That hit me in the gut, and tears gathered in my eyes.

"Don't you dare cry, or I'll slug you." Fab hugged me.

"Happy to see you unblemished and in one piece. I need a best friend, and it has to be you."

"Not going anywhere. You'd never find a good replacement."

"You shouldn't be here," Didier admonished.

"Oh piffle. Where else would I be? Tell me, did Fab kick in the window and swing in like Tarzan?" I beamed at her. "Where's Creole?"

"Right here." His arms wrapped around me from behind.

"Who's going to tell me what happened?" I asked, feeling annoyed that I even had to.

"I can't talk about the case until it's over," Creole said. "But I can listen while Fab and Didier fill us in."

"Help showed up at the kitchen door right behind me," Fab explained. "'Do you even know what stay put means?' he growled in my ear. Whether he liked it or not, though, I was going in. I was just about to kick him in the... Well, not there, but close."

Creole and Didier sucked in their breath.

"Then the maid yelped from the doorway, a soda flying out of her hand. Help is quick on his feet," Fab said in admiration. "I motioned for her to stay, and Help flashed his badge at the same time. Then another woman's voice screamed, 'Marta, get in here!'"

"That Marta is a tough one," Didier said. "I need to say thank you to her for her efforts. When I first got there, we had a moment alone, and she tried to undo the ropes. She succeeded in getting one loosened before Tina came back in the room."

"Well, we followed her when she answered Tina's call, and were able to see into the room where they were holding Didier without them spotting us. Do you know what happened next?" Fab looked at me pointedly.

"The doorbell rang!" I exclaimed.

"We suffered a few tense moments right before that, but I held off from shooting them. Tina was pointing a gun in Didier's face, shrieking about how he'd wrecked their plans. Balcazar cautioned her to wait until Nado delivered Madison and me. They argued over who would pull the trigger—he'd never killed before—always paying someone else to do the dirty work and dispose of the messiness. Tina was adamant that Nado be the one to dump our bodies in some remote location she knew of in Alligator Alley. He was in for a nasty surprise, though. Instead of payment, he'd get a bullet too."

I shuddered, remembering all the times we'd joked about feeding remains to the alligators, not to mention the vultures.

"Tina Balcazar. Brains, beauty, money—what a waste," Creole said in disgust.

"A frozen block of ice for a heart," Didier said.

"Then you-know-who was at the gate." Fab pointed at me. "Tina sent Marta to get it, thinking it was Nado. Balcazar followed, a gun jammed in the woman's back. Nado was already late and Balcazar got more agitated each time he called the man's cell phone and there was no answer."

"Everything happened at once." Didier shuddered.

"A shot rang out, then Balcazar was yelling he was dying. Tina was momentarily distracted, and Creole shot her from the opposite side of the room."

I smiled up at him, clasping my hands across

his arms.

"Tina's gun went off. Then I screamed." Fab looked haggard, reliving the moment. "Didier slumped to one side. I thought he'd been shot or worse, not realizing the bullet was embedded in the wall right over his head. Her gun clattered to the floor and she fell, and damned if she didn't try to crawl toward it, even though she was shot in the upper chest. Creole put his foot on her back and stopped her forward movement."

"Fab brandished a knife and cut the ropes, not a single nick." Didier held out his arms to show me, then leaned into her, brushing her lips with a kiss. I winced at the sight of the rope burns around his wrists.

Creole's phone alerted to a message. I groaned, knowing it wouldn't be good news.

"The chief is demanding my reappearance. We'll talk in the morning. I've got a few more questions." He hugged his friend, then turned to me. His lips met mine and turned the gentle contact into a demanding kiss. "When you roll over, I'll be there."

The blush started at my neckline and went straight up.

"Good thing you gave us a heads up. I'd hate to shoot you, thinking you're a prowler." Fab gave him a cheesy grin.

"I'm happy that another brush with death hasn't affected your sense of humor." He stalked off.

Fab grabbed my arm, tugging me around to the driver's side. "Didier isn't getting his car back tonight anyway. Do you mind driving?"

"Me?" I beamed at her, sliding behind the wheel.

"Try not to get a ticket this time," she said, shaking her finger at me.

Didier held the back door open, and they slid inside.

I checked the rearview and side mirrors. "Remember that cop, Watters? He showed up here. Creeped me out, the way he looked at me."

"We need to find out what he wants." Fab turned, looking out the back window. "Do you see him anywhere?"

"He disappeared again." I heaved a sigh.

I maneuvered around several cars. "You okay, Didier?" It worried me that he was so quiet. A first kidnapping takes a while to get over.

"I used to think I was good judge of character," he said on a low growl.

"Don't be so hard on yourself; some people are masters of deception. So good, they slip under the radar." Fab kissed his cheek.

Driving through the security gates, I adhered strictly to the posted speed limit. I didn't want to give Watters an excuse to pull me over, if he was still lurking around.

"Watching Fab in action, I can see why you like having her by your side in a tight situation. She never gives up, does she?" Didier combed her hair with his fingers.

"No, she doesn't." I smiled in the mirror. "Hang on back there, you're in for a wild ride."

"You don't need to impress us." Fab stretched out, laying her head in Didier's lap. "I can't believe I'm going to say this, but just be your pokey self. I'm lying down, and what I can't see won't bother me."

"I have your permission to not blow through yellow lights?" I asked.

Didier laughed. "After the day we've had, just get us home in one piece."

I inserted one of Fab's favorite CDs into the player and turned it down low. They could talk in privacy. As much as Fab liked to eavesdrop, she'd do the same for me.

Chapter Forty-Seven

The bed dipped, and I rolled into Creole's arms. "About time," I said sleepily.

"The boss gave me a few days off," he said in my ear. "You know what that means?"

"Hot sex at your house." I tried not smile.

Creole slid under the sheet. "Why aren't you naked?" he asked.

"You have to get dressed," I said, kicking off the sheets.

"Why?" he growled. "Expecting someone else?"

"You need to sneak me out and back to your house, so we can have loud, noisy sex." I smiled sweetly.

"Nice try." He rolled me away from him, removing my clothing with efficiency and sending it airborne.

"You appear to have practice removing women's clothing."

"Behave yourself," he barked a laugh. "We're not doing anything. You have a house full of people downstairs. Get some sleep; you'll have to face your mother in the morning." He wrapped his arms around me, tightening his hold. "You're not getting me in trouble."

* * *

I'd lucked out the night before. By the time we pulled up at the house, Mother and Spoon had left. No doubt, after finding out we were all safe, they hadn't seen any point in staying, knowing questioning by law enforcement would take an unknown amount of time.

"We're here. I feel compelled to warn you, Didier, that Mother and Spoon were not happy that we snuck out earlier."

Fab, who'd gone to sleep, had woken up when I cut the engine. "Looks like we lucked out. Spoon's silver Mercedes isn't here."

"I've got your back," Didier said flexing his muscles.

"Hurry up and get out." Fab pushed Didier's shoulder. "This is where she'll get all emotional."

Brad stood in the doorway, and I slid by first. "You're in the doghouse," he sing-songed as he hugged and twirled me around. Finally, he put me down and inspected me carefully. "Good thing you're in one piece."

"I followed orders for a change and didn't do anything life-threatening. I hope this means I can sneak up to my room?"

"Mother won't be back until morning."

I scooped up Jazz and left my brother standing there laughing at me.

* * *

Creole jerked into a sitting position. "What the hell was that?" He grabbed his pants off the floor.

"You don't need your gun. It's only Fab's idea of a wake-up call, kicking the hell out of the door," I said sleepily. "We've got a few minutes before she comes back."

"Like hell." He threw open the door and yelled, "You do that again, and I'll break your foot!"

"Look who woke up in a bad mood." Fab's voice came from down the hall.

She must have kicked and ran. I pulled the sheet to my nose, trying not to laugh.

"Breakfast is ready," Mother called cheerfully.

Creole, quick on his feet, managed to catch the door before it banged shut and closed it quietly.

* * *

Mother had brought a ton of food—enough to feed an army—and spread it out on the counter. As I entered the kitchen, Didier held out a blender container filled with his fresh green concoction.

I squeezed my eyes closed and shook my

head. I'd tasted it once and thought my mouth would fall out.

Everyone filled a plate, and we moved outside to the patio. Brad pointed to a seat next to Mother and mouthed, "Sit."

"I suppose this means the real estate deal is dead," Spoon quipped.

I'd never have guessed he'd be the one to break the ice and jump-start the conversation. Everyone had questions, but no one had wanted to be the first to ask.

"We'll find another one," Didier joked.

"You're quiet," Spoon said to me from the other side of mother. "You okay?"

"Not a scratch. Just tired." I squeezed Creole's leg under the table, thinking about his days off, and hoped he could read my mind and we'd leave early.

"I wish the two of you had stayed home and thought more about your safety." Mother glared at Fab and me. "And sneaking out!" she huffed.

"Would you have sat at home if it had been one of your family members?" Fab asked evenly. "As selfish as it is, I don't want to go on a job without your daughter." She reached across the table and gripped my hand.

I leaned over and kissed Mother's cheek, whispering, "I love you," in her ear.

"What she said." Fab flashed Mother a deranged smile.

Mother laughed and shook her finger at her.

"It's a damn good thing the two of you are okay."

Brad tapped a glass with his spoon. "Who's going first? We're here for details and, of course, food."

I kicked Fab under the table. "Fab can tell our part."

Fab started her story with how it was my idea to sneak out and she'd felt it was her duty to follow for my safety. She ignored my snort and continued, stopping short of confessing that she'd defied Creole and jumped the wall, impatient at the slow speed of Didier's rescue.

"How did you end up in the house?" Spoon asked, maintaining eye contact with Fab. "I'm surprised the cops would sanction you going anywhere near the property."

"The back door was open," she said.

I squeezed Creole's hand and hoped he wouldn't out her and tell them all that she'd had her own plan and taken off after being ordered not to.

Didier put his arm around her, a grin on his face. "I guess it's my turn to explain how *I* got there. It surprised me when I got a frantic call from Balcazar, begging me to come to a meeting at his office. When I got there, however, he and Nado were waiting for me in the underground garage. As soon as I got out of my car, both of those bastards had guns pointed at my chest."

I gave him a big smile, reminding myself to use his choice of language against him in the future.

He frowned, as though he could read my mind, then continued, "While Balcazar kept his gun on me, Nado shoved me in the trunk of my own car. Then Balcazar told Nado, 'Go pick up the other two.'"

He continued talking so eloquently, describing his conversation with Balcazar after he'd found himself tied up in his "friend's" mansion that I almost felt I'd been there.

"You forced my hand. If only you were in jail," Balcazar spit. *"Now that you're not the prime suspect, I have the cops breathing down my neck. I can't risk that you and your snooping friends have dug up too much dirt, and now I'll have to get rid of you all."*

"Murder? You'll never get away with it."

"Sure I will; I have before," Balcazar boasted. *"You, your girlfriend, and her redheaded friend are going to disappear — no trace. I'm very good at that, and it's a lot less messy than leaving a bloody body to be found."*

"You murdered Lauren?"

"Actually no, it wasn't planned, though it was going to happen eventually — some point in the future perhaps. Women are so damn nosey. My wife had a bug planted in my phone, listened to all of my conversations. Unfortunately, the one where I swore my undying love to Lauren and told her I'd be leaving my wife for her... Well, my wife didn't take the news well. She had no way of knowing that I would never

leave her; I just had to keep Lauren happy. She ran the office with efficiency and fulfilled every perverted fantasy of mine in bed."

"How did Lauren end up dead?"

"Tina confronted her. She assured me that she only went to her condo to threaten her to back off, not kill her. Lauren's confidence that she would be the next Mrs. Balcazar pushed my wife over the edge. Shot her. She did say she enjoyed messing up her face."

"Why try to frame me? Was I your first choice?"

"Nothing personal," Balcazar sneered. "You're just another pretty face in underwear. Who'd miss you? Your fault, really—you left your suit jacket in my car. The business deal is dead, was never going to happen. I'd have taken the money and given you a worthless title. This might surprise you, but I never liked you and your snotty European demeanor… Ah, but you have connected, wealthy friends. You were useful. I called in a couple of favors in your name. People are so stupid, never knowing when they're being used." He threw his head back and laughed.

"You won't get away with this."

"I already have." He continued to laugh. "I've sold that property four times in the last month. What a cluster when the docs arrived at the clerk's office all at once. I should've paid closer attention to the paperwork; Lauren didn't have the timing down yet. It's an art, you know, pulling off a multimillion-dollar fraud. The authorities can investigate all they like; they won't come up with anything. I kept my hands clean with layers of dummy corps. The only glitch to framing you is that I had to let all that beautiful

money slip through my fingers."

"You belong in jail. You think my partners won't track you down?"

"Where did you find such common people? They'll be kept busy chasing their tails, searching for you and those girls, and ultimately grieving."

Didier ground to a halt and shook his head. "It's my fault he was ever a part of our lives. I apologize to all of you." Didier looked around the table.

"Nonsense," Mother said. "This family knows only too well how someone seemingly sane can sneak into our midst and turn out to be a lunatic."

"Why did Balcazar want Fab and me?" I asked. "We were silent partners."

"I was ready to beg for your lives. Not that it would have done any good, but I'd have done it anyway," he said sadly. "The night you two went to Lauren's condo, the Hummer showed up on the surveillance tapes. That, plus an unidentified woman seen briefly on the same floor as Lauren's, made Balcazar suspicious; he'd bribed the security guard to let him know if anything out of the ordinary happened. He had the plates run, which led back to this house."

"Next time we park around the corner," Fab said.

Everyone at the table glared at her. I hung my head and smiled, *That's my girl.*

Didier continued, "Then the SUV showed up

again the night you broke into the corporate offices."

"No wonder he called to get info." Creole shook his head. "I knew he was up to something. At the time, I wondered, what?"

"He knew it was the same woman who showed up at Lauren's condo and the office, though he never got a clear photo. After a little digging, he figured you two were involved up to your necks."

Fab leaned into Didier, hugging him.

We sat in silence for a moment, each thinking of how badly it all could have turned out.

Finally, I stood and stretched, collecting dishes and stacking them on a tray as I contemplated various getaway plans. Creole's look let me know that he wouldn't be the one to tell Mother we were doing an eat-and-dash. I gave him a meaningful glance. If I listened hard enough, I could hear a margarita and the bubbles in a big tub with a water view shouting, "I'm waiting!"

Brad moved up behind me, reaching for the tray and carrying it to the kitchen. "I can hear you thinking. I'll do these while you go to your room."

"Remember when we thought that was the worst punishment? Now one of my favorite things is to lie in bed and read." I hip-bumped him away from in front of the dishwasher. He could rinse; I would load. "You're lucky you don't have a mind-reading superpower; you'd be blushing. Creole has three days off—"

"If you're going to sneak out *again*, let me know so I can leave first. That could pave the way for you to make an exit, but then you'd owe me and I'd have deniability later."

"This isn't about me." I sniffed. "You've got plans and you're also looking to slip away, drama free."

Brad and I had shared kitchen duty since we were in junior high and cleaned up in record time. I wrapped the last of the leftovers and was wiping the countertops when Fab skidded across the floor.

"How do we get rid of everyone?" she whispered hoarsely.

I shrugged in Brad's direction.

"Didn't see you standing there," Fab said.

"I'm leaving," he said, crooking his finger at me before hugging Fab.

"This is for Liam." I handed him a bag of leftovers. "His favorites."

"As hard as it is, have a few minutes of patience," he said to Fab before opening the front door and pushing me outside.

He grabbed me up in a smothering hug. "I wanted to thank you for handling the Striker situation and taking care of Julie and Liam and giving her a chance to tell me, even if she was slow about it. I was hurt by that, but she assured me that it wasn't because she didn't trust me. She was afraid that I'd leave her. I told her that I'd never hold some whack-job ex against her. Then I told her about one of my exes who ended up in a hospital for psychos."

"You don't have to worry about Striker showing back up. I sicced Spoon on the man."

"Do you suppose Striker's pushing up weeds somewhere?" Brad half-laughed, and I could see he liked the idea. "I did thank him but didn't ask."

"Spoon could be our stepdaddy one of these days."

Brad groaned, "I think if the two of us cornered Mother together, maybe we could talk some sense into her."

"Forget that. You'll hurt her feelings. We don't like her meddling in our sex lives, so we need to stay out of hers."

Brad clamped his hands over his ears. "Don't use that word again."

"What word? Sex?" I laughed. "The bright side is that Mother's really happy."

"In the interest of maintaining my best-brother-ever status, I told Spoon to take Mother home, Creole to make up a work excuse, and Didier that he should say he had underwear to go model. Not only did I tell them to lie, but I had their excuses all ready for them."

"Love you, bro."

"Yeah, right back at you."

Chapter Forty-Eight

Creole and I spent three days ignoring the world, only leaving once to go to the nearby outdoor market and buy our favorite foods from the local vendors.

Each night, we worked side by side in the kitchen prepping dinner, with Creole doing the barbequing. I wasn't sure why I'd bothered to bring clothes, as I spent the entire time in one of his oversized shirts, changing only to go down to the beach. I'd found the shirts in the back of the closet and chosen a white one, buttoning only the middle buttons and rolling up the sleeves. All my worry about not asking if I could borrow one melted away when I came out of the bathroom and his eyes traveled over every inch, returning to my face with a look of lust. He smiled and yanked me into his arms.

On our last afternoon, I lay on the couch reading, Creole's voice drifted through the patio door. I was unable to make out the words, but I couldn't miss his serious tone. I crossed my fingers that the call wasn't about work and that he wouldn't be announcing he had to leave.

At the sound of his chair scraping across the concrete, I closed my eyes, warding off bad news.

"You're not asleep, you little faker," he chuckled. "Here," he said, handing me his phone. "Text message." He lifted my legs, sat, and put them on his lap.

The message from Fab read, "Turn on your damn phone."

I made a face at the screen. "What's so urgent?"

"Didier and I planned dinner for the four of us at your house tonight," he informed me.

"Let's RSVP 'no thanks' and stay here and you know…" I waggled my brows.

"We can't do that. What kind of host would I be if I didn't show?" Not waiting for an answer, he scooped me into his arms, walked to the bed, and dumped me in the middle. "Besides, we have time to do both."

"No wonder Fab is texting. What are you two guys up to?"

He clasped his hands over his heart. "You wound me."

I wrapped my legs around his torso. "Please don't provoke her to shoot you. I don't want to have to audition a new boyfriend."

"I was a patient man, waiting for you to realize that we belonged together. You're all mine, and it's going to stay that way." The last came out as a sound between a growl and bark.

He was right, we were pretty much perfect

together, and I wanted it to stay that way too, the few hiccups along the way and all.

* * *

"We're here," I yelled, waltzing by Creole, who held open the front door.

Fab, Didier, and Jazz lay on the daybed. I loved that when I wasn't here, my cat retained his status as a very spoiled animal.

"About time," Fab snarled.

Hands on my hips, I leaned forward. "We've been busy," I snarked. "Same as you two, I suspect."

Fab's cheeks pinked. "I suppose." She jumped up, grabbing my elbow. "Excuse us," she said impatiently, then shoved me out the French doors and to the far side of the pool.

"Enough." I pulled away from her. "Why did you and Didier plan this impromptu get-together? Creole and I don't have enough do-nothing time."

"Nothing?" She glowered at me like an inquisitive mother when her kid comes home late from a first date.

"You know what I mean." I sank down on a chaise. "Did you two get bored with your sexy selves?"

"Hardly. I want to be engaging in the same kind of do-nothing as you, only more adventurous." She flounced down next to me.

"But the guys planned this. They're up to something."

"Don't you love the smell of the ocean air?" I inhaled, sucking in a lungful of air. "The fog's rolling in."

Fab snapped her fingers in front of my face. "Focus. Look at them over there, huddled together."

I glanced toward the barbeque. "We're huddled over here." I thought she was overreacting until they both waved at the same time. "So what's up? We can't be in trouble; we haven't left their sides in days. Or did you sneak off somewhere?"

She ignored me and asked, "What about Balcazar?"

"It's hardly our fault Didier got 'napped. By *his* friend, not ours. Okay, I shot the guy, but he's not dead."

"I smell a trap."

"You got a plan?"

"We stick together," Fab whispered conspiratorially. "I give you the look, you follow my lead."

"Which look? You need to show me."

Fab rubbed her temples. "You give me a headache sometimes." Didier wiggled his finger at her. "We can take them," she said over her shoulder as she walked away.

Creole took her place on the chaise. "It makes my neck hairs stand on end to see the two of you plotting. Do you have an unpleasant surprise planned for Didier and me?" He pulled me into his arms.

"Two minutes with her, and you're suspicious?"

He silenced further talk with a kiss.

They are up to something, I thought.

Chapter Forty-Nine

Didier commandeered the kitchen island, a black bib apron tied around his bathing trunks. Spread out before him was an array of freshly washed vegetables that needed chopping. Fab took a butcher knife to a head of lettuce, slaughtering it, bits of green flying everywhere, until Didier took it away from her and ordered us out of the kitchen.

Creole stuffed a dish towel into each side of his trunks, twirling and bowing, making me laugh. I offered to pour dressing out of a bottle into a gravy boat and got an index finger in the direction of the patio door for my gracious offer.

"Help me set the table?" I asked Fab, waiting for her to throw something in my direction.

She stalked to a drawer at the outside countertop, yanked out a handful of utensils, and dumped them in the middle of the tablecloth.

"Do you even know how to set a table? When you lived on your own, did you eat off paper and plastic?"

Fab turned up her nose. "I can set a table for fifty with the finest china, silver and crystal. It was a requirement for graduating from Miss

Marchand's etiquette classes along with the rest of the simps."

I clucked and pulled out a chair. "Sit—" I pointed. "—and tell me what's got you agitated."

"Did you know that a lady, when she sits, crosses her ankles ever so slightly? No crossing the legs, and certainly no manspread."

Laughing, I said, "I figured the latter out without having to be told."

"They're up to something." Her gaze flicked to Didier, who set a tray down next to the barbeque.

"What's the worst? They're not going to hurt us. I mean, maybe Creole might inflict bodily harm on you, but I'm safe."

She exhaled a long, breathy sigh.

The enticing smells from the barbeque made my stomach growl.

I pulled out the shell-embossed plates, setting them down, and Fab reached across and rearranged each one. She snapped her fingers, pointing at the small candle lanterns that she'd spotted in the seashell store she abhorred, but went to with me anyway. I put three down the middle of the table, flicking on the battery strands of lights inside each one.

Creole winked, setting a platter of salmon and grilled asparagus on the table. Didier served the mixed salad; he'd outdone himself, whisking together a homemade Greek dressing. He presented a bottle of white wine from some French vineyard where he knew the owner.

I prevented myself from responding, "It's okay; where's the tequila?" when asked what I thought of the wine. I wanted to mention the bouquet, but decided this wasn't the time to make a complete ass of myself.

Fab kicked me under the table, a hint of a smirk brushed across her lips.

The dinner was delicious, the small talk kept to a minimum. Trying to read Fab's thoughts made my eyes squinch. I looked away and picked through the salad, eating the good parts— the Greek olives and tomatoes—and wishing I had a dog for the croutons.

Finishing off my salmon, I leaned back in my chair, banging my spoon on the table. "What's for dessert?"

"Sorbet." Fab tried to hold back the laughter. "Didier picked it up at that trendy market that just opened."

I stuck my tongue out at him. "That's not even real ice cream. I'll have another glass of wine."

Creole laughed in my ear. "That's not nice."

Fab grabbed my arm. "Do not get drunk." She glared at me. If you looked carefully, you could see the gears turning. After a moment's hesitation, she changed her mind, "Go ahead. Drink up." She handed me the wine bottle. "Refill my glass."

I tipped the bottle, and a trickle dribbled out. "We're cut off." I put the bottle back on the table. "Since you two cooked, we'll clean up, won't we?" I looked at Fab and, to my surprise, didn't get a word of complaint. She jumped up and collected her and Didier's plates, and we escaped to the kitchen.

"See that stainless square right there?" I pointed. "That's a dishwasher. Would you like a quick explanation of how it works?"

Fab snorted and leaned across the sink, checking out the driveway.

"Any prowlers today?"

"Didier told me Nado's working a deal; everything he knows about the Balcazars in exchange for a shorter sentence."

"Creole says he's a professional criminal. I hope they think about the fact that if you hadn't snuck up on him, three people would be dead."

It wasn't long before we finished cleaning everything up. "What else needs to be done?"

Fab's answer was a non-committal shrug. There were no leftovers, and we'd put the plates in the dishwasher and cleaned the island. Mostly, Fab had supervised.

"You worry too much," I said.

"When do I do that?" she asked with a huff. "This party stays outside! If things go south, I'll push you in the pool."

I smoothed my short white skirt and cobalt sleeveless top with a deep V-neck. I'd worn the new lacy underwear that curved up over my cheeks with thoughts of flashing Creole when no one was looking, certain he'd go all caveman and drag me back to his hideaway. "You'll owe me."

Creole and Didier filled the doorway of the patio.

"We're moving inside," Creole said.

"Why?" I moaned. "It's a beautiful night outside. The lights just came on." If I didn't think it would look like a circus tent, I'd hang them everywhere.

"No more wine for you." Creole shook his finger at me.

"In that case…" I picked up my glass, downed the last few sips, and handed it to him. Fab had found an open bottle with enough in it for two half-glasses. "I hate to be wasteful."

"Do we have assigned seating?" Fab mocked.

Didier swept her off her feet and sat on the couch, deftly pulling her into his lap. "Yes we do."

I stretched out on the daybed, shoving pillows under my head, one leg hooked over the back. I hung my head over the side and waved at Fab.

Creole pulled me into a sitting position up against his chest.

"Dinner was delicious." I wiggled, and Creole's hold tightened.

Fab leapt up, or tried to anyway. Didier caught her and hauled her back into his lap.

Creole cleared his throat. "I've got several updates on the case, none of them good."

I wanted to cover my ears, but I wouldn't be able to stand not knowing.

"Tina Balcazar died this morning. Harder called with the grim news, and his only comment was 'saves taxpayers the cost of a trial.'"

Fab wrapped her arms around Didier's neck. I wasn't sure how the news was received by everyone else, as no one said anything.

"Balcazar's locked up. The Feds swept in and relieved Miami PD of the case with no explanation, which ticked the boss off. No arraignment as of yet."

"I haven't had a single call from a prosecutor. I'll testify. I don't want him ever getting out of jail," Didier said adamantly.

"Your friend Watters…" Creole blew out a frustrated breath. "He retired. Must have gotten wind that they were going to investigate him and his ties to Balcazar. Left Florida and directed all inquiries to his lawyer."

"Good riddance," Fab said, then changed the subject. "Dinner was great." She tried to stand, but Didier didn't relinquish his hold.

"Creole and I wanted to have a discussion with the two of you." Didier gave her a smile that didn't quite reach his eyes. "A few ideas that would make living together go smoother."

"You lied," I grouched at Creole. "Apparently you drew the short straw," I said, pointing at Didier. "There's nothing wrong with our relationship; we get along, never fight, why mess that up? You French ever hear about not fixing the broken wheel?"

"You got that all messed up." Fab rolled her eyes. "Besides, we're too sophisticated for such nonsense."

Creole stood and deposited me on the daybed before pounding his fist on the wall. "This come-to-Jesus meeting is called to order. I'll do the talking. Understand?"

Fab gave him the finger. "Ass…"

Didier, expecting that reaction, clamped his hand over her mouth. "Oww!" He jerked it back. Fab had sunk her teeth into one of his fingers.

Hard as I tried to contain it, the laughter escaped.

"We will be instituting rules that all of us—" Creole pointed at each of us. "—agree to."

"Rules?" Fab snorted, flashing her middle finger again.

I was the only one, who noticed, thoroughly enjoying her histrionics. I raised my hand.

"What?" Creole barked.

"I want to point out in our favor that we've been getting better." I honestly did work at keeping him updated. "Texting you from every location, for example."

"Every one?" Fab's brows shot up.

I ignored her. "The GPS hasn't malfunctioned in a while, and I agreed to have a GPS app installed on my phone."

"I'd like it if you texted me," Didier said to Fab.

"We're not suggesting a new line of work or

even an upgrade in clients. We just don't want you getting hurt, or worse." Creole brushed his fingers through my hair. "I suppose concern for your safety makes us crappy boyfriends."

Fab mimed rubbing her eyes with her fists like a baby.

"I feel the same way about your job," I sighed.

"After my experience," Didier said, "it's not a bad idea for us to know where you are for those just-in-case times." He sounded rattled. "Look at me—I texted Fab and it saved my life."

"Fab and I already talked about it," I said, "and agreed that someone knowing about our jobs is a good idea. Didn't we?"

She nodded. "Just don't call every two minutes and complain about the neighborhood. Sometimes it's unavoidable."

"Fine," Creole snapped. "Drive wherever you want. But don't jeopardize Madison's life. Leave her at an overpriced coffee shop and come back and pick her up if you make it out in one piece."

"*Chérie*, it's only because we love you that we're having this conversation," Didier did his best to placate Fab, frowning at Creole as a signal to lower his voice.

Love. I cocked my head and looked into Creole's eyes, which burned a deep blue. His face was blank, but he looked damned uncomfortable.

Neither of us had uttered those three little words. Did he love me? It had taken a while for me to admit my feelings to myself, and so far, I had only done so in my heart. The words had almost tumbled out a time or two, but I'd managed to catch them, not wanting to blurt them out. What if I did and he didn't feel the same way? Our relationship would never be the same. Ignorant bliss suited me for the moment.

"What are you thinking about?" Creole leaned down and whispered.

Knowing Fab and Didier weren't watching, I lifted my skirt and flashed him.

He stared, reached down and snapped the elastic of my underwear, then yanked my skirt back down. "You are so going to pay for that later."

"Is it later yet?"

He shook his finger in my face, and I tried to bite it. "Behave," he mouthed.

"Are we done?" Fab humphed.

"Fabiana…" Didier sighed heavily.

"Didier," I said, "would you like it if we turned into totally biddable women, always did what we were told, and never flashed anyone the finger?"

He smiled slightly as my words sank in. "Hell no." He stood and scooped Fab into his arms.

I licked the end of my finger and made a tic mark. "I'm keeping track of your vulgar language," I admonished him.

He laughed and kissed Fab, mumbling something I couldn't hear. She flashed him a huge smile, and he carried her upstairs.

"It's just the two of us now." I lifted my legs and wrapped them around his waist.

He lifted my skirt and kissed my stomach. "Let's take this somewhere more private."

"Your house?"

He winked.

Chapter Fifty

Creole carried me across the threshold of his hideaway and kicked the door closed. He strode across to the king-size bed and set me down, dispensing with my clothes first, then dropping his own in a pile on the floor. He lay down on the bed and rolled me over on top of his chest.

"You faded out earlier with this faraway look on your face. What were you thinking about?" he whispered.

My cheeks flushed. "About what a great boyfriend you are." I smiled against his lips, then looked back into his eyes. "How lucky I am that you were patient and waited for me to be available. How happy I am that you didn't give up. Most of all, how happy I am that you needed very little training."

"If your aunt was alive, I would wring her neck for not introducing us sooner. I've known for a long time that you're the woman for me and I don't want anyone else—ever."

"Have you factored in that I'm not well-behaved and I'm certain that, even with the best intentions, there will be lapses in the future?"

"I want you to know that I don't take one single text, one single call, for granted. And that I'm very thankful you're not the hot mess your friend is."

"Fab's coming around. Sometimes I'm a good influence," I laughed.

"About tonight." He paused, pushing me away and lightly brushing my lips. "I didn't want you to hear that I love you just because Didier blurted it out."

I caressed his cheek, reminding myself to breathe.

"I remember the exact moment I fell in love with you." He nibbled on my bottom lip. "You had staked out the driveway at The Cottages and slunk down behind the steering wheel of your car. The second I stepped into the driveway, I could feel your presence, and I scoured every corner until I found you. When I spotted you, I knew you could see me too. I winked and went inside my cottage with a stupid grin on my face."

"I was so annoyed and shocked that you'd spotted me in a second. I might as well have dragged out a beach chair and made myself comfortable. That wink…" I traced his lips with my finger, "…was the first of many delicious moments between us, even though at the time we were just friends."

"We will never be 'just' anything," he bit off in a growl. He put his hands on either side of my face and stared down at me. "I love you," he whispered and gave me a kiss that I felt in my toes.

"I realized I loved you when I was sitting by your hospital bed, your hand clasped between mine, willing you to open those beautiful eyes of yours."

"I love you, Madison Westin."

"I love you, Luc Baptiste, AKA Creole."

~*~

PARADISE SERIES NOVELS

Crazy in Paradise
Deception in Paradise
Trouble in Paradise
Murder in Paradise
Greed in Paradise
Revenge in Paradise
Kidnapped in Paradise
Swindled in Paradise
Executed in Paradise
Hurricane in Paradise
Lottery in Paradise
Ambushed in Paradise
Christmas in Paradise
Blownup in Paradise
Psycho in Paradise
Overdose in Paradise
Initiation in Paradise
Jealous in Paradise
Wronged in Paradise
Vanished in Paradise
Fraud in Paradise
Naïve in Paradise

Deborah's books are available on Amazon
amazon.com/Deborah-Brown/e/B0059MAIKQ

About the Author

Deborah Brown is an Amazon bestselling author of the Paradise series. She lives on the Gulf of Mexico, with her ungrateful animals, where Mother Nature takes out her bad attitude in the form of hurricanes.

Sign up for my newsletter and get the latest on new book releases. Contests and special promotion information. And special offers that are only available to subscribers.
www.deborahbrownbooks.com

Follow on FaceBook:
facebook.com/DeborahBrownAuthor

You can contact her at Wildcurls@hotmail.com

Deborah's books are available on Amazon
amazon.com/Deborah-Brown/e/B0059MAIKQ